An Allie B

DOG DRAMA

by

Leslie O'Kane

Book Six in the Series

This book is a work of fiction. The names, characters, places, and incidents are a product of the author's imagination or have been used fictitiously and are not to be construed as real. Although this book is set in the actual town of Creede, Colorado, and it is loosely based on Creede's wonderful repertory theater, changes were made to suit my story purposes. None of the characters are even loosely based on the staff, crew, volunteers, or actors that make the Creede Repertory Theatre such an extraordinary endeavor. Any additional resemblance to people living or dead, actual events, locales or organizations is entirely coincidental.

Dedication

To Pam Howell.
Thanks for being such a wonderful research-trip companion

Books by Leslie O'Kane

Life's Second Chances:
Going to Graceland
Women's Night Out
Finding Gregory Peck
By the Light of the Moon

Book Club Trilogy
How My Book Club Got Arrested

Molly Masters Mysteries:
Death Comes eCalling
Death Comes to Suburbia
Death of a Gardener
Death Comes to a Retreat
Death on a School Board
Death in a Talent Show
Death Comes to the PTA

Allie Babcock Mysteries:
Play Dead
Ruff Way to Go
Give the Dog a Bone
Woof at the Door
Of Birds and Beagles
Dog Drama (in July 2017)

Leslie Caine Domestic Bliss:
Death by Inferior Design
False Premises
Manor of Death
Killed by Clutter
Fatal Feng Shui
Poisoned by Gilt
Holly and Homicide
Two Funerals and a Wedding

Chapter 1

The scenery through the windshield of my boyfriend's Subaru was truly spectacular—golden-brown canyon walls, as steep and narrow as New York City high-rises, reaching up to a cloudless, deep blue sky. The late afternoon sun cast shadows on the brightly painted western-style shops and storefronts to either side of us.

"Here we are, Allie," Baxter told me. "Downtown Creede. The theatre is just at the top of the hill."

"What a cute little town," I said. "I'm a little annoyed at myself that I've lived in Colorado almost my entire life but have never been here before."

"It *is* pretty remote." Baxter gave my thigh a quick squeeze, and I scooted as close to him as my seatbelt would allow.

At age thirty-four, I had finally found my soulmate.

Though we'd been living and working together for over a year now, we both felt happiest and most productive when we were together, something that I hoped would last forever—

despite the inevitable fits and starts of any long-term relationship.

As we drove closer, the mountains' impressiveness increased. In Boulder, the Flatirons were a stunning backdrop. Here, the mountains so dwarfed the buildings, they seemed to be in the foreground. "From a bird's-eye view, this town must look like colorful dots within a mountain crevice." I paused, reassessing my statement. "That is, provided the bird was flying at extreme altitudes...an eagle, maybe."

"Or maybe a canary with a window seat in an airplane," Baxter quipped.

I laughed and managed to refrain from giving him a playful jab, not wanting to distract him from his driving.

We pulled into the dog-friendly hotel where he'd made our reservations. Dog-friendliness was going to be a lodging requirement for our foreseeable future. Baxter and I shared a passion for dogs. Our marvelous predilection was a blessing that had been handed down to us from generation to generation in both of our families.

My German Shepherd, Pavlov, hopped out of the Subaru. Baxter snapped her leash onto her collar and led her to an undoubtedly oft-tinkled-upon lodge-pole pine next to the parking lot. I grabbed our suitcase out of the trunk, along with my hip pack (which was technically a "fanny pack" but I always wore it on my right side). My little pack had become a staple during my work assignments. It contained treats, kibble, a clicker, scoop bags, and a small first-aid kit.

After I'd taken a couple of steps, Baxter traded me the suitcase for the leash and put his arm around my shoulders as we headed to the office door. His affectionate gesture chipped away the last of my restraint at exhibiting my joy. I took a couple of happy hops. "This is so much fun," I said.

Baxter chuckled.

"Not only do I get to spend a romantic week with you in the mountains," I continued, "but I *finally* get to work with a Border Collie. They're so darned smart and easy to train, this is the first time an owner has needed my services. Don't tell John this, but I'd have taken this gig for free."

"You've already given him tons of free hours these past few days."

"Yeah, but analyzing videos of your friend's stage-play, featuring a dog, is hardly a sacrifice. I've loved every minute."

"You *also* had to train Pavlov in stage acting." (My dog was perhaps going to be an understudy as I worked with the canine star of the play.)

"Also not a hardship. Besides, that will come in handy when I work with future clients. It didn't seem fair to charge John for something I probably already should have done with Pavlov." As a professional dog therapist, I'd been hired to help resolve an apparent case of severe stage-fright from the canine star of the show, John Morris's Border Collie. "In any case, he's paying me for a full forty-hour work week, plus expenses, even if I log fewer hours, so it should all come out in the wash."

"John's lucky to have you," Baxter said. "He even said so himself." He gave me a quick kiss on the forehead, then held open the door for me. My heart fluttered when our eyes met. I was head over heels for the man. To my never-ending amazement, he appeared to be equally smitten with me.

We checked into our room, which, as it turned out, the hotel owners—a friendly middle-aged couple—had dubbed the "John Wayne" room. The paneled walls were adorned with black-and-white studio photos and movie posters of the Duke, and they had a handful of his CDs stacked beside a plasma-screen television set with a CD player. The furniture was basic western—varnished- log bedposts and dresser legs, a green plaid bedspread, small nondescript nightstands.

"Huh," Baxter muttered. "The lady told me over the phone that they'd had a cancelation in John Wayne's room. I assumed some guy named John Wayne had cancelled his reservation."

"Is that why you didn't tell her I would have preferred an Audrey Hepburn room? Or a Lassie room?"

"Are you implying you won't be watching *Rio Grande* with me?" he asked, wiggling its CD case at me.

"Not unless Audrey Hepburn or Lassie costar." Pavlov raised her head and looked at me with her soulful eyes. "Better yet, Rin Tin Tin," I added, giving Pavlov a hug.

We set about unpacking and agreed we'd like to walk to the theater. After the eight-plus hour drive from our home in Dacona—twenty miles east of our office in Boulder—Pavlov, too, seemed to be eager to stretch. In anticipation of her perhaps having to fill in for John's dog in a performance or two this week, I had been training her in pedestal-and-target techniques. That was a highly regarded method for teaching dogs stunts on stage.

I grabbed my hip pack and my iPad. "I should have brought a dog whistle with me," I said. "I could have tested my theory during a rehearsal on stage."

"That someone in the audience is distracting Blue with a whistle, you mean?" (*Blue* was the name of the dog character in the play, as played by Flint, but after three days of training Pavlov to respond to "Blue" for the role, we had taken to using the names interchangeably.)

"Right. In the videos of the botched performances, Flint moves his head the same way Pavlov does when she hears an unexpected noise."

"Could be," Baxter said. "But didn't you say yesterday that they'd checked for you, and they haven't had any repeat customers for all four performances to date?"

"Right. But that doesn't mean it's not a group prank…teenagers passing around a dog whistle."

"Huh," he said, which meant that he'd heard me but was skeptical. I couldn't disagree. It *did* seem to be a stretch to think that a group of people would randomly decide to sabotage a theater production. Considering the Creede Playhouse was hosting the play's premier, what would motivate a batch of pranksters to focus in on this particular show from day one?

Baxter's friend, John Morris, had sent me links to his personal recordings of scenes in which his highly trained dog acted erratically on stage. Flint had been perfect in their many rehearsals, but in front of a packed house, he had ignored or forgotten his cues. My first question to John had been if he'd taken Flint to a vet for a thorough checkup, especially of his hearing and vision. He sent me a copy of the exam. The vet had run every test he could think of, but Flint had no physical problems whatsoever.

"All set?" Baxter asked as he and Pavlov stood by the open door waiting for me to lead the way. I didn't answer; the act of walking outside spoke for itself.

With Pavlov in perfect heel position at Baxter's side, Baxter took my hand and we laced our fingers. Pavlov had become thoroughly devoted to him, so much so that she was almost more his dog now than mine. On the other hand, his male KC Cavalier had compensated by making me the head of *his* pack.

"You haven't even mentioned how we left Ginger behind for the first time," Baxter said, all but reading my mind.

"Remarkable, isn't it? They're in good hands, though." My mother and her new husband were watching Ginger, *my* King Charles Cavalier, and my Cocker Spaniel—along with Baxter's Cavalier, and their own two dogs. It was quite a canine menagerie, but they had a huge yard and lived in the outskirts of Berthoud, in a rural area where no neighbors would object to a passel of dogs.

Ginger was gorgeous, with brown and white markings. She was not quite two years old. It made me smile just to think of her. Cavaliers are wonderful lap dogs. They epitomized the Charles Schultz saying: "Happiness is a warm puppy." If it was possible for a dog to have the perfect body temperature for sitting upon one's lap, *that* was the breed. Doppler, my seven-year old Cocker, did pretty well with the Cavaliers, largely because he enjoyed his moving up to the second in command in the canine portion of his pack. Pavlov was firmly number one.

We had told John—who was both the director and playwright—to expect us to arrive between four and four thirty. Having had short notice, we managed to leave our Boulder offices early this Sunday morning. We'd made good time and arrived at the Creede Repertory Theatre a few minutes before four.

John happened to be in the lobby as we entered. John and Baxter greeted each other with a semi-hug, semi-handshake. John was a nicc looking man, and he and Baxter had an immediate, easy rapport. After telling me that Flint was currently asleep on his dog bed on the second floor, John and Baxter made small talk about the rainy weather last month—May—at some lake they'd gone to last year. Baxter and I had attempted two camping-and-fishing overnight excursions. I wound up with poison oak at the first one and needing stitches in my neck at the second. (Let's just say that I'm *supremely* dreadful at casting the hook.) We'd agreed in the ER that, from then on, campouts were something Baxter would do with friends like John.

The walls of the lobby were covered with photographs and framed posters of past performances. Impressively, this little, remote theater had recently celebrated their fifty-year anniversary. What most captured my attention, however, was that every single poster for John's play had a red-and-white banner on it that read:

SOLD OUT. The posters themselves showed an adorable photograph of Flint—a black-and-white Border Collie—smiling as he gripped in his mouth a long-stem rose. The charming image perfectly befitted the name of John's play: *Good Dog, Blue!*

When their topic of conversation shifted to the business at hand, my interest perked up. The majority of dog owners tend to fib about their dog's misbehaviors. Few want to admit that *they* were the ones who instigated the phobias that their dogs now exhibited. For example, my dogs are trained to ignore dogs that we pass on sidewalks or paths. I can tell at a distance when owners have trained their dogs to be afraid of other dogs; they stop walking and grab their dogs. Then they further train their dogs to bark by calling out that their dogs aren't good with other dogs—which dogs interpret as their owner barking, so they follow suit. By the same token, it was possible that *John* was afraid of Flint performing in front of a large audience.

"So, yeah, like I told you guys," John said, meaning me and Baxter, "Flint is still spot-on during rehearsals, but has been tanking during the actual performances, every single time." All the enthusiasm had promptly drained from his voice.

"How did today's matinee go?" I asked.

He rolled his eyes. "Same old same old."

His frustration with what seemed to be a financial success confused me. "Do the 'sold-out' signs mean that only tonight's show is sold out?" I asked.

"No, the entire six-week run has sold out," he replied. "We're extending it another week, to try to accommodate the unexpected crowds. But, frankly, that's only due to my ingenuity. I wanted the actors to be prepared for anything...which is an unwritten rule of any and all live performances. All sorts of things can go wrong. Especially when you're working with dogs or children. So I wrote dozens of adlibbed lines for virtually each and every conceivable dog-related mishap."

I grinned. "You've practiced the art of feigning spontaneity on stage."

"Precisely." John rolled his eyes again. "The actors are prepared for poop, pee, whining, barking, puking, walking away, falling asleep on the stage, etcetera."

"Sounds good as far as it goes, but what about when *Flint* misbehaves?" I joked.

"Whoops!" He snapped his fingers, as if he'd had an epiphany. "So *that's* what I'm doing wrong!" His expression once again darkened. "That's another reason I wanted to be sure my play debuted right here, in my home town. All of the actors are practiced in the art of humorous improvisation. We have an audience-participation comedy show on weekends. It's called *Boomtown*. We're having a special kickoff show on Wednesday, though. You should attend, if you get the chance." He shifted his gaze to Baxter. "I'm hoping we can squeeze in a backpacking trip."

I fought away my mental image of Baxter climbing to a vertiginous cliff. (I have a fear of heights.) "John, why are you concerned about Flint—"

"*Good Dog, Blue!* is Standing Room Only because it's a relatively small theater," he said, cutting me off, "and it's funny. The cast jokes about whatever 'Blue' is doing on stage. The audience doesn't mind, because the play is being advertised as a not-to-miss event for dog lovers. Furthermore, all of the locals know Flint. That's what happens when you live in a town of, like, two hundred homes."

"But surely this has to be a huge success for a first-time production. It can't be all *that* critical to retrain Flint to respond correctly to his cues," I persisted. "The theater is selling out, and everyone's happy, right?"

"Not counting *me*." He put his hand on his chest for emphasis. "I wrote a really tight script that's hardly being used at all. It's like I've created a satirical sendup of my own creative endeavor. It's wrecking all of my aspirations for *Good Dog, Blue!* Plus, Flint is miserable. He's sensing that I'm not happy with his performance miscues."

"I see." In truth, having watched recorded scenes, I was skeptical about Flint being unhappy. The audience was roaring in the background. Furthermore, Flint had the bearing of a dog that is spot-on for his owner's expectations.

Baxter gave me a wink. He was keeping out of the conversation, perfectly willing to play second fiddle to me, despite his being much more knowledgeable about my client than I was.

"I want to take this show on the road," John continued. "Every producer and director of live theater is gun shy about putting dogs on stage...except for your basic 'how-cute-is-that' walk-on part for dogs. I wanted to create a show that flew in the face of that logic. My play is designed for herders...the most easily trained and reliable show dogs in the world."

"Oh, be serious, John," a woman someplace behind me scoffed.

I pivoted. A fortyish woman with a mid-length paisley dress and unkempt purple-streaked light-brown hair entered the lobby through a hallway to the right of the theater itself. "You see all kinds of breeds of dogs on TV in front of live audiences all the time." A Pug came trotting behind her and barked at us. Pavlov gave the little dog a wary look, but didn't return the barks. I suspected Pavlov felt superior. For one thing, the Pug was wearing a forest-green velvet dress with white lace around the collar.

"Felicity, this is Baxter and Allie, who are here to help coach Flint," John said, his voice and expression inscrutable.

"Hi, and welcome," she told me. "We've been expecting you." She smiled at Baxter. "Hi, Baxter."

"Hi, Felicity. Good to see you again." Baxter gave her a quick hug.

"Oh, right," John muttered. "You've met. Sorry."

Before I could put together when Baxter might have met her, Felicity won me over by beaming at Pavlov. "Wow! What a gorgeous Shepherd."

"This is Pavlov."

She held her palm out for Pavlov to sniff and asked, "May I pet her?"

"Absolutely."

While Felicity lavished attention on Pavlov and ignored her now-frantic-for-attention Pug, John told Felicity, "You're missing the point. Eddie on

Frazier had a studio audience, but it was *not* a live broadcast. The dog, Sandy, in *Annie*, is on stage for maybe two minutes. Yet *my* play is geared such that any herding show dog needs to treat four actors like four sheep. Since the actors all know their blocking and always hit their marks, it's like working with any other human actor on that stage."

"Except it isn't at *all* like working with a human actor, which is why you've had to hire a dog therapist." She picked up her dog, balancing him or her on one hip. (Come to think of it, considering the Pug's diminutive size and velvet dress, I was betting on female.)

"Only because someone is deliberately messing with my dog to prevent me from being successful," John countered.

Their bickering, along with Baxter and Felicity having met, reminded me that Baxter mentioned John used to have a longtime live-in girlfriend named Felicity.

"I hope you don't mean to imply that *I'm* the cause of Flint's problems," Felicity said.

"Why would I think that?" John retorted. "So that Pippa can take the lead, and we can make Flint the underdog? Or the understudy, if you prefer?"

"For heaven's sake, John," she scolded. "I'm just trying to be helpful. Casting a Pug to be bossing four adults around makes for a funnier visual." Her eyes darted from mine to Baxter's and back. "Allie, Baxter, you get what I'm saying, right?"

I did indeed get her point. But I could also see why John would prefer a Border Collie in the role.

And, regardless, I could safely assume *any* playwright would want all actors—human and otherwise—to perform the scenes he or she had created precisely as written.

Baxter simply shrugged. Both John and Felicity were watching me, awaiting my reply. "Is this Pippa?" I asked, grinning at the Pug.

"Yes, it is," Felicity answered, in somewhat baby-talking tones as she treated Pippa to an ear rub. "Isn't she absolutely adorable?"

"She sure is." Pugs were known as one of the natural clowns of the canine world. They are happy, friendly, amiable—and typically stubborn as a mule. Just then, Pippa started making a series of snorts and grunts, which was a side-effect of their breeding for that short face of theirs—a compromised respiratory system. "But as cute as your dog would be, bossing the actors on stage around, I can see why the role was designed for a breed with strong herding instincts."

"Exactly, Allie," John said. He snuck in a rather triumphant grin at his ex. "My play is a romantic comedy that's something of a *Parent Trap* from the Disney movie scenario, with 'Blue' serving the same purpose as Haley Mills' character. You know what I mean?"

"Yes. I saw the remake with Lindsay Lohan...playing twins," I replied. Not to mention having seen several scenes of his play that gave me the gist of John's creation.

"Right. Like the twins, Blue is trying to repair the rifts between his original owners, and to drive away the new love interests that each of his owners now have."

"All the action is comprised of three acts at three cocktail parties," Felicity continued, "which are held at the dog's two homes, now that the owners are divorced. The dog herds and/or separates the actors on the stage, according to the needs of the script. John has been advertising his play as being easily produced with *any* well-trained dog in the role."

"The operative word being 'well-trained," John said. "Hence the need to borrow your dog, Pavlov." He cast a look of disdain in Pippa's direction. "Our understudy isn't cutting it. Plus I should have said any medium to large dog can play the role. The actors could step right over the Pug."

"Which is why she was so cute in the role," Felicity said, crossing her arms.

"Pippa is incorrigible. Opening night was a disaster with Flint, but it was even worse with Pippa the second night. Both times the actors had to follow my pseudo-adlib-emergency plan." He paused. "It's time you met my dog." He winked at me. "Come, Flint," he called.

We heard the pitter-patter of paws trotting down an unseen flight of stairs.

John's remarkable dog trotted around the corner. "Uh, oh," I muttered as my heart all but skipped a beat. He was black and white with the signature thick coat and pointy ears. And his eyes! They were a brilliant blue. He focused those stunning baby blues on me, and it was love at first sight.

"This is Flint," John said, "and this is Allie. She's going to get you over your acting hurdles."

"Hi, Flint. You're one handsome dog." I let Flint sniff my fist, which is safer for me and less threatening for him, then greeted him side-by-side, also less threatening to dogs. I petted his shoulder. Pavlov was watching him warily. She'd seen me with so many canine clients that, as long as a strange dog didn't act aggressively toward me, she would not act aggressively to the dog.

"More to the point," John said, "he's an impeccably trained dog." He bent down and gave Flint a rather awkward pat on the head. "Let's show this dog expert what you can do, okay boy?" He then asked me if I'd mind putting Pavlov at a distance from Baxter and me. I had her lie down, then we moved several steps away from her. John pointed at Baxter and me. "Blue, separate."

Flint trotted toward us and squeezed between us. He kept pushing against us until he had room to turn around, then he sat down and looked at John. (No lie, it was cute as all get-out.) "Blue," John said, pointing at Baxter, then Felicity, and back at Baxter, "join."

"Hey," Felicity objected. "I'm holding Pippa."

"Set her down," John said.

Once again, Flint made short work of the command, pushing into Baxter's and Felicity's knees until they were standing beside each other, both laughing at how persistent and successful he'd been. Pippa, meanwhile, was barking nonstop, but Flint paid her no mind.

I clapped. "Bravo, Flint! You're amazing." Then I called Pavlov to come and gave her a treat. No sense making her jealous, after all.

"And adorable," Baxter said. He gave Felicity a pat on the shoulder. "Sorry, Felicity, but I for one would happily pay theater prices to watch Flint do that on stage."

"No worries," she said, "so would I. But I'd *also* rather watch Pippa than Flint *fail* at doing that on stage."

John gave her an annoyingly smug grin. "Allida here is a dog whisperer of sorts. I'm sure she'll have all of these dog issues resolved in no time."

I gave him an exaggerated grimace. "Nothing like starting work under pressure."

"I'm sure you can deliver the goods, Allie. My buddy Baxter would never steer me the wrong way. Would you, bro?"

"Never," Baxter echoed and winked at me with a big smile on his face.

I tried to return the smile, but in truth, my pulse rate was rising. I'd made a joke out of it just now, but John had just now ignored my caveats when I accepted this job. I had warned him that it could take me quite a while to get to the bottom of Flint's troubles. Meanwhile, the dog was even better trained than I'd imagined. I had absolutely no idea why he was messing up in front of an audience, and I was being very well-paid to come up with the solution.

My reputation and self-image were at stake. The curtain would be rising for tonight's performance in some three hours.

Chapter 2

"I'll abide by your decision on putting either Pavlov or Flint on stage tonight," John told me. "But the last thing I want is one more performance with Flint losing all of his training the moment he sets foot on the stage. From my own experience as an actor, the more times you repeat a miscue, the harder it is to correct the next time you're on stage. So I'd prefer we use Pavlov. But it's your call."

Neither choice appealed. Pavlov with no rehearsals, versus more-ingrained mistakenness for Flint. The latter would only be worthwhile if my being present helped me observe something I'd missed on the videos.

"Allie told me she suspects someone in the audience was blowing a dog whistle," Baxter interjected.

"I couldn't be certain," I added, "but Flint moved his head and took a step toward the same side of the theater at the start of his foul ups. So, I think the first thing we should try is having Pavlov backstage with Baxter monitoring her behavior while Flint's on stage. Both dogs will react to a dog whistle."

"And meanwhile, Allie can be keeping an eye on the audience," Baxter said.

We exchanged smiles. He was already doing a great job as my assistant. Baxter had his own dog-related business that was going strong. He designed and sold customized doghouses that doubled as outer-shells for dog crates. One design—his "Snoopy Dog Home"—was so popular, thanks in part to a friend of ours, he'd gotten a Trademark and was mass-producing it. Viewed from the side, Baxter's design looked identical to the *Peanuts* drawing. Viewed from the front—which the actual Snoopy doghouse never was—small, protruding ledges along the bottom of the roof were perfectly sized for small dogs paws, and the top of the doghouse featured a flat surface, with a waterproof pillow affixed. A Beagle-owning friend of ours had an enormous following in social-media. Photos of her Beagle, lying supine on his Snoopy Dog Home, had gone viral.

"Sounds good," John eventually replied, albeit with no enthusiasm.

"You're giving Flint his commands via a wireless one-way device, with a tiny speaker near his ear, right?" I asked.

"Right. I've been giving him the commands myself. I'm also an understudy for either of the two male roles. I have a printed script that I can give to Felicity or Valerie, the theater manager, if I need to be on stage. So far that hasn't been necessary."

"And you trained Flint to differentiate and interact with the actors on stage according to their costumes, I assume? So he won't get confused by an understudy taking over a role of his former owner?"

"Right."

"Have they been rehearsing with their costumes since day one?"

"Kind of," Felicity answered for him. "I decided on the fabric for the foursome's clothing, and they draped or pinned on the fabric during rehearsal. Once costumes were made, they'd wear at least one item. We've maintained that policy when the understudies rehearse."

"Is there a difference in the scent of the costumes between rehearsals and actual performances?"

"There *shouldn't* be," Felicity said. "Costumes have to be washed every single night after the performances. We wondered about their scent after opening night, so I took over the laundry duties myself. It made no difference whatsoever. Flint was just as boggled the next performance."

"To test the issue farther," John said, "we added a dress rehearsal prior to the third performance and didn't wash the costumes in between. Flint was spot on for the stage rehearsal. An hour later, he was a disaster. It was as if we'd pulled some clueless Border Collie off the street."

"Could it be stage fright?" I asked. "Could he simply be distracted by all the sounds and smells of a full audience?"

He sighed and lifted his arms as if in defeat. "Who knows? If so, maybe after a couple more performances, he'll snap out of it. But he's used to performing in front of audiences. He's an old hand at herding competitions. At the Denver Stock Show, he had all kinds of distractions. Albeit, he was working with sheep, not people, and in an arena, not a theater."

I caught Felicity glaring at John. He raised his eyebrow in reply. There seemed to be some unpleasant nonverbal communication between the two, but I didn't know how to ask about it politely, and merely hoped it had nothing to do with Flint's woes.

"It was nice meeting you," Felicity said. She slapped her thigh, and Pippa came toward her. "My Pugster and I need to get back to work."

I replied that it was nice meeting her, too, and waited until I could assume she was out of hearing range. "Sorry to ask a personal question, but you and Felicity used to live together along with Flint, right?"

His brow furrowed, and I held up a hand in apology. "Dogs often misbehave when there is a significant change to the members of their packs."

John grimaced. "Felicity and I broke up a couple of months ago."

"Are you dating someone new?"

"Um, yeah. But I doubt—" He cleared his throat. "I started seeing one of my two lead actresses. And we've really hit it off. So, geez, I don't know. I mean, yeah, it's crossed my mind as problematic, since Sally moving in with us and Flint barking at her on stage was more or less simultaneous. But Sally's crazy about Flint"

"That's ironic," Baxter said, echoing my thoughts.

"Flint could be basically acting out the very issues that 'Blue' in the play is experiencing," I told John. "He could be trying to keep Sally away from *you*."

John grimaced. "I hope not. He treats her just fine offstage and doesn't try to separate us. It'd be so much better if it was just some punk kid who's maybe passing along his dog whistle to his buddies at each performance."

"More likely it's a dog squeaky toy with a dog whistle in it," Baxter noted. "Squeezing a small toy would be easier to do surreptitiously than blowing a whistle." In addition to his doghouse/crate business, he also managed pet shows and events. He'd become familiar with every dog gadget on the market.

Flint sat up abruptly and stared at the front door.

A pretty, petite young blonde entered the theater, closely followed by a tall—if slightly paunchy—man. John's attention went directly to the woman. His face lit up. "Sally! Hi! We were just talking about you," he cried.

"How flattering. I was just thinking about you." She walked up to John and gave him a quick kiss. I studied Flint for his reaction. He gave none. No ears turning backward. No move to get up and intervene, as if to assert his placement as John's second-in-command. He was content to stay his ground and wait for Sally to come to him. I *so* admired dogs like Flint. They were such a credit to dog-kind. Even though he was now trained to "herd" Sally, he knew he wasn't on duty.

"Yeesh. Young love. Clogs the arteries." The man said, interrupting my thought pattern. He gave me a visual once-over. "We came over to meet our Wonder-dog fixer-upper."

"Hi. I'm Allie Babcock." I'd never been called a "wonder-dog fixer-upper." It sounded like a description for someone on a reality TV show.

"I'm late with introductions," John said. "This is Sally Johnson. Sally, Allie Babcock. Allie, Sally." John chuckled. He seemed almost giddy.

"I'm Hammond Davis," the man said, grabbing the reins. "Feel free to call me Hammie. My nickname, of course, proves that my parents knew from the very start they were raising an actor."

"Ah," I said, which, while meaningless, was better than voicing my thoughts. He struck me as possessing the "aren't I ever-so-charming" personality type that I disliked. That was probably highly useful for the stage, however, especially with those leading-man looks of his.

I returned Baxter's grin, realizing that he was reading my mind. Now *there* was a gorgeous man, if you ask me. I was so crazy about him, I would have thought of him as gorgeous regardless of his physical appearance—which, by the way, was sexy as can be. He's got a long, lean cyclist's build, adorable dimples, and sparkling blue eyes, with so many cowlicks in his light brown hair, he has a constant case of bed-head.

John introduced Baxter and made small talk. Hammond gave me a wry grin and said, "You're awfully quiet. Cat got your tongue?"

I forced a smile. "I'm on the clock. I'm here to observe."

"Come here, Flint," Sally said. The dog rose and came over to her. She gave him a big hug around the chest, which the dog accepted without complaint. That was a no-no for some dogs. From a canine perspective, she was signaling her dominance over him. "You are such a good boy," she cooed, in an accurate appraisal.

"Say, John, I have an idea," Hammond said. "Since Allie here is on the clock and busily *observing*, shouldn't we call Karen and Greg, and let her watch a live re-enactment of the first scene...sans costumes?" Hammond turned to Sally. "Would that be okay with you, my dear?"

"By all means. On matinee days, we can't really unwind, anyway. I think it's a great idea, if Allie's up for it."

"I *definitely* am, if the cast is," I replied, noticing that Sally and Hammond had failed to consult with John, the director.

"Allie will be able to see the scene as the author originally intended." Hammond paused and rocked on his heels, "As well as how *John* intended." He laughed and then winked at John. "Just pulling your leg, Captain."

Captain? Maybe John had military training I didn't know about. Or owned a boat.

"Allie's already seen the video of our first dress rehearsal," John retorted, his voice a semi-modified growl.

"Even so, it would be really helpful to me, John. I actually brought a recording of a restless audience with me, which I can play at full volume. It's on a ten-minute loop. I use it when I'm preparing dogs for shows. I can call that up on my phone and play it, and so on."

"We should get into some of our costumes and try to get someone to work the lights," Sally said. "Don't you think?" She looked at me.

"Sure," I said. "The more closely we duplicate tonight's performance, the better." My heart still seemed to be beating too fast. I took a deep breath and released it. Maybe I'd failed to admit to myself how anxious I truly was about this assignment. Then again, we'd been standing here in the lobby for a long time, and John hadn't thought to suggest that we go sit someplace, or to give us a tour of the building.

"Have you seen Sam around?" Sally asked John. Then she turned to me. "That's our stagehand-slash-crew manager who does all the lighting and sound and so forth for this show."

Judging by their season schedule, the Creede Repertory Playhouse was essentially a summer-stock theater that ran from late May through the end of September. Several shows were presented each season on their two stages, using actors in different productions at the same time. John's play was their headliner for the first half of the season.

"Does Sam just work on this one show?" I asked.

"Yeah, well, sort of," John said. "He's the muscle for changing the sets between performances, but he's also the jack-of-all-trades on my show. Kind of got him hired as a favor. I knew his brother."

"Sam charged out of here the moment the matinee curtains dropped," Hammond said. "He's probably three sheets to the wind by now," he added under his breath.

Sally gave Hammond a glare, but then cheerfully made a couple of calls and coaxed the other two lead actors in John's play to join us. Meanwhile, John ushered me down a narrow hallway to meet Valerie Devereux, the manager of the Creede Repertory Theatre.

"Here's the full scoop, Allie," he said quietly as we walked side by side. "There was a producer from a theater in Boston here for Wednesday's performance. He gave me a thumbs down. That's when I realized Flint's situation was urgent."

"I'm so sorry."

"So am I." He rolled his eyes. "He said it wasn't professional enough. That it was amateur hour, with all the gaffes." He forced a small smile. We stopped walking. "Valerie's expecting you. I'm sure she'll be in her office." John knocked on a cheap-looking door.

"Yep?" came a woman's muffled voice.

John winced. "When she says 'yep,'" he whispered, "she's in a bad mood. Give me a minute, okay?"

I nodded and gestured for him to go ahead, and he entered the room. "Hi, Valerie," he said, then shut the door behind him.

"The producer from Boston turned us down flat," John told her. The walls were so thin, I could hear him clearly.

"I'm sorry," Valerie said.

"*Are* you?" John snapped. "You'd never know it. You haven't put anything behind me and this play. I've been doing it all on my own. If I didn't know better, I'd think that you were trying to make it fail."

"That's not fair, and you know it," she retorted.

"Do I? Tell me how exactly you've had my back since I brought my work to life here?"

"I'm the one who put it on the schedule," Valerie said. "I'm the one who risked her career and the viability of this theater to stage this thing. Even though I knew full well what a risk a play that revolves around a dog is."

"And every action you've made since then is to bet against its success. You wouldn't give me a good reference when I needed it. You haven't said a kind word to the press. We've succeeded in spite of you."

"I've had just about enough of—"

Thinking nothing could be more awkward than listening to this argument, I knocked on the door.

After a pause came Valerie's, "Yep?"

I opened the door and leaned in. A thirty-something woman with light brown hair in an attractive bun was seated at a well-worn teacher-style wooden desk, with John standing in front of the desk, arms akimbo. "Excuse me, but I can hear every word you're saying, and I'm wondering if I could just reschedule our meeting for tomorrow."

"I'm so sorry," Valerie said, wearing that type of smile that makes it ultra-obvious she was angry with the other party in the room. "We were hashing out some things that...well, that aren't appropriate for public discussion."

"I didn't realize the walls were so thin," John muttered under his breath.

"My fault. I forgot you were coming," Valerie said, rising, with just the slightest edgy look at John.

"Valerie Devereux, this is Allie Babcock. Allie, Valerie."

We shook hands.

"Valerie is my boss, the manager of the Creede Theatre. We have some differences of opinion, as I'm sure you've gathered."

"That's what happens with group endeavors," I said.

"You can say that again," Valerie replied. "Were you in a drama club in school?" she asked.

"No. I was too busy playing basketball in high school and college to take part in theater productions. Sports teams have their fair share of disagreements, too."

"There's no 'I' in teamwork or in theater, but there sure are plenty of egos in both," Valerie rejoined.

If anything, this conversation was growing even more awkward.

"I just wanted to say hello and to thank you for hiring me, Valerie. I'll let you get back to work. The actors are going to assemble so I can see the first scene or two of the play."

"Splendid," Valerie, said. "I'll join you in a couple of minutes and work the electrical controls, and make noise from the seats."

"That's nice of you, Valerie. Thank you."

"Also unnecessary," John grumbled, "if Sam was doing his job right."

Not wanting to overhear more arguing, I practically raced off the instant I'd shut the door behind me. Flint could be hearing the staff here bickering over him every day. That wasn't conducive to good performances. It also wasn't good for my nerves.

I rejoined Baxter and the three of us entered the theater. Judging from the alphabetical lettering of the seat rows, they had over two hundred seats. I noted that they had a balcony as well, so somewhere around 250, upholstered in red velvet. We took seats in the center of the fourth row, and Pavlov lay down at Baxter's feet. There was one main aisle between seats; there were only four seats in the row to the left of the aisle, which led to short, four-step stairs onto the stage. There were curtains on either side of the three-wall set, which was an elegantly appointed living room. I could see that the curtains were angled such that Flint's trainer during the show could see the stage, yet be blocked from view by the audience. The setup would make it hard for me to watch more than a handful of seats, however. Someone sitting in the rafters above the stage could probably see the entire audience.

I told Baxter that we needed to recalculate which of us would spy on the audience. "You'll have to find a cat-bird's seat above the stage."

"No problem," he said.

I thoroughly enjoy live theater. John's play had a lot of energy and a good heart. It was an honor to know that I was going to be helping Baxter's friend with his production. As John himself had noted, a listing on my resume that I'd helped train the original *Good Dog, Blue*, would be impressive.

John nervously paced between the front of the stage and the first row of seats while we waited for the cast to enter.

"You're wearing a rut in the floor," Baxter told him.

John raked his fingers through his hair and looked at us. He gave Baxter a patient smile. "Seriously, guys, this represents more than two full years of my life. That's how long it took me to hone the script, as well as Blue's behavior—how Blue manages to wag his tail into the cocktails."

"'His cocked tail is in my cocktail,' I quoted. "I remember that pun well. It can't be used on a dog with a docked tail."

"Nor on a Pug's tail, for that matter. Although I rework the line for Pippa and had Pippa lick the glass. That was the one thing she did well. I put a smear of chicken baby food on the outside of the glass. She loves that stuff. We had to work around all kinds of things when Pippa was starring." He rolled his eyes. "Trust me," he said sotto voce, "Pippa will never make a suitable understudy."

A woman who—thanks to the videos and John's notes—I recognized as Karen Abbott, the second female lead, was approaching from the stage. She had black hair and was slightly pudgy. "Sorry to interrupt, John. My lemon water seems to have gone missing. Did I leave it on the floor of the second row of seats?"

He glanced at either side of us. "No, sorry," he said. "Did you check the fridge?"

"Of course I did. That's where I always put it."

Our eyes met. She gave me a big smile and came to the very front of the stage. "Hi, I'm Karen Abbott. You must be Allie and Baxter, the dog experts. Are we ever glad to see you!"

"Thanks," I answered. "I'm really hoping we can help."

"I'm confident you can. Your credentials precede you." Her eyes widened. "The restroom," she said, snapping her fingers. She met my gaze again and chuckled. "Sorry. I just remembered where I left my lemon water. Again, so glad you're here." She gave a friendly wave and disappeared behind the curtain, stage left.

"I hope my *credentials* aren't overselling me," I muttered to Baxter. He was watching John pace and didn't seem to hear me.

"Speaking of the Pug, I've got to tell you, John," Baxter said, chuckling, "I watched the one short video you sent us with Pippa in the role. I laughed my ass off at the pratfall when Hammond's dog-hater girlfriend kept leaning back in her chair to escape the dog licking her face. That's one big plus for having a little dog in the role."

I heard footsteps behind us. Valerie, who I now saw was wearing a Halloweenish floor-length orange skirt to go with her black top, was heading down the aisle.

I returned my attention to John. "Did you put baby food on Sally's face, too?"

"Yeah," he told me, then gazed at Baxter. "That fall is much riskier for poor Sally, though, than if she just gets a furry tail in her drink."

"Not to mention the risk to *Pippa*," Valerie said, "if she somehow winds up behind the chair while Sally's tipping it back.

"It didn't strike you as too slapstick?" John asked me.

I grinned. "I'm not usually a big fan of physical comedy, but I'm with Baxter on this one. I thought it was hilarious when she managed to keep her martini from spilling when the chair tipped over. And how, when Bluc kept licking her face, she deliberately dumped it on her face to kill the dog germs."

"With her feet sticking up in the air the whole time," Baxter added, laughing.

John chuckled as well. "That was all Sally. She can be a regular Lucille Ball. She has impeccable comedic timing."

Valerie, too, was laughing. "That was my favorite visual," she said. "Sally and Pippa stole the show." She grinned at me and said, "Allida, we never set up a time for our next meeting. Let's chat sometime early Tuesday morning, shall we?"

Apparently she wasn't willing to lose any of her day off; the Creede Playhouse, in keeping with tradition, was dark on Mondays. "Sure thing. Eight a.m.?"

"Good God, no. We're theater people. Early morning for us is ten a.m."

"In that case, ten a.m.?"

"Perfect." Her phone rang. "Sam?" she said into her phone, holding up her index finger to us, "are you on your way?" After listening, she said, "Yep," then hung up.

Valerie turned to me, "In case this has anything to do with Flint's problems on stage, Hammie and Sally were once engaged, not that long ago."

"Long enough," John said.

"That's how I got Hammie to commit to John's play," Valerie said. "I told him I had signed Sally Johnson, and he immediately signed on, as well."

"Right." John's eyes flashed as he looked at me. "More importantly, Valerie insisted that I cast Greg Gulligan in my play, and they went to high school together in Alamosa."

"That's true. We were friends and interned in the Creede Playhouse our junior and senior years."

"Yeah, that was a long time ago," an exceptionally nice-looking man with blond hair said, as he and Karen walked onto the set. "Greg Gullivan," he said. I introduced myself and Baxter.

His eyes flashed as he looked at me.

Sally leaned out from behind the curtain. "We're ready if you are," she said.

Valerie excused herself to "work the board," I think she said.

The opening scene began. I found it enchanting. Sally, indeed, struck me as a young star. She radiated a joy for life. Even though she played a germophobe totally creeped out by dogs, her character was immensely likable.

Frankly, I found it much less believable that Hammond was the dog lover his role demanded. Maybe it was just my particular sensitivities, but he seemed to be acting when he hugged "Blue." In contrast, it was utterly believable that Blue was completely correct to recognize that Karen—his character's first wife—had been his true soulmate. The two seemed to be meant for each other

Gregory Gulligan, frankly, was the weak link in the play. By a wide measure. His movements were stiff, and he didn't seem to have the connection and spark of his three fellow actors. Meanwhile, Flint was sheer perfection. With John sitting close to me, I could hear his instructions. Even so, Flint's reactions on stage seemed to be more natural than Greg's. Flint was always engaged, watching their eyes. The way he herded Sally farther away from Hammond every time Hammond's back was turned made Baxter and me laugh, even though I was trying to concentrate on John's verbal cues.

Some twenty minutes later, the scenes ended.

"So, what did you think?" John asked.

"As you'd said," I answered, "Flint was spot on throughout. He is absolutely amazing to watch."

"But what did you think of *me*," Hammond said, striking a comical pose with his fingers laced under his chin and batting his eyes at me.

"You were all excellent," I said, ignoring the fact that Greg had merely been pretty good. "I liked all five of you."

"You heard that, didn't you, Hammond?" Sally asked, crossing her arms and glaring at her ex. "Counting the dog, four other actors were on stage with you. Just in case you forgot."

"I do indeed remember," Hammond said. "We keep hearing talk of *you* being the next Lucille Ball. I'm simply trying to spread the butter on all of our buns."

"What does that even mean?" Sally asked. "It's a good thing you're an actor, not the playwright."

"Let's not argue, for once," Karen said. She gave Greg a small smile. "At least Greg and I don't bicker all the time."

You're my Best Friend Forever," he said in a Donald Duck voice, breaking the tension.

"Allie? Have you got everything you need from us two-legged actors for now?" Karen asked.

"I think so. Thanks. I'll see you all tonight." I rose. "Let me try working with Flint a little now." Once the scene ended, he'd taken it upon himself to lie down on his dog bed on stage, waiting patiently.

The actors started to leave the stage. "Did you find your lemon water, Karen?" Sally asked.

"I sure did. It was so stupid of me. I'd left it—"

Just then, a large, black metal beam supporting several lights crashed to the floor. Sally screamed at the sight. Flint yelped and leapt out of the way.

Chapter 3

All four actors had turned and were now staring at the debris on the stage in stunned silence. Nobody had been hurt. Flint had been the closest to the lights. He fled to the farthest corner of the stage, where he peed and trembled in fear.

John and Baxter both rushed to the stage, vaulting over the rows of seats and jumping onto the stage.

Like Flint, Pavlov, too, was shaken. She was now standing in a crouched, attack pose, barking and growling at the fallen lights. I said her name and offered reassuring words in a calm voice. Even as much as I trusted Pavlov, I moved toward her slowly. Any badly frightened dog is prone to snapping.

The stunned silence had quickly changed into angry exclamations. Valerie was running down the aisle toward the stage, cursing and then crying, "Is everyone okay? Anyone hit by broken glass?"

"No, though I'm not sure if I'm on the verge of a heart attack," Hammond said. "That damned thing just missed me!"

Valerie dashed down the aisle and up the stairs of the stage. Baxter had begun looking at the assemblage of broken glass from the lights. John had plopped down on the stage and pulled Flint onto his lap.

"How did this happen!?" Valerie looked and sounded fit to be tied. "How did a heavy light fixture fall onto the stage?"

Baxter had been visually scanning the stage floor as well as the lights from all angles. "There's one sheared bolt in the center that must have been holding up the entire heavy fixture. The full assembly is missing four nuts and bolts," he told her.

She grabbed her head. "Dear Lord. Somebody could have been killed! On *my* watch! This is utterly unacceptable!"

"It had to have been Sam, or one of his crew members," John said. He was rocking Flint on his lap and feeding him treats. "I made a mistake insisting you hire him."

A pair of stunned young men dashed onto the stage, followed by Felicity and Pippa. Her dog was barking at the fallen lights. It was unhelpful, but born from the same automatic startle mechanism that caused everyone else's alarm and raised voices.

"Cancel tonight's performance," Greg said to Valerie. "If this had happened a few minutes earlier, we all could have been killed. All four of us had been standing front center stage."

With her hands on her hips, Valerie was eyeing the two young men who'd rushed onto stage. "Who was in charge of maintaining the lights?"

The startled young men both cried, "Not me," simultaneously. A third man stepped onto the stage behind them.

"Sam!" Valerie cried at the short, stocky man in his forties or so. "Is this your responsibility? Have you done safety checks on the lights?"

"You told me I *couldn't*. Remember? We wanted to move the lights back a couple of feet last month. That electrician you hired did the work, the same week as when I came on board. If he forgot to fasten all the nuts but one, it sure as hell wasn't *my* fault."

"Valerie, you need to get the numbskull electrician back here and answer to me," Hammond exclaimed. "I have high blood pressure. I could have had a heart attack!"

"We all could have gotten taken out," Greg said again.

"Not unless you'd all been holding hands, precisely under the metal beam," Sam said.

"Such a distinct lack of empathy you have for your fellow man, Mr. Geller," Hammond told him, snidely. "And *you* aren't even a self-absorbed actor like me. What's your excuse?"

"The important thing is: nobody got hurt," Valerie said.

"The *second*-most important thing is that nothing like this ever happens again," John said. He glared at the three crew members. "I've seen all three of you up in the rafters one time or another. Someone must have loosened the screws...bolts...whatever. Unless the electrician that worked here last month was a total moron."

"It's a really solid bolt, though," one of the young crewmembers said. "It could have been like this since it was first installed. Maybe the electrician figured it was up to code."

"No qualified elec—"

"Look," Sam said, interrupting John. "Truth of the matter is the buck stops here. Bob and Jim work under me. It was ultimately my responsibility. If you want to fire me, go ahead. But I can also point out that nobody was scheduled to rehearse at this particular time. This *should* have happened on an empty stage." He gestured at the rafters. "You can see for yourself that nobody's up there now with a crescent wrench."

"That's true," Valerie said, her voice much calmer.

"You could get the sheriff out here to investigate," Sam said to her. "If you want to take fingerprints to see if there are prints on the nut."

"I'd need to get evidence from the *missing* nuts," she muttered. "And it's not like the electrician is going to cop to having found four nuts and bolts in his toolbox after leaving the theater."

"So you want me and my crew to get new lights installed?" Sam asked. "Even though none of us are licensed electricians? Cuz' that's the only way you're putting on a second show tonight."

"What do you think, John?" Valerie asked.

"You're the boss," he grumbled.

"I don't know what to do. But we definitely can't reschedule," Valerie said. "I guess we'll have to just replace the lights and carry on. If I'd been on the stage, I'd have passed out with fright. If anybody wants to bow out, I'll understand. We'll bring in the understudies."

John had risen and told Flint to lie down and stay. He was pacing with his fists clenched. "There's no way *Flint's* going on stage. Not under any circumstance. Not tonight."

All eyes turned to me and Pavlov. "We'll have to give Pavlov a shot, but we'll have to rehearse with her from now 'til curtain-time. She hasn't rehearsed on this or any other stage even once."

"Let's just take care of this right now," Sam said. "I'll get this rewired and functional." He looked at Valerie and grimaced. "I told you we should have updated the light fixtures."

"There's a big difference between saying something's out of date versus potentially lethal," Valerie retorted.

"Folks, you're all going to be working with Pavlov playing Blue tonight," John said.

I glanced over at Felicity and Pippa. Felicity was frowning and I think she would have much preferred getting to see her dog in the role again.

"Are you sure it wouldn't be better to try Pippa, John?" I asked. "Pavlov's never worked with the actual actors. All we've done is train her to understand the commands she'll be given. But she was in her own backyard, and Baxter and I were playing two roles at once, along with a couple of dummies we made out of two coats, stuffed with pillows."

"Perfect. Sally's always called me a stuffed shirt," Hammond quipped.

"I'm certain the *dummies* didn't try to eat the scenery," Sally rejoined.

"Pavlov will do fine," John said. "If she can hit her marks...or targets, as you call them, she can't possibly be worse than Pippa was on night two."

"Pippa brought the house down on night two," Felicity stated.

"And *Sam* just now brought the lights down on top of Flint. This is *my* play we're performing. *I'm* the director. Does anybody here have a problem with that?"

An uncomfortable silence ensued. "Aye, aye, Captain," Hammond said.

John's and my gazes met. "We'll get...an usher, a ticket taker, or whoever else we can find to rehearse the roles with you," he said. "I'm taking Flint home, and I'll be back as soon as I can. Certainly in plenty of time for tonight's show."

Baxter and I exchanged glances.

"Okay," I said. "As long as nothing else is going to fall from the rafters, we'll get Pavlov to do the best she can under the circumstances."

"Right," Baxter said. "If the audience is told in advance that Blue is played by an understudy, it will be fine."

"They will be," Valerie said. "I'll type up an insert for the programs and state openly that the part of Blue will be performed by Pavlov after an unexpected mishap."

"Good," John said. "Just be sure and tell the audience that Flint is fine and will resume his role on Tuesday." He shifted his gaze to me. "The theater is dark tomorrow. We don't put on shows on Mondays."

I nodded, already well aware of the tradition. Flint was still panting. I saw that he was also shedding. He was still in a state of duress.

"I do have quite a bit of experience in calming traumatized dogs, John. Are you sure you don't want to have *Baxter* train Pavlov for tonight's performance and have me work with Flint for a while? If Sam and crew can get everything cleaned up and functional again, we might still have time to check to see if Flint can handle being on the stage."

John looked down at Flint. He shook his head. "I want be with him when he's freaked out like this."

"Of course you do. I meant that the three of us should leave the building, then refocus his attention to something he excels at, such as a game of fetch. That will help him get his bearing."

"Then who's going to give *Pavlov* her instructions during the makeshift rehearsal?"

"Baxter," I repeated.

"Pavlov does well with me training him," Baxter said reassuringly.

"We'll help," Sally said. "Karen? Gentlemen? Anybody willing to help the show go on by rehearsing with our new understudy?"

"You all need to clear the stage," Sam said, already motioning at Karen and Greg to head for an exit. "I can't have anybody walking below us. Last thing we need now is to boink a wrench off one of y'all's heads."

"We can move the rehearsal upstairs," Karen said.

"Geez." Greg grumbled, "We already gave up a chunk of our afternoon to do an extra scene. Now we're supposed to work all evening and top it off with a second performance?"

"I'll pay all of you for your rehearsal as if this was an additional performance," Valerie said.

"That's very generous of you, Valerie," Karen said.

"I'm in, obviously," Sally said. Greg thanked Valerie and said he'd just need a couple of minutes to clear his schedule. Hammond threw in a: "Me, too."

"I hope this decision doesn't backfire," Baxter said. "Pavlov was traumatized, too. We're asking a lot of her. And you're the one who knows how to work with her."

I squeezed his arm. "Pavlov works just as well with you as with me. You just need to remind her to hit her targets."

"I just don't think this is going to work for either dog." John looked thoroughly rattled. "I don't think we'll get Flint to want to ever be on that stage again."

"Let's see how he does after I work with him. We have all day tomorrow and most of Tuesday to get him confident on this stage once again."

"Okay. If you say so." He turned his attention to Baxter and pointed at the spot where he had been cradling Flint. "I left my headset and Flint's clip-on speaker over there, by the flat. Felicity can show you how to hook it up. We also have a backup set, in case it breaks. The script's on the front-row seat where I was sitting."

So they had two *headsets for transmitting commands to Flint.* That was another thing that I wondered about. Someone might simply be hijacking the verbal radio signals John was using.

John joined Flint. "I'll meet you backstage, Allie," John said. "C'mon, Flint," I watched them walk away. Baxter, meanwhile, hopped down from the stage and joined Pavlov and me in the aisle.

"Sorry you're taking the yeoman's duty," I said to Baxter. "I'll get back here as soon as I can. Probably only in an hour. Flint's already stopped shaking."

"No worries." He told Pavlov to come, and she promptly obeyed. "We'll get right to work. Won't we, girl?" he said to her. She wagged her tail.

I found John's script and gave it to Baxter, gathered my things, and went to join John and Flint. There was neither hide nor hair of them. I went out the nearest exit, and all but tripped over Greg Gulliver. He was sitting on the metal grated steps smoking a cigarette, looking thoroughly relaxed. In the sunlight, it was quite obvious that he was younger than he appeared to be in stage makeup. He could still be in his late twenties or early thirties. "Oh, hi," Greg said. He held up his cigarette. "I'm full of bad habits." He took a long draw on his cigarette and puffed out a smoke ring, which quickly dissipated. "Too bad the poor dog had such a big scare. Good thing it was just lights and not a piano."

"Too bad it wasn't a pillow. Have you seen John and Flint?"

"Oh, right. Sorry. He said to tell you he'd be right back. He needed to take care of something before he forgot." He took a final puff, then stubbed out his cigarette. "Have a seat." He scooted over and patted the step beside him.

Now that we were talking one on one, he struck me as laid back and likable, and I quickly complied. "Did you get things cleared for the impromptu rehearsal?"

He made a comical grimace. "I didn't actually have any conflicts. A white lie. I needed an excuse to justify grumbling about extra work."

"Ah. I see. Can't say as I blame you. I'm sure you don't normally still have rehearsals during the run of the show itself."

"No, but then, this is the first time I've worked with a dog in such a pivotal role."

"Have you ever seen a big lighting fixture fall before?" I asked.

"Well, that's how they bumped off a character in *Birdman.* But in real life, no. I've seen mishandling of guide wires, cables snapping and the actors falling, electrical units shorting, background flats crashing down in the middle of scenes. Things happen all the time." He snorted. "Yet another reason a dog actor isn't a good bet." He chuckled sardonically. "John told me he was going to hype his show for high-school stagings, but with a kid in a dog costume."

I let that image set in my head for a minute. It would never work for a professional troop. The majority of the humor was the interaction between the actors and an actual dog. "What's your take on Flint? Do you think he's just getting overstimulated on stage and forgetting his training?"

He shook his head. "I'm not really a dog person." (No surprise here. And I'd bet anything Hammond was of the same mind.) "So right off the bat you've got to take that into consideration. But Flint rocks his part in rehearsals. Seriously. You can take that dog, go through your blocking assignments, run through your lines, every movement perfect. In the second act, I have this one line where I say: 'I don't know what you're talking about.' Then I'm supposed to trip over Blue. Each time, Flint's in perfect position. One time he *wasn't*...but then I realized, I had jumped the gun...delivered my line several lines too early. Flint hadn't been given the cue through his earpiece. Our eyes met—the dog's and mine—and he ran up behind me, to the exact spot on stage where he *should* have been for that line if I hadn't screwed up."

"So what could be causing this behavior in front of audiences?"

He paused and looked behind him. "If I didn't know better, I'd think *John* was giving him all the wrong cues."

"I know what you mean, but that wouldn't make any sense. Maybe Flint isn't hearing John's commands," I said. "It's possible someone has hacked the sound system...intercepted the signal." John was driving up in his Jeep Cherokee. I stood up and turned to say something cordial to Greg, but he'd also risen and was heading back inside the theater.

John pulled up to the bottom step, along a dirt road between the building and a river.

"Let's go," John said through the rolled-down window. From my angle, I could see that Flint was lying down with his eyes closed. I didn't know if his falling asleep so quickly was a good sign or a bad sign.

"See you later, Greg."

He held up his hand in acknowledgment.

I descended the stairs. "Can I ride in back with Flint?" I asked. "It's a bad precedent to set, but I want to—"

"No need," John interrupted. "He's asleep. I gave him a tranquilizer."

Chapter 4

"What?" I was stunned that John—that *any* dog owner, for that matter—would medicate their pet simply because he'd been badly startled. For a moment, I actually thought he was joking, but his expression didn't change. I struggled to hold my voice down, because Greg was in earshot. "Why did you do that?"

"He was going bananas when I put him in the car. Like nothing I've ever seen. I was afraid he was going to hurt himself."

My heart was pounding. "But, John, you *knew* I was going to help him work through this. And you knew I was right here." I looked up at Greg, who was staring straight ahead as if he couldn't see us. "All you needed to do was tell Greg, 'Get Allie.' He's been sitting right there."

"Yeah, but...you should have seen Flint!"

I managed not to growl: *I would have seen him if you'd just spoken up!* "Why did you even *have* tranquilizers on hand?"

"From Felicity. She left them when she moved out. She asked me to bring them to her a while back. I stuck them in the glove box and forgot about them. She used to have to give Pippa one in order to fly with her. I figured Flint is two and a half, three times bigger than she is. It's like giving him a third of a dose."

After considering my limited options, I decided to get into the car. I got into the passenger seat. "The thing is, John, *now* it's meaningless if I try to divert his attention and get him to play with me. It's also meaningless if he goes on stage tonight, because, even if he's flawless, he's been doped. He will behave differently in subsequent performances when he isn't under the influence."

While I was talking, John had set his jaw and was driving, obviously not agreeing that what he'd done was highly irresponsible. Maybe *this* was the cause of Flint's performance anxiety. Maybe he was being doped on a regular basis. "Have you given him any un-prescribed drugs before?"

"No, Allie. Of course not. This is the first time ever. I swear."

"So be straight with me. A tranquilizer would normally take at least fifteen, twenty minutes to take effect. You *had* to have had it on you. And given it to him almost immediately after the lights fell."

He was grinding his teeth now. I said nothing, staring at him in profile.

"Okay, fine, Allie. You caught me. The truth is, yeah, Felicity asked me to return Pippa's tranquilizers, like I said. That's what put the thought in my head. I was contemplating giving him a fraction of a dose tonight. To help him get over his stage fright."

I balled my fists and tried to keep my voice steady and low. "I see. Surely you realize, though, that doing so would have undermined my work completely. Is there any reason for me to be here?"

"Yes! I was going to discuss it with you first, Allie. I was going to wait and see how things went. And if everything really is as big a mess as I think it is, I was going to get your approval prior to giving him a tranquilizer."

"Well, it was not a wise thing to do under today's circumstances. We'll have to wait and see how he seems to be handling the dose you gave him. At least he's not going on stage. But I'm not a fan of drugs to manipulate a dog's behavior. If that's what's necessary to get a dog on stage, he shouldn't *be* on stage to begin with."

I had only met John once in passing several months ago. Baxter liked him, though, and that was always good enough for me. Until now. At the moment, at least, I no longer trusted that John was telling me the whole story about Flint.

"I'm concerned that we're not on the same page, John. If it hadn't been for the heavy fixture terrifying Flint, you anticipated that today I would get acquainted with your dog, give you any training tips I could, and either keep a close eye on how he followed directions in tonight's performance, or put Pavlov in the role. Right?"

"Right."

"Did I leave anything out?"

"No. That was it. Frankly, I thought this would end up being like my typical doctor visit. I wait 'til I think I'm going to keel over to schedule an appointment. Then by the time I see the doctor, I'm feeling fine."

I looked back at Flint, who was sleeping with his back to us. "And that exact scenario—Flint being as good as he is in rehearsals—would be the ideal thing for you, Flint, the theater, and all the actors? Despite the current sellouts that you're getting without sticking to the script?"

He winced so quickly it was more like a nervous facial tic. "Yes."

"You sound somewhat less than certain. Do other people agree with Felicity that it's just fine if the dog louses up and the actors adlib?"

He hesitated. "In the long run, I think everyone's onboard with me—that we'll be best off when performances go as well as rehearsals. Short term...not so much. Actors love to show up the playwrights. Makes them feel all the more important."

I decided to let the matter drop, for the time being. "What do you hope to see come out of *tonight's* performance, now that Pavlov is stepping into the role?"

"I hope she'll do a reasonably good job filling in, considering you had no notice and next to no rehearsal time."

"That's all? If she does everything perfectly, would you want her to replace Flint?"

"No. I want you to help Flint be comfortable on stage. Like I've said. More than once." His voice was a little testy.

"Then I guess we are on the same page after all. I just had my doubts considering your haste in giving your dog downers."

"I just...don't want him to get hurt. That's all. That beam barely missed him."

"You don't think someone intentionally rigged that fixture to drop, do you? Nobody benefits from hurting you or your production, do they?"

"Not beyond petty differences. Jealousies. Bitterness. That sort of thing. Nothing so terrible someone would want to injure an actor, or a dog."

"Yet you and Sam Geller aren't on the best of terms."

"Did someone tell you that?" he asked.

"No," I said, a little surprised, considering how obvious that had been to me. "It was because of your body language. Tone of voice. That sort of thing."

He shrugged. "I felt indebted to his brother, but Sam and I rub each other the wrong way."

We pulled into the dirt driveway of a little cabin. "Here we are. Ten minutes out of the booming town of Creede."

"Come on, boy," he said, opening the hatchback. Flint awakened, but was still clearly drowsy. While John was shutting the hatchback door, Flint peed on the dirt driveway. With John and I following closely, he trod inside, headed straight to his dog bed, and dropped down as if he'd been asleep on his feet.

John rubbed his face. "So. Looks like you were right. He's had a bigger reaction than I figured he would."

"Indeed. Obviously there isn't anything I can do with a fast-asleep client."

"Sorry to waste your time, Allie. I just lost my head for a minute there."

I suppose I should have said something reassuring, but in truth, I remained annoyed. If he wasn't a friend of Baxter's, or if our relationship wasn't still in the opening phase, or even if I hadn't made such a long drive to get here, I'd have seriously considered saying thanks but no thanks to this job.

"How long do you think he'll be groggy like this?" John asked.

"I have no idea. But at this point, my time would be much better spent working with Baxter on Pavlov's training."

He sighed and looked at the sleeping dog, then back at me. "I'll give you a lift back to the theater. Then I'll head back home and let you know the moment he's back to his old self again."

***

We made inconsequential small talk during the return trip. He dropped me off in front of the theater, waved, and drove away. I went straight to the stage, even though I knew they had moved the rehearsal upstairs. Sam Geller and two other men were clearing up the debris. If nothing else, I needed to feel confident that Pavlov was safe from a repeat incident before I would okay her returning to this stage. I decided to chat with Sam.

As I walked up the four steps, he gave me a quick glance, and returned his vision to the floor.

"Hi, I'm Allie. Here to work with Flint's training."

"Yeah. There's nothing wrong with Flint that a good owner couldn't cure."

I silently gave him some credit. He, too, knew that the owners typically lead to the bad behavior in their dogs. "You think John's been mistreating his dog?"

"*Mistreating?*" He paused from using his push broom and peered at me, tilting his broom to an upright position. "That's an interesting question. I think John considers his dog a goose that's going to be laying golden eggs."

"So...that's a no?"

He snorted. "Sure, lady. John treats Flint like a royal goose."

His voice was so nasty, he could be capable of sabotaging Flint's performance. "Border Collies are worth their weight in gold to ranchers," I said. "It's not a huge stretch to train them to herd actors instead of cattle or sheep."

Sam laughed heartily. "Actors are a lot like livestock. You got a point there." He returned to his sweeping. "John doesn't like me talking to anybody when I'm supposed to be working."

"Okay. Nice meeting you," I said.

He made no reply.

I found my own way to a staircase and climbed up to the second floor. At the top of the stairs, I could hear one of the actresses' voices from behind a closed door. Taking care to be quiet, I turned the knob and tiptoed inside. A dog bowl and water dish were stationed along the wall near the door. As I tiptoed past them, the odd shapes of the kibble in the dish caught my eye. Some of the pieces looked eerily similar to chunks of dark chocolate. I picked one up and scraped it with a fingernail. A thin dark-brown sliver stuck to my nail that looked and smelled chocolaty. Alarmed, I tasted it and, sure enough, it was dark chocolate.

I swept the bowl off the floor and cried, "Who did this? Who put chocolate in a dog's bowl?"

Karen stopped in the middle of her soliloquy. She and Sally were doing a scene together while the men were offstage, sitting in chairs along one wall of the large space. "*I* put dog food in there. Pavlov was sniffing at Pippa's stash of kibble in the Tupperware, so I assumed she was hungry and put a couple of handfuls in the dish. She backed away from it, though, so I just left it there."

"Pavlov is trained not to eat anything in a strange setting unless I give her the okay. This would have made her really ill."

"I'm sorry, Allie." Karen walked up to me and looked at the contents of the bowl. "Those chocolate pieces weren't in there when I put the dog food in the bowl."

"Are you *positive* about that?"

She hesitated. "No. I wasn't paying a lot of attention. They are the same color as the kibble, and all I did was grab two handfuls and drop them into the bowl. We'll have to ask Felicity, but someone must have sabotaged Pippa's dog food by mixing the chocolate pieces in."

"Did you ask Baxter if it was okay? Or Felicity if you could give Pippa's kibble to Pavlov?"

"She did," Baxter said. "I thought she meant the food in your hip pack."

"I still have that with me," I said, touching the pack.

"I knew Felicity wouldn't mind," Karen said. "It was such a small helping. And I was worried with all the drama about the lights crashing down, Pavlov's dinner might get overlooked. John's always careful to feed Flint two hours before the show begins. I used to have a dog myself, so I was...on autopilot."

As she was talking, I poured most of the pound or so of kibble onto a shelf so I could sort through it. There appeared to be only three pieces of chocolate left in the square-shaped container. There were eight pieces in the dog bowl.

The other actors had joined us and were watching me. I removed the chocolate pieces and swept the kibble back into its container. I needed to cool down a notch. No damage had been done, and we had to get Pavlov on stage in a couple of hours. "I'll have to discuss this with Felicity. How's the rehearsal been going?"

"Fine," Karen answered. "Pavlov is a regular Rin Tin Tin. She's following her instructions almost as well as Flint. In rehearsals."

"Felicity is here if you want to talk to her," Sally said. "Just knock three times on the wall. That's the combination costume storage and sewing room."

Hammond obliged. His face looked a little pale, and his forehead was dotted with perspiration. "Are you okay?" I asked him.

"Feels like my heart's in arrhythmia," he replied. "Happens when I'm stressed out."

"This is nuts," Greg said. "Why are we putting on the show tonight? Someone here obviously wants to destroy the show. What if we're all sitting ducks?"

"Chocolate in a dog's bowl would probably only make a dog ill for a couple of hours," Hammond said. "And chances are the lights fell by accident. Don't argue with my logic or I'll need to breathe into a paper bag."

A door in the opposite wall opened. "You rang?" Felicity said, Pippa trotting into the room by her side. "Wardrobe malfunction?"

"Nothing like that," Baxter explained. "There were several chocolate pieces mixed in with Pippa's kibble. Allie spotted it in the dog's bowl."

"I put it there," Karen said. "I just scooped it out of the Tupperware."

Her face fell. "Someone sabotaged Pippa's food?" she asked.

To my surprise, John appeared in the doorway behind me. "What's going on? What's the matter with Pippa's food?"

"It's been laced with dark chocolate," Greg said.

"What the hell is happening, all of a sudden?" John shouted. "A steel beam falls on us in rehearsal. The dog food bowl is filled with something that will make the dog sick! Not even an hour ago, our worst problem was the minor annoyance of a nervous dog in front of an audience. Now we've had two narrowly averted catastrophes!"

I felt my cheeks warming, wondering if anyone was going to accuse me or Baxter of being a bad-luck curse. I looked at Pavlov. She had realized that nobody was delivering their lines anymore, so she lay down, keeping her eye on me. I smiled at my sweet dog and patted my thigh. She quickly came over to join me. I gave her a hug.

"Somebody is trying to hurt my Pippa," Felicity said.

John balled his fists. "Are you sure it wasn't *you*, trying to make *Pavlov* too sick to go on tonight?"

Felicity gaped at him. "*Please* tell me you're not serious, John. You've known me for five years! I would never do anything of the kind! You have to know at least that much about me."

John lifted his palms. "Nothing bad has happened to your dog, just everyone else's."

"Flint's as much my dog as yours, you stupid jerk!" Felicity shouted. "For all we know, you staged all of this yourself. Maybe you're afraid your play is a dud, so you're shooting yourself in the foot to try and sue the theater for breach of contract when they dump it."

"That's bullshit!"

"Two dozen people have likely walked by the container today alone and could have dropped a handful of chocolate in there with none of us being the wiser."

"Stop!" Hammond cried. His face was flushed and he was panting.

"What's the matter?" John asked. "You don't look too good."

"I'm not. It's my heart condition. Ask Sally if you don't believe me."

"It's true," Sally said. "His heart goes into arrhythmia, and his blood pressure goes through the roof." She went over to him and grabbed his arm. "For heaven's sake, Hammie, sit down and do your breathing exercises."

Her tone was gentle, almost loving. John shot Hammond a vicious glare.

Hammond followed Sally's instructions, bending forward to rest his elbows on his knees as Sally rubbed his back.

"That's it," Hammond said, panting. "I've had enough for one day. I'm having a panic attack. I can hardly breathe. John. You're here anyway. You'll have to go on in my place tonight."

"Seriously?" John asked

"I've got post-traumatic stress."

John groaned. "Fine. I'll take your place, Pavlov will take Flint's place, and we'll just have to hope for the goddamned best."

"Nice, John," Felicity said sarcastically. "We should have Valerie add that to the program insert tonight," Felicity growled. "'John Morris as Steve Gadfly, Pavlov in the role of Blue, *and we'll just have to hope for the goddamned best.*'"

"Catchy," Hammond intoned.

"Allie," John said, "you'll have to give Pavlov his cues during tonight's performance." With undisguised disdain, he added, "Welcome to show business."

Chapter 5

Baxter and I discussed watching the audience to try to spot someone blowing a dog whistle. He told me that he'd followed the pair of young stagehands to see if there were any clues that indicated someone had recently tampered with the light fixture—patterns in the dust or nuts that might bear fingerprints. There weren't—it was surprisingly low on dust—but he *did* discover that there was a safe corner for him to sit that gave him a full view of the auditorium seats. He would be in the shadows and the audience wouldn't realize they were being watched. Due to my acrophobia, I asked him not to even let me know when he was going to be climbing up there.

I was starting to get really nervous for Pavlov's sake as we drew closer to the 7:30 curtain time. Pavlov is a very smart dog, and I'd taken her to perform in agility contests as a three-year old. I also frequently had her perform for me at presentations at pet stores and so forth, plus the occasional birthday party for friends' children. A stage performance of a full-length play was way out of her wheelhouse, however.

To give myself something to do besides fretting, I popped into the dressing room. A wave of aromas hit me as I opened the door, and it occurred to me that maybe Flint was being overwhelmed by scents during the live performances. They surely would not have worn their stage makeup for rehearsals. Maybe the smell of greasepaint had so greatly overtaken his senses that he'd been unable to focus on his commands.

At the opposite side of the room, Sally was chatting with Felicity. Sally appeared to be already in makeup and costume, ready to step onto the stage. Karen was seated at one of the mirrored vanity tables applying her makeup. I did a double take at the vase of wildflowers beside her. "Hi, Allie," she said, catching sight of my reflection in her mirror. She turned to face me with a big smile on her face.

"Hi, Karen. I was wondering…during your dress rehearsals, were you in full makeup?"

"Yes, we wore our makeup for both of them," she said. "I was thinking that it could have explained Flint's troubles if he'd had allergic reactions to our makeup. But we used all the same products in our hair and makeup."

Her flowers caught my eye. "Is this bouquet yours?"

"Yes, it is. That was given to me by a secret admirer at Wednesday night's performance. Isn't it lovely? I love that they're wildflowers, instead of the old standby…roses."

"Yes, they're lovely. But I just want to warn you to be extra careful not to place them anywhere the dogs can get to. Monkshood is poisonous."

"Really? I've kept this bouquet here for the last few days. I'm certain that *Flint* can't get into them here, but I suppose Pippa could hop onto the table. But…I really thought those purple flowers were Larkspur, not Monkshood."

"They're Monkshood. Since I work with pets with less-than-perfect behavior, I need to be able to recognize flora that could make dogs sick. Monkshood contains aconite, which is highly poisonous, either by ingesting it or getting it ground into an open wound on a paw. If Pippa were to jump up on the counter and drink from your vase, it could make her really sick."

"What a terrible thought," Karen said. "If Pippa were to get poisoned due to my carelessness, I'd never forgive myself." She grabbed her vase. "I'm going to move this to a higher surface."

Sally and Felicity glanced in our direction. "Why are you moving your wildflowers?" Felicity asked.

"Allie just warned me they're poisonous. I don't want to take any chance of one of the dogs lapping up the water in the vase."

"It's the Monkshood," I explained.

"Thanks, Allie," Felicity said. "I had no idea those flowers were poisonous. That's such a scary thought that my Pippa could have gotten deathly ill from them."

"No problem. To be honest, I'm not a hundred percent sure that aconite could leach into the water. I just wouldn't want to risk it."

"Speaking of risks," Felicity said to Karen, "How do *you* feel about appearing in tonight's show?"

"In the wake of the light falling on stage, you mean?"

"Of course. Are you in Hammie's camp? Wanting to back out of the show?" Her voice was slightly snide to my ear, and Karen immediately answered, "No. But then, *I* don't have a heart condition. I think Hammie is feeling a little snake-bit lately. In any case, I can't really blame him for wanting to be careful with his heart condition."

Curious about his being "snake bit," I asked, "Has he been injured on stage or something? Snapped at by Flint?"

"No," Karen replied, "but things certainly haven't been going his way."

"She means that he took the role under false expectations," Sally said. "He wanted to rekindle our relationship. Which, I have to admit, has happened before. We've broken up and gotten back together twice already, thanks to our romantic roles on stage." She got a wistful smile on her face. "This time, though, I fell for a young, dashing playwright instead."

Personally, I didn't consider John Morris "dashing," whatsoever. He wasn't even all that young, but rather in his late-thirties or early forties. Nevertheless, I smiled at her. Heaven knows we are all better off loving rather than hating.

"I think John believes his play is being sabotaged," Sally continued. "He seems obsessed now with who put the chocolate in the container of kibble."

"Maybe it was one of the interns," Felicity said, "who dropped it on the floor and figured they'd give it to the dog for a treat. Not everyone knows how badly dogs react to chocolate."

"I wish I'd minded my own business and hadn't tried to feed Pavlov," Karen said.

"Oh, it's all right," Felicity said. "Allie noticed in plenty of time to save the day." She gave me a small smile and headed for the door. "Time for me to get back to work. 'A stitch in time' and all that."

Karen rose and also left the dressing room, calling out that she was heading to the green room to get her lemon water before curtain time.

Alone together, Sally took a seat at the vanity counter and met my gaze. "This must seem like quite the rag-tag operation we've got here. Dark chocolate in the doggie bowl, falling lights, poisonous bouquets. We're a regular dog-and-pony show, minus the pony."

I chuckled. "As long as you avoid being stricken by locusts and/or the plague, I'm happy. I'm a huge fan of live theater. My mom and I have season tickets to the Denver Center of Performing Arts. This is pretty much my first time seeing a production behind the scenes, though."

"Ah. Well, frankly, this is pretty much the way life in the theater always goes."

"Really? Are you being facetious?"

She flashed me a truly winning smile. I could certainly see why she was so appealing to men. "Oh, half and half, I suppose. The more time I spend in this business, the more jaded I become. It's systemic in the very nature of this profession. We endure such intense competition for jobs every time we try to do what we believe we were *born* to do. Over time, it gets easier and easier to lose sight of your moral compass."

I studied her pretty features. With her black hair and light blue eyes, she was truly striking, yet gave off a "girl-next-door" vibe. "So...you don't necessarily trust Felicity's or Karen's stories about mistaking chocolate for kibble?"

"To be honest with you, Allie, you probably shouldn't put *anybody* past doing something underhanded to get closer to whatever spotlight they're seeking."

"You're dating the writer/director of the play. Doesn't that make *you* something of a target?"

She gave me a sad smile. "Bingo."

I waited for her to continue, but she held her tongue.

"Are you suggesting someone has already double-crossed you?"

"That's the feeling I've had ever since I got the part." She searched my features. "Didn't John describe Flint's first scene on opening night?"

"Not specifically. He sent me some recorded outtakes, but the recordings didn't start until the second act."

"That surprises me. The opening scene was quite striking, actually. Flint started barking every time I opened my mouth. I couldn't get a single line spoken without having to shout over his barks."

"That must have been awful."

"Awfully annoying, for sure." She grimaced. "*I* suspect this whole mess with Flint's performance was intended as a way to ruin *my* performance, not the entire production."

"And if that's the case, Felicity had a second reason to throw a monkey wrench into the works. She might be jealous of your relationship with her ex, plus want to see her Pug in a permanent starring position."

Sally fidgeted with the tissue in her hand. "Right. And yet, when I hear you say those words aloud, they sound so petty. I could easily be mistaken about Felicity. She's been truly sweet to me. It isn't *her* fault that I've become so jaded. If I force myself to be honest, at one time or another, I've suspected all three cast members of having deliberately messed with Flint's behavior on stage in order to upstage me. For all I know, they feel exactly the same way about *me*."

I gave her a sympathetic nod to show I was listening. But her words were causing my stomach to clench. This theater company was chockfull of raw feelings and prickly relationships, any one of which could potentially wreak havoc on Flint's performance.

"I keep thinking Hammie has been tampering with Flint's performance. I know for certain that he's seething with jealousy over my choosing John over him. I also know Greg had left the theater world many years ago and is trying to make a comeback. He accused me of upstaging him just this afternoon in our matinee. On the other hand, Karen's so nice, it rubs against my jadedness. And yet *she* was originally supposed to be cast in my role, which is the showier and bigger part. But, again, maybe *I've* just got a raging ego and have invented all of this unseen *Sturm und Drang* so that it's all about me.

She paused and stared into her own eyes in the mirror as if trying to discover a hidden truth there. "Still, I adore Flint. We've had a wonderful relationship on and off the stage, since the moment we met. And it all fell apart on opening night. Why would a dog decide on his own suddenly to bark at my every line?"

Maybe it was Flint's reaction to a particularly piercing whistle that only he could hear. She'd spoken as if it was a rhetorical question, however, so I kept that thought to myself.

She glanced over at Karen's flowers. "Did Karen mention if she's learned who gave her the flowers?"

"No, why?"

She flicked her wrist. "I'm suspicious about *everything* now. It worries me that Karen received them from a 'secret admirer.' Especially now that I know these flowers are poisonous to dogs."

Chapter 6

I was disconcerted as I left the dressing room. I'd already been on edge by the falling lights and finding chocolate in a bowl of kibble. Sally's words made me wonder if everyone on the cast and crew was out to stab one another in the back.

Pavlov was making little whining noises, picking up on my nerves. This was the last thing I should be doing some fifteen minutes before the curtain opened. Backstage, I sat on the floor beside her, playing a tame game of fetch—rolling her favorite ball to the opposite wing of the stage. The lighting assembly had gouged one of the floorboards, but otherwise there was no sign that the incident had ever occurred. The supports had been dented but had been reattached using new nuts and bolts. The lights themselves had all been replaced.

Baxter rounded the flats—the large canvases built to form the backdrop of the scene. In this case they were walls of the room in which a party would be staged He grinned when he spotted me.

"Hi, Allie. I've been looking all over for you."

"I was in the dressing room chatting with the actresses. Trying to calm my nerves. Let's just say it was less than successful."

"That's doesn't sound good."

Pavlov had risen, her tail wagging as Baxter gave her an ear rub. "How's our future star doing?" he asked as she wagged her tail even harder. I was so blessed to have such a wonderful man and wonderful dog in my life.

I looked over and saw John watching us from the wing. He approached. "The seats are filling. I should have taken a doggie tranquilizer myself. I haven't been on stage in a couple of years."

"You'll be great," Baxter said, giving him a fist bump. "I'll bet you know the lines better than anybody."

"You'd be surprised," he grumbled. He eyed me. "Are you ready? Do you know all of Blue's commands? Whatever else happens, you don't want to lose your place in the script." His words came at me in rapid fire. It was somewhat endearing that John was so nervous.

"I'm pretty confident I can follow along and cue Pavlov at all the right times," I said.

"Good. Good. Let's just get you to your station, then."

"I have an actual *station*?"

He started ushering me toward the stage-left wing, so I patted my thigh, and Pavlov fell into step in heel position. "I've positioned the director's chair over here." He gestured at a metal folding chair positioned behind the curtain line, stage left. He switched on the floor lamp next to the chair. "You can see the entire stage and all of Blue's marks from here. Let me just angle the overhead light for you."

I sat down dutifully while he adjusted the lamp's flexible arm so that the light shone directly over my shoulder and onto the first page of the script. Pavlov, meanwhile, lay down beside me.

"If, God forbid, an actor forgets his lines, you can cue them, but just know that's a last resort. All the actors are experienced enough to stall and/or cue one another effectively." He put his hands on his hips and gave me a long, studious look. "Do you need a pillow, or anything?"

"Nope. I'm all set."

He rocked on his heels. "All right, then. I'll just—" he broke off and started to look at his watch. "Crap! I forgot to take this off." He unfastened his watch. "Hammond's got freakishly long limbs. Felicity had to baste new hems in my cuffs. The sleeve catches on my watch."

A red light flashed above us. "That means 'noises off,'" he whispered.

He pivoted, and I whispered, "Break a leg." He didn't acknowledge my remark and might not have heard.

I patted Pavlov and crossed my fingers briefly, silently wishing her a good performance. I found it curious that John had given Pavlov no notice whatsoever. It seemed odd that a dog owner wouldn't notice the dog he was about to share the stage with—where he'd be pretending to be that dog's devoted owner.

I donned my headset and tested it by quietly giving Pavlov a few commands: sit, shake, lie down, and roll over. All was working well, yet my pulse was still racing, and I had butterflies in my stomach.

The opening scene began with John and Sally chatting about tonight's dinner party. Their dialogue informed the audience that Sally's character had recently moved in with John's character, and that his ex-wife and *her* new love interest were coming for dinner, much to Sally's chagrin. The conversation then turned to her dicey relationship with Blue, and how she wished John's character would agree to have his ex-wife keep Blue, as opposed to their current arrangement of sharing ownership between their two houses.

I followed along with the dialogue until John said, "Come here, Blue," and I said into the mouthpiece, "First target, Blue." Pavlov promptly trotted up to John. I breathed a sigh of relief. One thing, at least, had gone perfectly. Now she just needed to obey my commands for another twenty minutes, then there was a short intermission before Act Two.

As the scene progressed, Pavlov misbehaved in perfect accordance with the script. She herded Sally and Greg toward each other and away from Karen and John. Pavlov was following my every command, although she looked precisely like a dog that was following a command, as opposed to moving on her own accord. Still, the audience seemed to be enjoying themselves, laughing in all the right places.

Suddenly, Pavlov's ears perked up, and she looked at the front-left corner of the theater audience. I jumped to my feet and followed her gaze, and caught sight of an elderly man lowering his fist from his lips. He could have been stifling a cough, but he also could have been gripping a dog whistle.

I waved at Baxter on his high perch above the diagonal corner of the stage. I caught his eye and indicated the suspicious man. I tried to pantomime that the audience member was wearing a plaid shirt. Baxter held his hands over his eyes to indicate that he couldn't make out who I'd tried to point out to him.

I struggled to keep up with the actors and missed a cue. I winced at my gaffe and gave Pavlov a better-late-than-never command, "Blue, target three." Meanwhile, Baxter made his way to my side. I held up a hand so he wouldn't distract me until Pavlov was able to lie down for a couple of minutes.

"Did you see someone blow a whistle?" Baxter asked in a whisper.

I nodded and yanked off my microphone headset. "Maybe. White-haired man. Third row, aisle seat, wearing a plaid shirt."

"The one who's been coughing?" he asked.

"Or pretending to."

"I'll go talk to him as soon as the performance ends."

"Be subtle about it," I whispered. "If he's deliberately distracting Pavlov, he won't admit to it. Just start a conversation with him, and get his name and address for a free ticket or something."

Baxter started to reply, but I held up my hand.

"Blue, target one," I said into the microphone.

"Will do," Baxter said.

I refocused, and the scene progressed as written.

With a little over a page of dialogue remaining before the first intermission, something went wrong on stage. Sally's character had grabbed John's wrist and pulled him aside, where they were supposed to have a private conversation. But John had all but screamed, "Let go! You're hurting my wrist!"

Sally followed his adlib with one of her own—an off-color remark that she'd forgotten about his repetitive-motion injury after his ex-wife had forced him to sleep on the couch.

The audience roared at their banter, but they weren't on script. All I could think to tell Pavlov to do was to cue her early to perform a "separate-them" command. It worked well-enough. Sally then returned to her scripted lines, and I gave Pavlov the "jump-up" command. The timing was perfect this time; Blue danced with Sally just as John had turned on romantic music, intending to dance with her himself. The look on John's face was reminiscent of Johnny Carson's, as he kept trying in vain to cut in, only to find himself dancing with Blue. Oddly, however, John continued to keep a grip on his wrist. Apparently she truly *had* injured his wrist.

The stage lights were switched off as the first act ended. The actors left the stage. John stormed off stage brushing past me. He ripped off his shirt. Blood was running down his right arm.

Alarmed, I rose. "John. Are you okay?" I asked.

He continued past me and toward the door.

Grimacing, John gestured emphatically for everyone to follow him as he marched out the door, wadding his shirt in the process. I put Pavlov into a "lie down" and "stay" next to my pseudo director's chair and complied, along with the three actors. Felicity headed toward us through the passageway behind the stage. Pippa was trotting after her, making curious little grunts. She was now wearing a purple satin gown with purple feathers on a boa around her neck. The little dog sat down near the wall, watching John expectantly as if she knew to expect a dramatic scene.

John flung the bloodied shirt on the floor and was pacing, squeezing his right wrist with the fingers of his left hand. Suddenly, he stopped pacing and growled, "Somebody did this to me deliberately!"

Baxter was approaching. He undoubtedly wanted to report on whether or not he'd seen anything suspicious in the audience, but his brow was furrowed as he looked at John.

"Oh, come on, John," Greg scoffed. "Someone accidentally left a pin in your shirt. Stuff like that happens all the time."

"That's not possible," Felicity declared, snatching up his shirt. "I altered this shirt myself less than an hour ago." She proceeded to examine the cuff. Her eyes widened. "It's a tack," she exclaimed. "The point has been pushed through the fabric."

"Did *you* put it there?" John asked, positively seething. "Did you use *tacks* to shorten the sleeves of Hammie's shirt?"

"No, I didn't, John. *Obviously.* I basted a fold into it. I guarantee on Pippa's life that the tack was not in the sleeve when I altered it."

At the sound of her name, Pippa stood up and barked at John.

"You're lying!" John stomped his foot. "You wanted to sabotage my play!"

"John, I'm telling you the truth! And you know me well enough to realize I would never sink so low!" She refocused her energies on examining the sleeve. "My stitching is still here...but it's been partially undone. There's an inch gap in the basting right where the tack is." She inserted her finger between the layers and fabric and pushed at the tack. "The head was glued into place."

John grabbed the shirt away from her. "That's precisely where Sally grabs my wrist in this scene." He mangled the fabric as he picked at the alteration, ignoring that his actions were once again causing his puncture wound to bleed. He removed the tack, then once again chucked his shirt against the wall. "Why didn't you check my costume before you dressed me?" John shouted at Felicity.

"I'm supposed to know to check for a *tack*?" Felicity fired back.

"Maybe the tack was meant for Hammond," Karen suggested.

"No, it wasn't," John retorted. "The fold wouldn't have been there in the first place if Hammond had been on stage. He has arms like a monkey."

"Nice, John," Greg scoffed. "Maybe it's *you* who has alligator arms."

Pressing against his wound once again, John gestured with his elbow at Greg. "Need I remind you that *I'm* your director?!"

Valerie was rushing toward us from a connecting hallway. "What is happening? The set's been changed, and none of you are even in costume!"

"Hammond was injured," Karen explained. "Someone planted a tack in his sleeve."

"Oh, for Pete's sake!" Valerie said under her breath as she marched to a cupboard in the corner. "What the hell is happening to my theater?" She grabbed a first-aid kit. "Felicity! Light a fire under any and all minions to bring us the act-two costumes. You dress John yourself."

"Make sure to check for razor blades," John snarled at Felicity. Meanwhile, Valerie was tightly securing a cotton ball to his wrist with adhesive tape.

Valerie patted his back. "Try to keep your right hand elevated as best you can. Okay? I'll put in a call for Hammond just in case we have to replace you."

Within what seemed to me, at least, to be less than sixty seconds, Felicity and three stage crew folks, dressed all in black, arrived with costumes and accessories, yanked the clothes off all four actors down to their underwear, and had them redressed.

"All set for Act Two," Felicity said, panting a little.

John feigned a kick in Pippa's direction. "Get your little mutt out of here before she runs on stage and ruins everything."

Baxter, like me, was remaining silent throughout, but his eyes widened, as did mine, at John's nastiness toward Pippa. Felicity merely pursed her lips and swept up Pippa into her arms and left the area.

"It's going well, John," Sally said in a sweet voice. "Pavlov has been almost flawless."

"Maybe too much so," Valerie said. "It's not getting the usual laughs."

Again, John jerked his elbow in the direction of Karen and Greg and glared at Sally. "That's because the three of you must have thrown out your notes. You've forgotten all of my directions!"

"The biggest laugh was when you kept telling Sally, 'Ow, you hurt my wrist,'" Greg noted—accurately.

"That's because it was the only line with authenticity to it," John retorted. "I had to say something to explain why I was applying pressure to the wound I shouldn't have so that I didn't bleed out in front of a Standing Room Only crowd. Especially *you*, Greg! You're the weak link in this play. I should fire you on the spot!"

"You're the one who's sleepwalking through his performance!" Greg said. You're wrecking your own play, even though *you're* the one who's so freaked out about the doggie going rogue during the performances."

"Guys, please!" Karen said.

"Let's just nail it in the second act," Sally said. She gave John a quick hug, which he accepted as if he was a scarecrow—with one arm lifted at a right angle.

"Someone probably *will* drive a two-inch nail into me next," John grumbled.

Baxter widened his eyes at me. "He's not normally like this."

"*Sure* he is. You obviously have never had to deal with the guy at work," Sam Geller said as he brushed past us, carrying a coil of cables.

After watching him leave the vicinity, Baxter said to me, "Huh. Sam might have a point."

Baxter returned to his lookout spot. I returned to my seat. Pavlov was still quietly awaiting my return, though she did appear to be greatly relieved, judging by her exuberance as I greeted her.

The second act began smoothly. All of the drama surrounding John's bizarre injury had enlivened the actors. Pavlov, too, was doing fine. I followed along with the script and gave her the instructions.

After a few minutes, the timing was off. John had gone off script again. Something seemed to be wrong with him. He was looking wobbly and sweat was dripping off his face. His lines were coming out in a slur. Deeply worried about him, I rose, wondering if I should try to help him somehow. We were not even halfway through the second act. I didn't know what to do.

Pavlov was standing still, staring at me. I'd made what John had warned would be my worst possible mistake—I had lost my place in the script.

Chapter 7

On stage, John pulled his sleeve down and stared at his bandaged wrist. "Still bleeding," he murmured.

"Did Blue bite you?" Sally asked. Although she kept her face tilted toward John, her eyes darted toward Karen and Greg, clearly discombobulated as to what they should do.

"I don't feel so good," John said.

"I faint at the sight of blood," Sally said. Then she promptly swooned, in what I hoped was simply an act.

The audience laughed.

"I think I'll join you," John said, then dropped to the floor. The line sounded like a joke, and the audience laughed again.

"Steve? Georgia?" Greg said—the character's names for John and Sally—the conked-out actors.

"Oh, dear," Karen said. She bent over John and put her hand on his neck, feeling for a pulse on his carotid artery. She did the same thing for Sally. When she rose, her face looking less tense; I surmised that neither of them had actually lost consciousness. "They're both out cold. I guess Steve was right. He and Georgia *do* have something in common. They both faint easily."

Once again, the audience laughed.

"This is awkward," Greg said. "Maybe they'd wake up if we threw water in their faces."

Sally shook her head. "That sounds unpleasant."

"Okay. In that case, let's get the dog to lick their faces." He pulled a dog treat out of his back pocket and placed it on John's forehead.

"Come on, Blue." He gestured at Pavlov to come toward him. "Treat! Yum, yum! Go ahead, Boy."

Having trained her not to accept treats without my or Baxter's okay, Pavlov stayed put.

"Blue is a girl," Karen said.

"Is it?" He bent down to look at Palov's underside. "So it is. I hope I haven't caused her a case of gender confusion."

"But that's why she won't listen to you. I'll bet I can get her to give me a kiss." Without waiting for his reply, she knelt down and brought the dog biscuit up to her lips. Gripping the biscuit between her teeth, she knelt and said as clearly as she could, "Come give me a kiss, Blue,"

"Grab it, Blue," I said, not actually having a command for this circumstance.

Pavlov gently took the dog biscuit from her teeth. The audience gave a collective, "Aww!"

"See what I mean?" Greg adlibbed. "You *do* love Blue more than me!"

Karen was giving me the nonverbal signal for a canine to lie down behind her back. I gave that verbal command, which Pavlov promptly obeyed.

"Now the *dog's* fainted, too," Greg said. But he was looking at John as if concerned. "He touched

John's forehead. "He's burning up. Is there a doctor in the house?"

The audience took it as a joke or part of the play, laughing and applauding. Greg turned his back to the audience and mimed pulling a cord. Sam saw it and closed the curtain. The audience gave a huge ovation, obviously believing this was the end to the second act.

Baxter rushed onto the stage to John's side. Pavlov started wagging her tail at the sight of him. I told her to come, pointed at a dog bed near the stage door and told her to lie down.

"John?" Baxter said. "What's the—"

"I'm sick as a dog. Heart's racing. Can't feel my arm. Got to get to a bathroom."

"Greg, give me a hand."

Sally sprang to her feet. She was starting to cry. "I think he's truly ill."

"He's got the symptoms of aconite poisoning," I said. "The tack must have been tainted with poison. It's gotten into his bloodstream."

"Oh, geez," Karen said. "Did we jeopardize his life by continuing the scene? Has anyone got a cell phone on them?"

"I do," Sam said. He promptly dialed.

"Tell the dispatcher that the doctors need to do a blood test and check for aconite poison," I told him.

"Will do," Sam said and moved away to a quieter spot.

Greg returned, while Karen, Sally, and I were listening in silence to Sam's voice in the background. He called the poison "anocondite," and I corrected him and added, "It's from Monkshood wild flowers."

"Allie thinks John was poisoned," Karen explained to Greg. "Sam's calling nine-one-one."

Greg gave a solemn nod. "That's what Baxter thinks, too. He's calling nine-one-one, too. Valerie already joined them."

Sam hung up. He took a couple of steps toward us and said, "The dispatchers just figured out someone already called it in." He walked over to Pavlov and gave her a quick tummy rub, then headed for the door. "I'm going to go see if Val's cancelling the performance, so I can go home."

Sally snorted and crossed her arms. "Great work ethic *he's* got."

Nobody spoke. I glanced over at Pavlov, who was watching me with sleepy eyes.

"The thing is," Greg said, "we don't have an understudy to the understudy."

"At least if we have to end the show," Sally said, "I can go with John to—"

As if on cue, Hammond stepped through the door. "I'm here," he said, striding toward us. "I got Valerie's call and came right over. My blood pressure is under control, and I started to feel like a heel for leaving you out here on the stage I was afraid to be on myself. I'll reclaim my role, and Valerie can make an announcement that he's taken ill from a twenty-four hour flu bug."

"So we'll just carry on as if the muddled scene never took place?" Sally asked.

"No," Karen said, "we'll start it from where it ended and joke about it being too strong alcohol. And we'll pick it up from where we went off script."

"But...what if he's truly been poisoned?" Sally asked. "With a lethal dose?"

"Then I'm sure he'd want us to carry on and complete his show for the audience," Hammond replied. "*He's* the one with the determination to take this show on the road. And sell it all over the country."

"Technically, *I'm* the one who poisoned him when I grabbed his wrist," Sally said, hugging herself, her lips trembling.

"We don't even know for certain that there was poison on the tack," I countered. "Even if there was, whoever put it inside his cuff is guilty of a crime, not you."

Valerie arrived. "I've been with Baxter and John. The ambulance is on its way, and as physically fit as John is, I'm sure he'll be just fine. Put him out of your minds for the next forty minutes or so, shall we?"

Sally was crying softly, and Valerie pulled her into a hug. "I meant what I said. My mother was a trauma nurse. She's told me about the miraculous recoveries she's seen. He'll be fine. The best thing we can do for John is to knock everyone's socks off. Okay?"

Sally nodded and dried her eyes.

"I'm going to make a brief announcement to the audience," Valerie said calmly. "We'll start from where you left off, and you can all make a couple of jokes about how different Steve looks. Got it?"

Nobody said a thing.

Valerie pursed her lips, then straightened her shoulders. "Okay, folks. Let's give it your all. Hammond, your shirt and slacks are close enough to Steve's costume in the second act."

"That's why I wore them," he said under his breath.

"Actors, take your places," Valerie said as she headed off.

I physically accompanied Pavlov to the spot where she had been and commanded her to play dead, thinking what a miserable command that was, given John's circumstances. I was worried for Baxter's sake, too. I had no idea what it must be like to see your close friend crumble in front of you from a homicide attempt. He must be beside himself.

Sally and Hammond sprawled on the floor, and Karen and Greg resumed their standing positions. As Hammond rose and went over to Sally, I gave a "release" command into the microphone. Hammond shook Sally, and she let out a death-curdling scream, then cried, "Steve! What happened to your face?" The audience laughed and clapped.

I told myself to concentrate on Pavlov, to follow the script that listed her cues and targets. She was panting and kept glancing over at me. Picking up on my mood, Pavlov was both tense and distracted. It occurred to me that, in the previous shows, both John and Flint had also been carrying heavy emotional baggage. *Good Dog, Blue!* represented an enormous opportunity for John. Maybe I'd been overlooking the obvious dog/owner simpatico.

The remainder of Act Two went well. They shortened the second intermission and commenced with the third act. By then, the actors were in full stride. The audience was enjoying the performance. Hammond was clearly a better actor than John, and Greg was much better than he'd been in any of the scenes I'd seen him perform to date. Toward the end of the third act, I threw in a "hide your eyes" trick, when Greg made an especially bad pun. The audience roared. The play ended, and the actors left the stage.

"That covering-your-eye thing with your dog was a nice touch," Hammond told me.

"Thanks. It's a trick I learned from Kyra Sunshine's book. You put a piece of sticky tape on their nose to train them the command."

"Clever." He gave me a hug. "This has been a great show. You've done an awesome job with Pavlov."

"Thank you. Although having the director be carted off to the hospital in an ambulance was hardly great."

"There's that, of course. But I'm sure Valerie's right, and that he'll be fine."

"I hope you're right."

The actors went out for their ovations. Although I'd forgotten the protocol for Blue in the ovations, Baxter remembered and gave Pavlov a pair of roses. The actors turned and called, "Come, Blue!" And I told Pavlov to go to marker two, then gave her a "drop it" command, right in front of Karen. I then gave her a "grab it" command. She was supposed to pick up one of the roses and bring it toward Sally. Instead she looked at me and wagged her tail.

Karen picked up her rose, and when Pavlov failed to pick up the second one, she patted her on the head, gave it back to her, and said, "Good dog, Blue." The audience laughed and applauded with abandon.

Pavlov and the rest of the cast returned backstage. I smiled at Baxter who was heading toward us. He looked tense and merely gave me a nod.

"Has anybody heard how John's doing?" Sally asked.

"Valerie said she was calling the hospital just now," Baxter said.

My thoughts raced. Now that the performance had ended, it felt so heartless for us all to have continued with the play, not knowing if its creator was even still alive.

Both Valerie and Felicity joined the cluster of actors and me. Pippa, still wearing her purple gown, was trying in vain to get Pavlov to play keep-away with some tattered rags that someone had knotted together for her. The rest of us waited silently for Valerie to give us an update.

"I called the hospital, and they admitted John," Valerie said as she strode toward us. "Strictly for observation. He's out of danger. He's been doing better since they've been giving him intravenous fluids."

We all spontaneously applauded.

"Oh, thank God," Sally said.

"Crisis averted," Greg said.

I sighed with relief.

"Pavlov is an excellent understudy for Flint," Valerie then said to me. "Too bad she's only here for a week."

"We can always ask Pippa to hold up the tent post," Felicity said.

"All Pippa does is bark at everybody on stage," Hammond grumbled.

"It worked perfectly well on opening night for Blue to be barking over Sally's lines," Felicity snapped. "That's really the most John had to do with the dog's role. It would have been easier to stage that way, which is precisely the way I'd written it to begin with."

"*You* wrote *Good Dog, Blue!*?" Valerie asked.

"I sure did," Felicity replied, her features now in deep scowl. "He bought it from me. For a dollar. Back when I thought he was the love of my life." She spotted Pippa still trying to get Pavlov's attention. "Come on, Pippa, let's start collecting the costumes." She strode down the hallway.

Baxter and I exchanged glances. He looked at least as surprised as I was at Felicity's statement. We followed her to the dressing room, Pavlov trotting toward us.

"Felicity, can we ask you something?" I called after her.

She stopped and waited for us.

"Did you really sell your script concept for a dollar?" Baxter asked.

"I sold him the whole shebang. My first draft. He wrote up a contract and everything. All freehand, while we were in bed. We both signed and sealed the deal by making love."

"And then John rewrote it and took it from there?" I asked.

"Yes. But, like I said, I'd envisioned the two couples sharing a small, headstrong dog like Pippa, who would bark whenever the husband's new love interest tried to speak, and would try to get in the way of the wife's love interest and trip him. I trained her so that, when she was on one of our two stages, she would bark at anybody who took a big step toward her. Then I planned to train her to lie down at actors' feet whenever I gave her a special command, "Lie down feet." But John said he was going to get himself a pet herding dog to play the role. And that's what he did."

"The Blue Heeler he used to own?" Baxter asked.

"Right. The original 'Blue.' But Blue was already eleven when John got him from the Humane Society. John decided that he needed a younger dog to play Blue in the play. That's why he got Flint."

"Huh. I didn't know any of that," Baxter said. "It sounds like you really got the short end of the stick."

"Sometimes that's the way it goes," Felicity said. She opened the dressing room door and forced a smile. "Excuse me. I have a lot of costumes to wash."

***

I studied Baxter's handsome profile as we drove to the hospital. He'd been silent for a while, and I suspected he, too, had been stunned by Felicity's revelation. We'd had one harrowing experience after another since we'd arrived this afternoon. In the backseat, Pavlov had fallen asleep, although I always marveled at dogs' ability to wake up within an instant of a pack member leaving the area; she would undoubtedly awaken the instant we arrived. Flint, too, would be anxiously awaiting his owner's arrival in vain.

"John never mentioned that Felicity had written an original version of the play to you?" I asked, as a conversation opener.

He shook his head. "I'm a little surprised *she* told us about that. Their past history makes her look guilty. Give the position he apparently put her in...dumping her and taking up with the lead actress...she'd be a prime suspect in wanting to make him massively sick. If it turns out she's guilty, I hope she didn't actually want to kill him."

"And yet, just after he'd gotten jabbed by the tack in his sleeve, she was telling John the opposite...that he should know her well enough to realize she'd never do such a thing."

Baxter grimaced. "That could have just been words. What else was she supposed to say under the circumstances?"

"True. The jilted lover...who he'd exploited."

"We don't know John's side of the story. We just know that John worked for over two years on this play."

"We know that John *said* he worked on it for two years," I corrected. Truth be told, I was getting a bad feeling about John and was beginning to worry about his character in general.

"Point taken." He paused. "He's a friend, though. I'm trying to give him the benefit of the doubt."

"I understand. Maybe all Felicity did was come up with the concept of a jointly owned dog that barks whenever his owners' new lovers tried to talk. Which probably was worth only a dollar or two."

"Right." The muscles in his jaw were working, though.

Felicity apparently came up with the dog deliberately tripping the significant others, as well, though. If John truly did cheat Felicity out of the proceeds of a hit play and then dumped her, he might be lucky, karma-wise, to come out of this ugly incident with merely an overnight hospital visit.

"How did you meet John?" I asked.

"At the canine sheep-herding competitions at the Denver Stock Show, three or four years ago."

"Was Flint competing in the herding class?"

"No. He had a Blue Heeler then that was getting up there in years. I happened to be managing the event that year. John helped me to calm down a pair of irate owners."

"Why were they irate?"

"There was a gate in the arena that had a squeaky latch. They blamed the squeak for wrecking their dog's performance. John told me he was writing *Good Dog, Blue!* clear back then."

"So that must have been closer to just two years ago."

Baxter paused. "It was two and a half years ago. I offered to buy him a beer. He told me he owned part of a ranch near Creede. Suggested I bring my dogs... join him for some hiking and fishing. Up until now, he's always been really laid back around me."

"Just not at work," I muttered, thinking about Sam's statements this afternoon.

***

We managed to arrive shortly before visiting hours were over. We entered his room, which was built for two patients, but the second bed was vacant. John looked pale and as if he'd aged ten years. He forced a feeble smile and promptly switched off the television set. He managed to sit up and gave us both fist bumps in greeting. We made predictable chatter about how he was feeling and this having been a close scare.

"How did the rest of the performance go?" he asked me.

"Really well."

He nodded. "Allie. The doctor said you're the one who alerted everyone to check for poison. You saved my life."

"That sounds heroic, though it wasn't. But the important thing is that you rest and get better," I said.

"What's *most* important is that we find the person who tried to kill me. I already told the police that it's Sam Geller. He's had it out for me for years now."

"You think it's Sam Geller?" I asked, surprised. If anything, I would have expected him to be positive that Felicity had done this. "You've known each other for years?"

"Quite a few," John said. "He's behind Flint's troubles on stage. He's doing everything he can to get back at me."

"For what?" Baxter and I asked simultaneously.

"We got into a big argument over a poker game between me and him and his brother. It was a long time ago, when I was young and stupid. I was real low on money, and I'd been running a tab I couldn't pay, so I palmed an ace. Even so, when he called me on it, I insisted he was nuts, because I knew the guy was going to clobber me. I even threw the first punch, but the police believed *me* and not him or his brother. *He's* the one that spent the night in jail. So a couple of years later, we run into each other out of the blue, here in Creede, and he recognizes me. Brings up the whole thing. I apologized and gave him a job. The guy just won't let it go. And I can't ever seem to catch him red-handed."

Baxter and I exchanged glances. "You told that to the police?" I asked.

He nodded. "Just a short time ago. I don't remember what happened to the tack. They said they needed to see if they can find traces of the poison on it. He said he'd go to the theater and track it down. But I don't think they're doing anything. I don't know if they're taking any of this seriously."

"Of course they are," I said. "That's their job."

"Has the doctor said when you're going to be able to leave?" Baxter said.

"Probably tomorrow, thank God. I mean, they had the hospital test my blood, so they know I was poisoned. But Felicity doused the wound in antiseptic and washed it. So Sam's going to get away with it. And there are tacks on the damned message board in the hallway. They probably won't even get the right tack!"

A nurse stepped into the doorway. "I'm sorry, but visiting hours are over now."

"You have to keep my dog," John blurted out. "I don't want Sam to steal him."

"Why would he steal him?" Baxter asked.

"It's bad blood. His brother used to own Flint. He got cancer and died though, and I bought

Flint. Sam's so delusional he thinks I cheated him"

"Dude," Baxter said, "why did you hire a delusional man to work with power tools and heavy overhead lighting and so on?"

"To get him off my back." He sighed as if impatient with us. But his story wasn't making any sense. "Look, I took some shortcuts to get Flint. I kind of shortchanged his brother. I can get a little carried away with competition sometimes. But the important thing is, I know Sam is out to kill me. And I have to keep Flint from him. Maybe you can take him to Boulder with you. I'll take good care of Pavlov, and once Sam is arrested, we can get everything straightened out."

"Mr. Morris," the nurse said, her voice more emphatic this time, "you need to get some rest. It's well past visiting hours. I'm sure things will clear up and look differently in the morning."

"Go to my house," John said, ignoring her. "Don't leave Flint alone. I need to get you the keys. They're in the pockets of my pants, but I don't know where my things are."

"They should be in the closet," the nurse said.

"Wait. Never mind. My costume is in the closet. My pants are still in the dressing room. But it's easier if you guys just use the spare. The key's in the hanging planter by the front door."

"Fine. We'll get Flint right now," I said.

"Just stay at my place tonight. Take Pavlov with you, and stay there. Promise me."

"Promise," Baxter said. "Get some rest, bro. We'll see you tomorrow."

"Take care, John," I told him. I gave his hand a gentle squeeze. John's grip was so strong, I had to pull my hand free from his grasp.

Baxter and I left the room with the nurse. John's weird stories about Sam and his brother had left me unsettled. His lack of coherency was probably due to whatever drugs they'd given him to treat him, or perhaps a side effect of the aconite.

"Our friend wasn't sounding like himself," I said to the nurse as she escorted us toward the front desk. "Is he lucid, do you think?"

"I didn't hear all of what he said to you, but it's not unusual for patients to get paranoid and alarmed. He's been under a lot of stress today."

"That's probably all it is." I looked at Baxter, but he didn't meet my gaze.

We thanked her and left. We were silent as we made the drive back to John's house. Pavlov was also silent, but a little restless in the backseat. "Is it just my imagination," I said, "or is our romantic getaway in the mountains off to a really bad start?"

Baxter gave no reply.

Chapter 8

"I wish I knew what was going on, Allie," Baxter said with a sigh after another minute of silence.

"Me, too." Feeling forlorn, I stared out the window at the shapes of the foothills in the darkness. "I warned you about this, you know. It's my curse. I have a ridiculous knack for winding up on the periphery of murder investigations."

"At least this is just an attempted murder." After a lengthy pause, he added, "Do you want to bail on this job? Tell John that all this animosity makes it impossible for you to help Flint?"

I mulled the question. "No. I haven't gotten the chance to work with Flint even once. For that matter, we haven't spent more than fifteen minutes in our hotel room. We had to scarf down our takeout dinner so fast during our rehearsal I'm not sure I even tasted it." I studied his features. "But is that what *you* want to do?"

"No. I'd feel terrible if I just deserted John while he was in the hospital."

"Do you think he's right about Sam Geller?"

"Hard to tell." He grimaced. "I've never heard John ramble like that. I'm thinking his brain was still feeling the crazy-making side effects of the poison."

"The whole story was garbled, but if the gist was correct, Sam could be the type of person who thinks if he can't have something that's rightfully his, he'll make damn sure nobody *else* can have it."

We parked in front of John's front door. Baxter found the spare key in the planter, while I let Pavlov out of the Subaru's hatchback and waited for her.

Meanwhile, Flint watched us through the front window. Baxter let him outside to join us, and soon enough, the two dogs had lifted our spirits. We shamelessly ran around John's property with them like we were kids. I'd recently taught Pavlov how to play "tag," and Flint immediately figured out the rules of the game. Although both Baxter and I are athletic, the dogs could literally run circles around us, and their antics made us laugh heartily.

A police car pulled up behind our Subaru. John's one-acre property was on a dirt road with just a couple of houses nearby, but my first thought was that a neighbor had complained about our whopping and hollering at this late hour. A moment later, I realized that it was far more likely the officer was here to investigate the poisoning.

We stopped our game. Wordlessly, Baxter took my hand, and we walked toward the officer who'd emerged and stood waiting for us at his vehicle. He was bald with wire-rimmed glasses.

"Evening, folks. I'm Sheriff Caulfield. I'm looking into some matters concerning the owner of this property."

"John Morris," Baxter said. "He's a friend of ours." Baxter then introduced himself and me, and we shook the sheriff's hand.

"John told us to use the spare key and to dog sit for him," I explained. "We just returned a few minutes ago from visiting him in the hospital."

"Can I see some IDs, please?"

We handed him our driver's licenses, which he examined under his flashlight while we explained how we knew John and that I was here to train Flint.

The sheriff listened, then said, "Mr. Morris is of the opinion that he was poisoned during his performance this evening. Did you witness the incident?"

"Yes, although I didn't realize he'd been injured until he left the stage," I said.

"Neither did I. I was up above the stage in a back corner," Baxter added, "and couldn't always see his face from my angle."

"The actress was supposed to grab his wrist, and when she did so, a tack in the cuff punctured his skin," I said.

"He went back on stage for the second act and became ill about twenty minutes later," Baxter said. "I helped him until the medics arrived."

"Do you have any idea who put the tack in his sleeve?"

"No," Baxter answered. "The costumes are stored in a room upstairs, and anyone who works at theater has access to it."

"Though it would have taken a while to put the tack inside the cuff," I said. "The seamstress shortened the sleeves an inch and basted them, so the person who put it there would have needed to poke the point through the fabric enough to keep it in place, but not enough to scratch him as he fastened the buttons."

"He gave me your names as friends of his," the sheriff said. "You two just got into town today?"

"Right," Baxter said, simultaneously with my: "Yes."

"Thank you for your time. I'll probably have some follow-up questions, but right now I'm simply trying to gather some information." He smiled down as he looked at Flint. "Good luck training that dog. I saw the show opening night. The dog was clueless. It was pretty funny, though."

"So I've heard," I replied.

"He was barking in the beginning, then darting around in the second act. It made me appreciate the actors. They were really quick witted. It wasn't until I read the program that I realized the dog was supposed to do more than just sit there throughout the third act."

"Pardon?" I asked.

"Yeah, he just plopped down in the middle of the stage. Then he lay down and went to sleep."

"That's not what happened on the video recording I had. This was opening *night*?"

"Oh. No. Not officially. It was an early showing. Kind of dress rehearsal in front of an audience."

"Huh. I was told Flint did really well in the dress rehearsal."

I looked at Baxter, who was obviously as surprised as I was. Greg had also raved about Flint's performances in rehearsals. Maybe the difference in opinion was simply semantics of what was or was not a "rehearsal." Either way, John was proving to be suspiciously unforthcoming with information.

"It sounds to me like the dog had been given a tranquilizer," I said. That would have made today's tranquilizer the *second* he'd had, which called into question why John claimed to be surprised by the severity of Blue's reaction to the dosage. Not to mention his lying to me.

"Yeah, you know, that's what I thought, too, but my wife thought they just deliberately picked an old, mellow dog for the role." He headed toward his vehicle. "Have a nice evening."

"Thanks. You too," we replied in united voice.

"If you think of anything significant that you might have seen or heard, don't hesitate to call me." He got into his car, and we let the dogs back into the house.

The moment the door shut behind us, I told Baxter how alarmed I was that John lied about Flint's never having had one of Pippa's pills before today. "His entire premise of needing to calm Flint down before he hurt himself made no sense," I told Baxter for at least the second time. "He knew I was right there. That's like self medicating on your way to a doctor's appointment. What the hell do you think John's doing?"

"I have no freaking idea. I really thought I knew the guy better than this."

"I was willing to write off his actions today as bad judgement when something heavy had nearly flattened his dog. But not even mentioning that Flint had been listless during their first actual performance before a live audience? Something strange is going on. He's not telling us the full story."

Baxter grimaced. We both stared at Flint, who was lying on his dog bed in the corner of the living room. "If only dogs could talk."

"You haven't noticed any bumps or scars on him, have you?" I asked timidly. "I know Flint doesn't show any of the emotional worrisome signs. He doesn't flinch if you raise an arm suddenly or anything."

"I don't think there's any chance that he's been beaten. But it won't hurt to check."

We knelt in front of his bed. "Flint, sit."

He promptly followed my command. I petted every inch of his fur, finding nothing suspicious—no healed scars or bumps. I had him stand, as well; he had a solid physique with no signs of joint pain. As I kept assuring him he was a very good dog, I gave him a roll-over command and gave him a belly rub, palpitating his lower abdomen in the process. I then batted a chewed tennis ball around with him.

"He seems fine. John sent me his veterinarian records. His blood panel results were all normal. The vet couldn't find anything at all wrong."

"Right," Baxter said.

Pavlov had quietly joined us and was now taking turns panting into each of our faces as we sat on the floor. I told Baxter that both dogs deserved treats for this long, demanding day. We searched the kitchen and found a pair of rawhide strips.

As we watched them both happily gnaw away at them, I said, "Please don't tell John this, but I'm going to talk to Sam about this brother of his.

I want to hear his version of how John got his brother's dog."

"That's not a good idea, Allie. What if John's right about him? What if he's unstable and tried to murder John?"

"If he doesn't want to talk to me, I won't press him. I just..." I sighed. "I'm sorry, Bax, but I no longer trust John. I hope to discover that I'm wrong. But if John did something really unethical to get Flint away from his rightful owner, Flint could be at risk."

"I hear you. I want to be there when you talk to Sam, though."

"Good. I'd feel safer that way, too."

John's house had two-bedrooms. We found a set of linens and made the queen-sized bed in the guest room. Baxter nodded right out. Too jittery to fall asleep myself, I grabbed my laptop and researched the participants at the Denver Stock show for the last couple of years. Even though I was native Coloradoan and had spent most of my thirty-two years within an hour's drive from Denver, I'd never once been to the annual stock show, which took place every January.

I spent an enjoyable time watching YouTube clips that featured working dogs competing for best sheep herding and cattle herding. Afterwards, I located an article in a tiny publication that captured all of my attention. Flint, as it turned out, had done badly in his most recent competition, despite being heavily favored to win. Baxter had told me to wake him up if I found anything major, and I took him at his word.

He sat up when I called his name, making my heart flutter. He looks adorable when his hair is suffering from bedhead. "Did you find something?" he asked.

"This is from an article written last year about the outcome of the sheep herding competition at the stock show. It tells about the first three finishers and their owners, then it says, 'The big surprise was that the odds-on favorite, Flint, owned by Roger Geller, finished second to last. Throughout the competition, Flint was uncharacteristically distracted, almost dazed, in this reporter's opinion. Afterward the visibly upset owner replied 'No comment,' to my questions about what went wrong. A person with close access to Mr. Geller, however, told me confidentially that there was good reason to suspect tampering. Because none of the fellow competitors were considered conspirators, there was little point in airing anyone's dirty laundry. Of particular regret was that this was Mr. Geller's and Flint's final competition, due to Mr. Geller's declining health.'"

Baxter held my gaze. "You're thinking that's what John was talking about at the hospital."

"Exactly. I think *John* was the one who tampered with Flint's competition for his own benefit. He drugged Flint or distracted him with a dog whistle. And in order to atone, he hired Sam Geller to work on his play. And now Sam is getting back at John by wrecking Flint's performances."

"So why would John let Sam stick around?" Baxter asked. "Why not pay him off, or settle the matter in court?"

"I don't know. Maybe it's because he figures the consequences for confronting Sam would be even worse."

"But how could that be? John basically told both of us that *Good Dog, Blue!* is his one real shot at the big time."

"Yet now he's all googoo eyes over Sally Johnson."

"'Googoo eyes?'" Baxter repeated, smiling.

"Head over heels, let's say. So maybe he doesn't want Sam telling her how he connived to get Flint away from a dying man."

Baxter yawned. "I'll buy that for now. We'll see if we can get any information from Sam in the morning. Okay?"

"Okay."

"So you can come back to bed now. Okay?" He added teasingly.

"Okay," I said.

I turned out the lights and let myself be folded into his arms. I could hear the chirping of crickets in the night air, which was normally such a peaceful sound to my ear. Tonight, however, they were ringing like a warning siren.

Chapter 9

In the morning, we divvied up six scrambled eggs among ourselves and the two dogs. Flint had been able to eat his kibble as well, but Pavlov waited until Baxter drove all of us to our hotel so we could give her her accustomed brand. With the theater dark on Mondays, this would be my first opportunity to work with Flint on stage. If he was experiencing any lingering after-effects from the tranquilizer, I sure couldn't detect them.

The problem now, though, was that John was supposed to let us in this morning, yet his keys, like his pants, were in the dressing room of said theater.

I located Valerie Devereux's contact information. Just as I was texting her, she sent me a text that read:

I talked to John. He's on the mend. When should I meet you at theater to let you in?

I erased my own note and sent back:

10 a.m. Thanks, Valerie.

She texted:

Yep.

At ten a.m. sharp, we entered the theater. We exchanged some small talk with Valerie. She was holding John's clothes—a pair of jeans and a light-weight brown-plaid shirt, both on hangers as she spoke to us.

"Did John sound okay to you?" I asked. "He was out of sorts last night. He was saying the stage manager poisoned him. But that might have been the drugs talking."

"That's what he told me this morning, too," Valerie said, "as well as the sheriff, last night. I'm sure they'll get to the bottom of it. By the way, I had a building contractor I know and trust come to the theater first thing this morning and make sure the overhead lights are all securely fastened now. He can't tell, of course, how long ago the extra bolts have been missing from that one fixture, but he assured me everything now is snug and up to code."

"That's good to know," I said. "And it's nice that the theater's dark tonight anyway, so everyone has an extra twenty-four hours to recuperate from yesterday's trauma."

"True." She smiled at me, then said, "Since we're both here anyway, why don't we hold our official introductory meeting right now?"

Eager to work with Flint, I was of two minds. "It's fine either way with me. I know it's your day off, so if—"

She made a vague gesture in the air. "Come on back to my office, both of you."

As she hung John's clothes on a hook on the inside of her door, she offered to put on a pot of coffee for us, which we declined. We took seats, letting the dogs accompany us as we all sat down in her small, drab office. After Baxter filled Valerie in on John's physical condition and the visit from the police officer, I asked, "What do you know about bad blood between John and Sam?"

Judging from her furrowed brow, I should have allowed her to guide the conversation. Nevertheless, she answered, "All John told me about Sam was that he was currently down on his luck, and John wanted to make amends for some bad judgment he used in dealing with Sam's brother a few years ago. So I hired him. Point of fact, though, I'm not all that pleased with him. We'll probably never know if Sam was the one who *removed* the bolts, but he should have checked the entire stage for any safety issues."

"Did John ever tell you that his...shady path to acquiring Flint was what he meant by 'bad judgment'?"

"No. It didn't seem germane to ask about *John's* behavior, and he never got into any specifics."

"I think it's very possible that's somehow behind Flint's problems on stage."

She paused as if to let this sink in, then said, "I see." She tented her fingertips. "And what about the understudy, Pippa, screwing up on stage?"

"I haven't worked with her at all, but I've seen how she and Felicity are together. My educated guess is her troubles might be due to inconsistent training."

"Ah." Valerie began to rhythmically move each of the fingertips of her hands together and then apart. "Can you resolve Flint's problems and also train Pippa for the role this week?"

"That's the plan, at least. I won't know how much time either task will take until I get the chance to work with them."

She nodded, peering into my eyes. I got the uncomfortable feeling that she was trying to assess my confidence in my ability to succeed. "John and I are both hoping that he'll be able to return to work tomorrow and direct the show," she said, still holding my gaze.

"Will Sam Geller be working during tomorrow's performance?" Baxter asked.

She arched her brow at Baxter's question. "Barring his confession or resignation, yes. I...find it hard to believe it was legitimately attempted murder. This is a small town, where everybody knows one another. When you come right down to it, we're talking about a pin prick coated with some nasty sap from a wildflower."

"They had to give him a transfusion last night," Baxter said. "It was hardly a 'pin prick.'"

Once again, Valerie furrowed her brow. "Maybe I'm just not seeing this clearly, because I'm too close to the situation. Running this theater is my passion. I love this place, and everyone in it. Especially the dogs. But I just can't believe anyone truly believed putting a dot of sap on a pin could have killed a full grown man."

I sighed. Last night, Baxter had told me things could look different in the morning. Indeed they did. I was now worried for Flint's safety, and I had decided that I couldn't trust anything anybody at the Creede Playhouse told me. "The policeman...sheriff, rather, who spoke to us said that Flint had seemed half-asleep during a dress rehearsal that was open to the public."

She nodded. "John lost his patience. He decided the best thing to do, considering it was just a rehearsal, was to put the dog into a sit-stay during the third act." She spread her hands and stared directly into my eyes. "There was nothing nefarious about it."

I bit back the temptation to reply, *I didn't say there was*; it served no purpose to get myself into an adversarial position with the manager. "Maybe the poisoned tack was just a warning or something," I conceded, truly hoping that was the case.

"Did the sheriff talk to *you* last night?" Baxter asked.

"Yes. He asked a few questions. I did tell him I was skeptical about the whole idea of a murder attempt. I'm not—"

Someone knocked on her door.

"Come in," she said.

It was Sam. "Hey, folks," he said. He stayed put in the doorway.

"Morning, Sam. You're here on your day off?" Valerie asked.

"Yeah. Wanted to double check all the stage's ceiling fixtures. Can't have anything else fall from the ceiling on my watch. Wouldn't help my resume." He grinned.

"That's true. Although I hired a competent professional to do that for you, earlier this morning. Furthermore, Mr. Geller, you'd best brush up that resume of yours. I'm putting you on notice as of this minute. One more incident, and you're out of here." Valerie lifted her chin. "That said, let me accompany you out of the building. Ms. Babcock is expecting to have the theater all to herself today. Clearly the place is going to the dogs." She gave me a self-satisfied grin.

I rose, feeling awkward for Sam's sake; it hadn't been necessary—or appropriate, in my opinion—to talk to Sam like that in front of us. "We'll get to work right away." I said.

She pulled a set of keys from her pocket. "These are John's. Lock up whenever you leave, even if it's just for a minute or two. I'll leave it to you to arrange returning John's keys."

"Thanks, Valerie," Baxter and I said in unison.

"Yep." She stood in the hallway, waiting for us to get out of her office, and she locked the door with her own set of keys.

"It was nice chatting with you," I added. This time, she didn't even give me a "yep," but rather strode away with Sam as if she hadn't heard me.

***

My first order of business was to do some simple aversion therapy with Flint. Although he walked onto the stage with me, he froze and stared at the spot where the light fixture had landed. I walked on a diagonal route across the stage with him in a heel position, distracting him by singing "dee-dah-dah" to the tune of Baxter's dial tone. We pivoted at the corners to walk from back to front stage, then diagonally across again. Next we walked right across the very spot the lights fell. After fifteen minutes of heeling, sit-stays, and lie downs at various places on the stage, Flint seemed at ease on every portion of the stage.

The next few hours flew by. Part of me felt guilty for having such a great time, all the while knowing that the person who'd hired me for this job was in a hospital bed. It was so much fun, though, to have an entire theater to Baxter and myself, plus two brilliant dogs. I was probably fooling myself, but I sensed the dogs loved every minute as well. Baxter read the lines for both male leads, and I read for both females, and we moved a pair of folding chairs around whenever "Blue" needed a physical stand-in for the absent actor or actress.

By the time we called it a day, I felt good about Flint performing as Blue tomorrow night, with John at the helm. We called John and asked if we could bring him a nice dinner, or if that would break hospital rules.

"You bet," he replied. "And I don't care if you have to sneak it here in a bed pan." He also told us that he'd gotten a slight rash on his abdomen, so the doctors were keeping him there for an extra night, just to be cautious.

We wound up feeding both dogs and leaving them at John's house, despite our promise we made when he was paranoid last night. We then splurged on three excellent steak dinners to go, and we all three jammed ourselves atop John's little bed and ate our sirloin steaks, mashed garlic potatoes, and roasted Brussel sprouts, assuring the nurses that the wonderful pinot noir was cranberry juice.

Not a word was spoken about Sam, poison, or even Flint. John and Baxter regaled me with tales of their hiking exploits. It was a wonderful ending to a wonderful day.

***

A little after ten a.m. on Tuesday morning, we again brought both dogs to the theater. Someone was whistling on the stage. I leapt to the conclusion that it was John and rushed onto the stage a few steps ahead of Baxter, with a big smile on my face. Instead of John, however, I was greeted with a: "Hey," by Sam Geller. He was coiling a pair of long black cables.

"Hi, Sam," I replied. "It's nice to see you."

"Nice for me to be back at work, considering yesterday morning's conversation," Sam grumbled. "Yeesh. The boss-lady must've gotten up on the wrong side of bed."

I gave Baxter a quick glance. This was an opportunity to ask Sam some questions in private. Baxter met my gaze, which I took as a good sign.

"I heard about your brother's death from cancer earlier this year," I said. "That must have been hard to take. I'm sorry."

He stopped working on the cables and stared at me. "Who told you?"

"John gave us the gist when we visited him in the hospital on Sunday night. Then I researched past herding-competitions at the stock show online. I learned about Flint's troubles performing at the Denver Stock Show competition two years ago. How Flint was supposed to win. And he lost due to someone's interference with his performance."

"Yeah?" he said.

"I'm assuming that was John."

He gave both Baxter and me long looks. "So you're probably *also* assuming I've been lousing up Flint's performance. And tried to kill John, as well."

"*Should* we suspect you?" Baxter asked firmly, squaring his shoulders. He was taller than Sam, although Sam was really muscular. I would hate to see Baxter have to defend himself—or me—against him.

"Nope."

I studied his features. He stared right back at me.

"My job is simply to get Flint to respond on stage like he does in rehearsals," I told him. "I merely have to eliminate his distractions, or eliminate his response to those distractions. I'm strictly on Flint's side. If there is a tug-of-war between you and John, because John cheated you out of owning your brother's dog, I wouldn't blame you."

No comment.

"It wouldn't necessarily mean you loosened the bolts on the light fixture or poisoned John," Baxter added.

After another fruitless pause, Baxter asked, "How *did* Flint wind up in John's possession?"

"He bought him."

"Fair and square?"

Sam snorted. "Let's say that someone got plastered and made a ridiculous, stupid bet at a freaking bar."

"When John cheated you in a game of poker?" I asked.

"Poker? No way. This was a bet about the sheep-herding contest. Not realizing the contest was rigged. And that nothing could be *proved* about its being rigged."

"You bet your brother's dog on the contest?" I asked in surprise. I couldn't imagine anyone ever doing that with their pet dog, let alone a working pet that helped increase their wages.

Sam's features darkened. "My *brother* made the damned bet. I was just too drunk as well to stop him." He shook his head. "Ownership of the dog if he failed to medal, versus ten grand if he medaled."

"Then he distracted Flint with a dog whistle?" Baxter asked.

Sam shrugged. "I was there, watching him like a hawk. Couldn't see a thing. More likely, he had an assistant doing the actual distraction. But, nobody saw anything. We filed a protest. It went nowhere."

"What about the sheep he was trying to herd, though? Did all of them seem normal?" Baxter asked.

He snorted. "Normal for a sheep, I guess. But one of them was skittish and couldn't be controlled for the life of him. Might have been drugged. My brother was just too appalled with himself over being goaded into making the stupid bet. He decided not to press the matter. And John promised he'd take great care of Flint. He handed Roger five hundred in cash, saying something like 'so there'd be no hard feelings.' As if the top sheep-herder in the state was worth a measly five-hundred bucks."

"That had to be infuriating," I said. "It's making me mad on your behalf, even though that happened a year and a half ago."

"Hell, yes. It rankled me plenty. But I sure as sh...ooting didn't try to poison the jackass. And, at the time, Roger decided it was just as well if Flint went with a theater director. He figured he was going to be dead in another six months, and his top dog deserved a chance to show off his smarts. It was his decision to make, not mine."

"But John told us the other night that he'd cheated you in a card game and wound up in a fist fight with you, and you spent the night in jail."

Sam shook his head. "That happened to me, but with someone else in the fist-fight. Last month, when I came into town, he asked why I waited so long to find Flint if I wanted him back. I was having legal troubles."

My thoughts were racing. I was getting angry at John. I believed Sam. He had no reason to lie about the poker game. Whereas *John* must have been spinning tales while he tried to make a case so that we would be compelled to defend his ownership of Flint. Even when John knew he had valid reason to fear retribution from Sam. So much so that John wanted us to keep Flint in our sight.

"John is a friend of mine, Sam," Baxter said. "He's a good guy, by and large. Maybe someone else cheated, and John just wasn't enough of a mensch to admit it. The show-winner's owners could have been behind it."

"That's what John claims happened. Says he never would have made the bet if he'd been sober himself."

"Did you offer to buy Flint back from him?" I asked gently, hoping he would say no.

He nodded. "After my brother died. Offered him six hundred bucks, as much as I could drum up, being unemployed and all. Turned me down flat. 'Not for sale,' he said. Going to be a big canine star on Broadway."

"So John got you the job here," I said.

He shrugged. "It gave me the chance to be around Flint and get some bank. The job comes with a rent-free room. Not such a bad deal, all in all."

"Yet you *aren't* sabotaging Flint's performances?" I asked.

"Why would I want to hurt Flint's chances as a cushy life? Getting gigs like eating dogfood in TV commercials?"

"Maybe because you hoped to frustrate John into giving up on him," I replied.

"I ain't underhanded like John. I'm just trying to stay below the radar for a while. As long as John keeps his end of the bargain, that is. If I can save up enough money, I'll get my own business up and running—training dogs to herd. Hell, I trained Flint in no time."

He pointed with his chin at Pavlov. "Your bitch is okay on stage. She just doesn't lock eyes with her sheep. Probably why she ain't making eye contact with the actors. You want your doggie to act on stage, you should make sure your dog's strong-eyed toward the actors on stage."

I was confused for a moment.

Sam added, "I mean she's naturally loose-eyed. She figures it's okay not to maintain eye contact. Flint, though, looks sheep right in the eye. Let's 'em know he's keeping an eye on 'em at all times."

"Oh. Right. That was in a video on sheep herding," I said, now realizing Sam deserved respect for his dog-handling skills. He had made an excellent observation. *That* was why Pavlov's performance seemed flat last night. She had performed one simple trick after another, following my directions, but never making on-stage eye contact. "And you're saying dogs are naturally inclined, one way or the other."

He nodded. "Herders work upright or crouched. Loose eye, or strong eye. And that's that. It's kind of like our being born left-handed or right-handed."

"Interesting. Thanks."

"You at least inherited your brother's ranch, didn't you?" Baxter asked Sam, which snapped me back into the conversation at hand.

Sam shook his head. "The ranch went in order to pay his medical bills. Prob'ly why he was dumb enough to accept the ten-kay bet. Left me with nothing."

"It's so unfair," I blurted out.

"You're telling me. But the last thing I'd want to do is scramble with Flint's performances. I got me a signed contract with John that I'll be in charge of training new dogs in the role, once the play starts selling to multiple theaters."

"Why aren't *you* the one training Flint, then, instead of me?"

He snorted. "John didn't trust me, I guess. Once Flint started screwing up, he said I was cutting off my nose to spite my face. He was dead certain *I* was the one messing with Flint. So he called Baxter, and here you both are."

"In that case," I asked, "why did he trust that you should be the official trainer when the play got produced at other theaters?"

"There's a clause that makes the contract void if this here world premiere doesn't go smoothly," he replied.

"I see," I said. "Though, again, if he didn't trust you, I still don't understand John's motivation for striking that deal with you."

"I think he figured he'd help me out with no skin off his nose. He was just going to be offering my training skills as, like, a bonus to theaters that didn't have access to herders. Plus, that way he had me over a barrel, if I were to try and even the score between us."

"Hmm," Baxter muttered.

"The way things are turning out," Sam added, "I should have gone with my gut. Told him to take this job and shove it."

Chapter 10

Baxter and I had formed a tacit understanding not to discuss any of our conversation with Sam yet. We had lots of work to do. Baxter had somehow managed to win over Flint in addition to Pavlov. They flanked him wherever he went. I pointed out that he'd won their devotion.

Out of curiosity, Baxter walked across the stage. Sure enough they both trotted after him, tails wagging.

"It's like they expect me to pull a pork chop out of my pocket," he said.

"Yeah, it's probably time you got rid of that *Eau d' Sautéed Pork* aftershave you're so fond of."

"It's my animal magnetism," he replied, wiggling his eyebrows.

"I hope you can use it on some of the staff here. We could use some volunteers to rehearse with us."

He looked at Pavlov. "We should probably just work with Flint today," Baxter said. "Don't you think?"

"Sounds right." *Although Pippa was probably upstairs.* I wondered what Felicity had dressed her in today. I decided a tennis outfit would be fun.

Both Valerie and Sam were here, so I asked Baxter to talk with Valerie about filling in herself or suggest a suitable stand-in, and to also mention that I wanted Sam to read lines with us, unless she objected. Both dogs put themselves into a heel position and trotted alongside him as he headed toward Valerie's office.

I located Sam. He was fixing a wobbly chair in the theater's enormous storage room. "Would you be willing and able to read one of the male-lead's lines with us, while we rehearse with Flint? Provided pulling you away from your job is okay with Valerie?"

He scratched at his cheek, where he had a two- or three-day beard. "I guess it's all right with me, as long as it's all right with the boss lady."

"Great. Baxter is checking with Valerie now, so I'll let you know if she objects. In any case, thanks for agreeing to help me out."

"No problem. Mind if I take a cigarette break first, though?"

"Of course not. See you on the stage in five or ten minutes."

I heard soft music coming from the green room. Hopeful of getting one more recruit so I could sit offstage and rehearse via the audio system, I ducked into the room. Sally was sitting on the oversized couch, which, though ugly, was dark green velvet—an appropriate color. I said hi and glanced at her knitting. "Making a scarf?" I asked

"For John," she answered. Her eyes were red and puffy. I took a seat beside her.

"Are you worried about him? The doctor said he's recovering. He'll be leaving the hospital today or tomorrow."

She nodded. "I know. I went to see him as soon as visiting hours were open this morning." She grimaced, but kept her eyes on her knitting. "We had a little spat."

"I'm sorry to hear that. He probably wasn't himself, though. He was cranky when we saw him on Sunday night. The nurse told us it's not uncommon for patients to get a little delusional, even."

Her expression remained glum. "I can't blame him for being angry at me. He's right. I should have been fawning all over him Sunday night and rushing him off the stage. That would have been in keeping with Georgia's character. She's supposed to be infatuated with him. But all I could think to do was faint. As soon as I planted myself on the floor, I had no options. I had to just lie there, while everyone else figured out what to do." She abruptly stopped knitting and searched my eyes. "What kind of a girlfriend does that? Chooses to pretend to faint in order to keep a show going...when her boyfriend's on death's door?"

"You're asking the wrong person. I thought it was brilliant of you to swoon. And I don't think you should feel guilty in the least for the three or four extra minutes until he got to the hospital. He'd have been in precisely the same physical condition."

She grimaced again, and retrieved her knitting needles. "Tell that to John," she muttered. "Although Sunday's performance *was* extra stressful to me, too. My dad was in the audience. And, by the way, he told me that, not counting me, your dog was his favorite actor in the production."

I couldn't help but grin. I adored it when people complimented one of my dogs. "That's nice. Has he seen the play with Flint or Pippa in the role?"

"No, he's been recovering from a case of pneumonia, actually. This was the first time he felt well enough to come out in public. He's been coughing up a storm."

That sounded familiar. "I noticed a man coughing, seated in the third row. White hair, wearing a light green T-shirt. Thin. Glasses."

"Yeah, that's my dad. He and my mom always reserve the same seats in advance of any of my shows. I like to know where they're sitting. They're close to the stage and off-center, so those particular seats are slow to sell out." She grinned. "Dad claims my roles always cause me to spend more time on the left side of the stage. I think it's just his imagination. It's sweet of them to always be so supportive."

On the other hand, maybe nobody in the box office was keeping track of the actors' parents attending all of the performances. Did it make me a bad person to entertain the notion that Sally could be in cahoots with her elderly father to sabotage John's play? "So that was his only time seeing the performance?"

"Yes, but they're coming back tonight. Fortunately. I'd objected when they first told me that, thinking they already knew all the jokes and wouldn't enjoy a repeat. But considering Sunday's fiasco, I want them to see me in the role without my boyfriend getting massively ill."

"So they know you two are a couple?"

She winced a little. "Sort of. I told them it wasn't anything serious. Which was probably a good decision, since we're already at odds with one another."

"Allie, Valerie said it was fine," Baxter said, from the doorway. "We're ready to rehearse."

"Great. Thanks." I hopped to my feet.

"Do you want me to help you out in my role again?" Sally asked.

"That would be really helpful, if you're sure you don't mind."

"Not at all." She stood and gave me a sincere smile. "I'll just say my lines and walk through my blocking assignments. It's not going to strain my voice or anything."

Baxter waited for us and asked me if Sam was going to pitch in. "Yeah, he's probably out back. He's taking a cigarette break."

Much to my surprise, John was in the auditorium when we arrived; he and Valerie were chatting.

"Hey, John," Baxter said. "You're up and at 'em! Good for you!"

He gave us a feeble smile. "What's a mere poisoning? The show must go on." He looked a little haggard and as if he'd lost weight. His light brown plaid shirt appeared to be hanging off him. Valerie must have gotten the clothes he'd been wearing Sunday night back to him yesterday.

"There's been a minor change in plans," Valerie said. "You're going to be rehearsing a new scene first. So John says he doesn't need me to read lines."

"Okay. Thanks anyway, Valerie," I said. She strode away without another word.

John and Sally, meanwhile, locked gazes. "I'm so sorry about this morning, Babe," John said. "I was talking myself into being miserable. Maybe the poison did a number on my brain."

"My poor darling," she said and rushed into his arms.

John gave her a passionate kiss. Their embrace ended, and Sally giggled as she glanced at Baxter and me. "Sorry for the PDA. Let's just all pretend John was directing me how to kiss for the play."

"No worries," Baxter said.

For my part, I was happy they'd made up. Maybe the ill will now would blow over like a bad thunderstorm. I was optimistic Flint would be able to perform tonight. Every now and then, my canine clients' behavioral problems resolved themselves merely by my being there to observe and reassure the afflicted pets and their owners.

Sally put her hand on John's cheek. "I'm also checking his temperature," she said. "I don't know if our director is up to being back at work so soon."

Hammond and Greg arrived.

"What great timing," Sally said. "Allie could use our help again with a read-through for Flint's rehearsal."

"Actually, we came because John sent us a text that he wanted to work on the new penultimate scene," Hammond explained. "When Blue has his soliloquy."

I looked at Hammond, confused, imagining Blue delivering a to-be-or-not-to-be speech comprised of yowls and barks.

"Greg, you're not even in that scene," Sally said. "But *I* am. Why didn't I get a call?"

"I stopped by your place, and you weren't there, so I assumed I could talk to you here, in person," John said.

"And *I'm* supposed to be here 'just in case,'" Greg said, putting air quotes on the final phrase. He sounded surly.

"Allie's bound to need you to run through your lines for the whole play," John said, matching Greg's surliness.

Meanwhile, Hammond gestured for me to come closer, then said, "I bumped into Sam a minute ago. He said to tell you you've obviously got plenty of actors for the rehearsal, but he'll check in with you later."

I nodded and thanked him. Meanwhile, Sally was telling John he should simply watch tonight's performance and have me cue Flint. She noted that would be a lot wiser rather than to risk making himself ill by taking on too much too soon.

John smiled lovingly at her. "I'll see how I feel around six or so, and if I get dizzy or whatever, I'll sit out the performance."

"Just be careful not to sit on a tack," Greg said, chuckling.

Sally clicked her tongue. "That's in bad taste, Greg."

"By all means, Greg," Hammond said, with a theatrical lilt in his voice. "Try to be more *tack* full."

"For pity's sake, guys! Can't we save the stupid puns for *Boomtown* Improv? John nearly died!"

Greg smirked at Sally. "You're oversensitive because *you* feel guilty to have unintentionally jabbed him with poison."

"If anybody should feel guilty, it's *you*," Sally said. "You're the one who's been so busy flirting with Felicity you've been distracting her. It wouldn't have happened if the costumes were closely monitored."

"Enough," John growled. "Save your picayune jealousies for tonight's performance, people. Tonight has to be flawless. I'm recording the entire performance and sending it to my agent to shop around in Broadway theaters. This is your big chance to show the world how good you are in these roles."

Hammond let out a derisive laugh. "John, my dear boy, only *you* could suggest that we need your play to boost our careers. It's clearly the reverse."

"It's a two-way street, you asshole!" John fired back. "The boat rises with all tides." He paused. "The rising tide raises all boats, I mean."

Sally shot Hammond a fiery look then said something under her breath into his ear.

Hammond stared at her for a moment, then turned to John, his palms upraised. "I spoke out of turn. You're in charge of this production, not me. I'm a bit out of sorts today. The sheriff has a nasty habit of knocking on doors in the wee hours of the morning. I couldn't get back to sleep."

"We all got door knocks," Sally said. "The sheriff told me he was talking to everybody in theater housing."

"I'm surprised you were able to arise, after last night's exploits," Hammond snarled at Sally. With John having been in the hospital, I had no idea what he meant. John must have wondered the same thing; he glared at Sally.

She blushed. "That was hardly a free-for-all. I was just visiting my parents."

Greg continued to smirk at her, but she never met his gaze.

***

We worked on a scene that John had planned to use as soon as Flint had all of the rest of his performance down pat. Obviously, incorporating that scene in the next couple of days was premature, but John said he'd like to take advantage of my expertise while I was in town.

The scene was risky because it called for the dog to be alone on the stage. While Hammond's character was offstage—ostensibly getting dressed—Sally calls to him that she was leaving to go to the store. Flint then had to nip at Sally's feet to hasten her exit. (Nipping at one's heels was a standard herding technique; hence the name "Blue Heelers.") Flint then "shuts" the door in her face, which was rigged; Flint merely needed to get close to the door and an offstage crew member pulled a string to shut it. Next, Flint had to shove a chair under the knob of the door, actually accomplished by a wire; the dog had to simply follow the chair and appear to be pushing it.

Far trickier, Flint then needed to seemingly place a phone call in front of a live audience. We trained Flint to grab a handset—upon which was dabbed baby food—and then set the phone on the floor, with the baby-food-spackled button-side facing up. Flint had to push the keypad with his nose a couple of times. Dial tones and then Karen's "Hello?" were heard over the audio system. Finally a "Speak" command instructed the dog to bark into the phone.

At this point, Karen's broadcasted responses to Flint's barks let the audience listen in as she convinced herself that something dire had happened to Hammond, and assured "Blue" that she was on her way to rescue Hammond.

Karen had been late to arrive at the theater, but John had prerecorded her lines of dialogue. She arrived at the theater just as John was telling us this would be their final run through for today. He assured her that she might as well watch from the audience and give him her opinion.

She took an aisle seat right behind Baxter and me; Pavlov was sprawled across the aisle, having been sleeping on her side. Her tail thumped a couple of times, though, as Sally rose long enough to give her a belly rub. John, too, was in the audience with us. He was sitting in the front row, dead center, giving Flint his commands into a headset. He also called to Sally, "Take it from the top."

"Darling?" Sally called through the set door. "Can I get you anything from the store?"

Flint, who was in "Play Dead" mode, leapt into a "Sit" position, his tail wagging. I could sense at once that he was going to be spot on. It made me so happy, my eyes immediately misted.

A few minutes later, we were all clapping, having watched Flint perform the scene to perfection.

"What do you think?" John asked, springing to his feet.

"It's an absolutely amazing scene to watch," Karen said.

"It truly is," Sally said. (After "Blue" had shut the door on her, she had come around to a side entrance and watched from the seats.)

"But more than a little risky to do live," Baxter said.

"That's why I needed Flint in the role." John was grinning ear to ear. He stood next to the stage, rocking from foot to foot with energy. "Sorry, guys, but we've just *got* to run this one more time so Valerie can see it." He strode up the aisle, chuckling. "Watch," he told us. "Bet you everything goes wrong once Valerie's in the audience." He then shouted, "Crew! Set us up for one last run-through!"

Just as the door swung shut behind him, Sam rounded the stage flats and hopped down to our level. He grinned at Baxter and me. "Did that scene look as good from the seats as I think it did?" he asked.

"It sure did," I said. "We were just talking about how amazing Flint is. I wouldn't even *dream* of training Pavlov to do all of that in less than a month."

"No kidding. That's Flint for you. The smartest dog I ever met."

"I can't argue with you," I said, "and I've met literally hundreds of dogs."

"I just wish my brother had lived to see this. Once we get all the kinks worked out, I mean. And once Flint's on Broadway."

"From your lips to God's ear," Karen said.

A hinge on the door squeaked. I turned to look. John strolled down the aisle toward us. Flint had spotted his owner returning, and leapt to his feet, his tail wagging. He started to trot up to the front of the stage, but froze when he assessed his owner's mood. Although John had been smiling at first, his expression morphed into an angry glare. He marched toward Sam. A few steps behind him, Valerie was following him into the theater, looking worried. This must have been John's first encounter with Sam since getting out of the hospital.

He pointed at Sam. "You're fired!"

Chapter 11

Valerie picked up her stride. "Actually, he *isn't*," she said to John. "I put Sam on notice yesterday morning. Which I decided was the appropriate response to *my* employee's actions to date."

"And I intend to be a model employee from here on out," Sam told her. He shifted his gaze to John. "I'm turning a new leaf. Coming in on time. Checking all the nuts and bolts and loose screws around this joint."

John glowered at Sam. "Valerie's your boss. So I can't fire you from the Creede Playhouse. But I *am* revoking the contract you and I have. It's now null and void. You tried to kill me!"

I had to all but literally bite my tongue. John was leaping to conclusions again. Sam struck me as by far the most *convenient* person for John to suspect, which did not make him guilty—or innocent.

"Give me a break," Sam protested. "I had nothing to do with the sloppy work on the overhead lights, or your poisoning-by-wildflower."

"I don't trust a single word you say."

"Whatever, dude. I'll have a lawyer contact you."

"Like *you* could afford a lawyer."

Sam snorted. He turned toward Valerie. "I've got to go meet that guy in North Creede...with the railroad ties he wants to donate to us."

"Thanks, Sam," she said, watching John all the while.

Sam stormed up the aisle.

"You and I need to talk," Valerie said to John under her breath. She trotted after Sam.

The actors took it on themselves to leave the stage. Flint was watching John with his ears back. He was ready to jump between his owner and anyone confronting him. Pavlov had sat up, also alert. I kept telling myself to keep my mouth shut. Sam might indeed have been behind the poisoning, but it seemed just as likely that Felicity or one of the actors was guilty. Furthermore, John had just now validated my suspicion that he'd planned to give Sam short shrift all along.

"What are you doing, John?" Baxter asked quietly, as all the actors found other places to be and wandered offstage. "You can't be certain he was behind the poisoning."

"Maybe not, but I *am* certain he's making me miserable. I tried to help him out. This is the thanks I get."

"You think you deserve thanks for cheating Sam's brother out of the victory he deserved in the herding competition?"

"Flint lost because of lousy luck...and being off his game. There was this one sheep that—"

"Enough B.S., John!" Baxter growled. "I thought you were a standup guy, all this time! The least you can do is *not* lie to my face!"

For a moment, John looked pale and unsteady on his feet. He dropped into the nearest seat on the aisle. “Look, Baxter. There’s a lot of rancid water under this bridge. Truth is, I’m not proud of myself for what I did two years ago. The way I acted back then...that isn’t me.”

I studied Baxter’s face, wondering if he was reminding himself that he and John had met and became friends three years ago, when John was or wasn’t himself.

“I got into some real bad habits,” John continued. “Snorting cocaine, for one. So, yeah, I was desperate for the money I felt Flint alone could help me earn. I was too broke to pay what he was worth. So I took the only way out I could find. I bribed some roadie who was feeding and cleaning up after the pens to make sure Flint didn’t win. I had him plant a dime-sized electronic speaker near one of the sheep’s ears and take it off right after the event. I’ve hated myself long enough. Once I found out his brother died, I tried to make amends. I gave Sam the chance to get his feet back under him. That’s more than most people would do. And I’m the guy who can make Flint a bigshot on stage. I’m telling you, he’s so smart he can be right up there with that dog, *Eddie*, on Frasier.”

I couldn’t stop myself from growling in disgust. Both he and Baxter looked at me. “Dogs don’t care about fame and money. Only the people in the dog’s pack care about that stuff.”

John spread his arms. “That’s why I wanted the Geller name to be famous for training him. Along with training all of the future ‘Blues.’ But that obviously isn't in the cards. Sam hates me and wants me dead."

"Sometimes that's the way it goes," Baxter retorted. "Sometimes when you cheat someone, they don't forgive you...and their lives remain screwed up permanently."

"That's *not* what's happening here. Sam has always been a screw up. He didn't need my help to get him there. His brother was the one with all the smarts and the class. *He's* the one I'd give anything to set things right with. I didn't know he had a terminal disease. I swear to God I didn't. I got the damned ball rolling, and I just...I just didn't know how to stop it."

"I have a couple of ideas," I said, getting to my feet. "How about contacting the Denver Stock Show and telling the officials what you did? How about contacting the reporter who wrote the story about Geller's dog's unexpected loss and explaining that he *hadn't* lost? You can let the man have his competition record restored posthumously, like he'd deserved!" My righteous anger was morphing into tears. I was too choked up to continue talking. I turned on a heel and left.

I went to the women's room and collected myself. I also chastised myself for leaving both Baxter and Pavlov in the lurch just now. Maybe Baxter would better understand than I could how his friend got to such a nadir. And why he'd ignored the chance to atone. All John had ever needed to do was hire *Sam* as "Blue's" trainer, from the very first minute he'd arrived, seeking employment.

***

I returned to the auditorium and quickly found Baxter. He was standing in a back corner, looking at his cell phone. I walked up to him. He grabbed my hand and gave it a gentle squeeze. "You were right about John. Sorry I got you into this mess."

"That's not your fault. Besides, I'm not sorry I'm here. Working with Flint has been a joy."

"Which is a lot more than we can say about his ruthless owner."

"Even so, I'd like to see if we can get Flint through at least two flawless performances, like we originally agreed when we took this job."

"Me, too."

"Let's see if we can get the actors back out here for at least one run through of all the scenes that Flint's in."

Baxter shook his head. "John told them all to leave, and to be back here at six." He put his phone in his back pocket.

I couldn't resist giving Baxter a hug. "Where's John now?"

"He said he was going to try and track down Sam and have a long, honest conversation with him."

"Maybe they can come to terms. Maybe he'll see fit to hire Sam as Blue's permanent trainer...meaning both Flint and Pippa. We'll be gone in another five days. He could take over then."

Baxter gave me a look that meant he was more cynical than I was. "That'd be nice. If the police get to the bottom of the poisoning, and Sam's cleared."

My mood picked up when I saw Flint was sharing his bed with Palov. The dogs were facing opposite directions, their backs pressed together as they snoozed.

"John also said he'd leave it up to you to decide if you want to give Blue's cues tonight, or if you'd rather he do it."

"*I'd* like to. We'd better get something to eat. Then let's take the dogs out for a hike. The fresh air will do us all some good. Besides, it's therapeutic for Flint, and that's what I'm here for."

"Preaching to the choir," Baxter said with a grin. "It was getting late, so I already ordered a couple of pizzas. I figured there'll be somebody else who missed lunch. It shouldn't be hard to find takers for a few slices."

"Good idea." I headed toward the stairs. "I'm going to go ask Felicity if she's hungry. I want to see Pippa's outfit."

I must have said Pippa's name too loudly. She was already barking and running down the stairs. She was wearing a dark-brown fake-mink cape, and a matching pill-box hat.

***

Less than an hour later, I'd proven to myself that Flint knew the role of Blue backwards and forwards. All I had to do was say the right commands at the right time, keep my voice level and enunciate carefully. He could do the rest.

Greg's and my eyes happened to meet as I was trying to gauge what I should do next. He had some tomato sauce on his cheek, which he realized on his own. He shook his head amiably. “Another late lunch eaten while standing on my feet in a dusty, dark wing of the stage.”

“Sounds fun.”

“Yeah. It is.”

“Allie, when’s the next run through?” Karen asked.

“Maybe never,” I said. “Certainly not today.”

“You’re calling it a day?” Greg asked.

“Yeah. Just doesn’t look to me like the dog needs another rehearsal, and you all certainly don’t need one.”

“Great,” Greg said. “I’ll tell Sally and Hammond. I’m sure they’re arguing somewhere. This will cheer them up.”

He left.

I looked at Baxter. “Good decision, Allie.” He grabbed the dogs’ leashes and proceeded to snap them onto their collars. Both dogs were wagging their tails so strongly that their rear ends were also moving from side to side.

“Border Collies need a lot of daily exercise, and it strikes me as possible that his having been fully exercised prior to going on stage in his role could be really helpful to his performance.”

“All the better, then,” Baxter said, handing me Pavlov’s leash. “Oh, actually, let’s switch leashes. “Seeing as you’re on the clock, you should—”

“Hey, guys,” Karen said. I wasn’t sure if the “guys” referred to the dogs or Baxter and me. She was already joyfully greeting both dogs with ear rubs and exuberant praise. She straightened. “I hate to rain on your parade, but we only have two hours.”

I glanced at my watch. "It's not even two p.m. The play doesn't—"

"I went out front to grab a coffee a few minutes ago. I bumped into John on the way back. He said we're all meeting at four. He claimed he just needed a nap, then would be right back." She took a long look at Flint, then at me. "Are you already planning to be giving Blue's commands tonight, I hope?"

"Yes, I am."

"Oh, good. I hope John gets some rest. He was all sweaty and ashen looking, and I had visions of him passing out again."

"We'll be ready. And Flint seems to be on top of his game."

"He did great on that scene John added toward the end of the play. Are you going to try that on for size tonight?" Karen asked, smiling. "I love that scene."

"We're going to talk to John about it first. Probably tomorrow or Thursday night would be better."

We started to head for the exit. "Are you taking the dogs for a walk?" Karen asked. "And if so, can I join you?"

"Yes, to both questions," I said. I was eager to get a chance to know Karen better. We'd spoken only a little, and I felt that of everyone in the cast, she might give me the most unbiased take on how John behaved around his dog. Maybe I could swing the conversation around to John giving his dog tranquilizers.

"We were talking about more of a hike than a walk," Baxter said. "John told me there was a nice path up to the original location of Creede and toward Inspiration Point."

"Great idea," Karen said. "I know exactly where that is. John and I took Flint for a walk there just last week. There's a nice view. We'll just avoid going up to the rim. He told me he didn't want Flint near it. They did a lot of surface mining there, and it's pretty much an open pit. He was afraid Flint would fall and hurt himself."

Chapter 12

Karen explained that dirt road we were walking along was taking us into the silver mining district of Bachelor Loop, which I decided was a less daunting name than Widower's Loop. From the moment we started walking, Flint seemed to be tracking some familiar scent. For my part, as soon as I saw how sandy the soil was along the fairly inclined path, I could see why John didn't want his dog running to the edge of a steep drop-off. Not to mention me and my stupid fear of heights. I had no intention of going near the thing.

"Does John take Flint on this hike often?" I asked Karen.

"At least three times a week," she said. She pointed at what looked like a dilapidated building ahead of us. "That's the Commodore Mine. But that's another site to avoid. All of those yellowish, jagged boulders are waste rock that's contaminated Willow Creek with heavy metals. John doesn't like to have Flint climb on them."

"I don't blame him," I said, even though there was something truly majestic about the site. The view appeared to be broadening into a breathtaking scene. We headed along the trail to the right instead.

Flint was really pulling, whatever scent he was following seemingly stronger here. He clearly wanted me to break into a sprint. Pavlov, too, was not maintaining her heel position, eager to keep up with Flint.

"Do you mind if I hold his leash?" Karen asked. "I really miss Sandy, my Collie."

Baxter had Pavlov's leash, so I was going to have both of my hands free, and frankly, that was probably wise. Her mention of a "rim" made me worried that I might need to lie flat and hug the ground at some point. I gave her Flint's leash. "My mom has a Collie named Sage," I told Karen.

"Aren't they just a wonderful breed?" she asked.

"One of my favorites. I have a Cocker and a King Charles Cavalier at home. At my mother's house, actually. Along with her new husband's Golden, they have four dogs."

"Where do they live? Boulder?"

"Berthoud."

She nodded as if she knew that small town's location.

"Are you a native Coloradoan?" I asked.

"I am, actually. Born and raised in Denver."

"I'm a native Coloradoan, too."

"How about you, Baxter?"

"Moved here from Chicago," he answered with a grin.

"Did you know anybody in the cast or at the theater before you took the role?" I asked Karen.

"Only by reputation. Both Hammond and Sally are much better known than I am. I've been a member of the Actors Guild for longer, though."

"What about Greg?"

She hesitated. "He was making a big name for himself on the stage as a young actor. Unfortunately, he got into some trouble with the law. Drunk driving. He was a real natural, from what I've heard. He's been remaking his image, though."

"Huh," I said. If we knew each other better, I'd have told her that he was the weak link in the play. "From the performances I've seen, he gave his best performance last night in the final act."

"Stage magic," she said with a nod. She smiled, while keeping her eyes focused on the path ahead of us. "That's one of the reasons I've hung in there with my spotty career. I live for the exhilaration I get when I and everyone in the scene with me catches fire. It's like nothing else. You no longer feel like you're reciting lines. You're simply speaking your mind. You've melded with your character so completely, you're one and the same."

Our conversation lagged as we made our way around a craggy jag in the path. It appeared to me as if the dogs were leading us off course, but I assumed that was due to John avoiding the rim; Flint was striding with the confidence of a dog on a familiar trail.

"How's John as a director?" Baxter asked.

Karen peered at him and chuckled a little. "He's getting the job done, let's say. I imagine that it's hard to direct your own work. He's chosen not to get the perspective of an experienced director."

"I would imagine getting an outsider's opinion with lots of experience would have been wiser," I said. "Just in terms of being logical."

Karen made no comment.

"There is certainly plenty of backstage drama going on," I prodded. "Is that typical for stage productions?"

"Thankfully, no. But, drama *is* the lifeblood of all of us. So things *do* tend to get blown out of proportion in this business."

"A jab from a tack actually *was* an attempted murder," Baxter said.

"You do know I had nothing to do with that, right?" Karen asked both of us. "I mean, I know you saw my flowers, and the police took them in to their lab to examine them further. But no matter what the tests show, it wasn't *me* who tried to hurt John."

"I'm sure of that," I said. In truth, I wasn't *completely* sure, but of anyone I'd met at the Creede Repertory Theatre, I considered her the least likely to be guilty.

"John's a personal friend of yours, right, Baxter?"

"He *was*. I guess he still is. Can't say I have a whole lot of respect for how he cheated in order to win ownership of Flint."

"I know. That was pretty disturbing. I don't think that would have ever come out, except for the police investigation and all." She gave Baxter a sympathetic smile. "John can be a great guy. When his ambition doesn't get in his way. It probably has something to do with his childhood."

"He had a rough childhood?" I asked.

She shook her head. "That's just me, playing amateur psychologist. I only met him a few months ago when I auditioned. I know next to nothing about his childhood. Common knowledge about *all* of us actors is that we felt deprived as kids...that we were so love-starved, we need the fix of an audience's applause."

"Do you know Sam Geller personally?" I asked.

"No." She studied my features. "Why do you ask?"

I gazed at Flint. He was sniffing the ground and the air, happily keeping ahead of us. "For Flint's benefit. I'd like to know whether or not John's claim that *Sam* is the one sabotaging the dog's performances has any validity."

"I think someone acted irrationally...in the heat of the moment," Karen said. "I can picture someone being so mad at John, they grabbed a tack from the corkboard, jabbed it into the stem of the Monkshood, and affixed it to the sleeve. But I honestly don't have any idea *who*."

"Sam never grumbled to you or to your fellow cast members about how little he thought of Sam?"

She shook her head. "He's not much of a talker." She grimaced. "He's more the...silent ogler type."

"He ogles you?" I asked, alarmed. I'd enjoyed his company today.

"During costume changes. Sometimes you really don't have much time for modesty. And we're always wearing underwear. He probably watches because he's a newbie to theater."

"Does *John* strike you as a good dog owner?" Baxter asked, somewhat surprising me. Maybe he was souring on John Morris as much as I was.

"Absolutely," Karen answered. "He always treats Flint well. In my presence, at least."

Our incline grew steeper. I was beginning to get nervous. I needed to talk to get my mind off this incline. "Did Flint ever appear to be stressed because John was near?"

"Well, he was panting quite a bit when he was backstage during his performances. But not during his rehearsals. So I don't know what that was about." She grimaced. "It seemed like classic stage fright to me."

"Did he ever appear to be drugged...dazed or anything?"

"No, I just...can't say. I was in my character's head. Even when I'm backstage, I'm trying to stay in character. During a performance, I'm always looking at him as if he was my new husband's fondest other. When—"

She broke off and cried, "Whoa!"

Flint suddenly went into hyper-drive, trying to race up the slope. Karen was jerked off balance and lost her grip on the leash. "Wait! Stop!" she hollered.

"Flint, Come," I called. "Come, Flint!"

Pavlov, too, started straining against her leash and whining, which was unlike her. Baxter was having to put his full strength into keeping ahold of her leash. She paused to sniff at a rock, near where Flint had decided to bolt.

Karen chased Flint up the slope. I was frozen, helplessly yelling, "Come!" The rim was just a few strides away.

There was a red stain on a portion of the rock that had darkened the sandy ground alongside it.

"Is that blood?" I asked Baxter, as I stared at the reddish splatter on the ground and the rock.

Baxter was too busy holding Pavlov back from charging ahead to look.

"Pavlov, sit," I said. She stopped pulling and sat down, though she continued to whine. I took the leash from Baxter and wrapped it once around the narrow trunk of an aspen tree, to make sure I could prevent her from pulling free from my grasp.

Flint was barking continuously. He had stopped at the highest elevation—at what must be the rim that John had felt was too treacherous for Flint to get near.

"Karen, wait," Baxter said. "Let me get Flint. Stay with Allie."

Flint had stopped just twenty yards or so ahead of us. "Flint, come!" I called once again. He made no move to obey me. He gave me just one glance and then turned his head back to the mine entrance. A second later he took a wide-legged stance and barked at me.

"Something is up there. He wants us to come see," I said, thinking out loud.

Karen returned, and I had her grab the handle of Pavlov's leash, in case Pavlov chose to zip around the tree and unwrap it. I followed Baxter partway up the incline, needing to be careful not to get too dizzy.

Baxter raced up to where Flint was standing. He grabbed Flint's leash and stood staring into the pit below.

"Aw, crap. A man's down there. I think he's dead. He's not moving at all." He seemed to sag as he continued to stare. "Call nine-one-one," Baxter called to Karen.

"It's not John, is it?" I asked, climbing toward him.

He shook his head and took a couple of steps toward me. "Wait there," he said.

I was confident I could meet him halfway. "It's not a steep drop off, is it?"

Flint stopped to tinkle. Baxter shook his head. "Less than ten feet, and it's graded. I need to get down there, though. He could need CPR."

"There's no signal—no cell coverage here," Karen said.

I took a deep breath and strode to where Baxter stood. I took two more steps, and took a glimpse at the supine figure below us, his head cranked to one side, his neck at an unnatural angle.

I returned to Baxter's side and grabbed his arm. "That's Sam."

Chapter 13

"It isn't anybody we know, is it?" Karen asked. She continued to hold Pavlov's leash.

We pretended not to hear her question.

My head was spinning. This all felt too hideous to bear. We had been on a simple hike with the dogs! Sam had been alive and well just an hour or two ago. Maybe none of this would have transpired if I hadn't told Karen that there were highly toxic flowers in her bouquet from an anonymous fan.

Baxter said in a half-shout, "Flint, heel."

I stared again at the body, willing my eyes to stop seeing that this was really happening. My vision swam. "There's something in his hand," I said, so woozy now that I took a seat on the hard-packed dirt. I sunk my face into my knees.

"Yeah. It looks like it's a small piece of cloth," Baxter said.

"I'm going down there," he said, breaking into my silent self-flagellation. "He could still be alive. You've got to hold onto Flint's leash and keep him up here. Okay?"

I sat up and took the leash handle. Flint sat down beside me, panting. I tried to take deep, even breaths.

Baxter's footfalls were noisy as he descended the hardscrabble slope. "It's plaid," he said. I knew at once that he was talking about the piece of cloth in Sam Geller's hand. "A light-brown plaid."

"Damn it," I muttered to myself. John had been wearing a light-brown plaid shirt today.

"Are you okay?" Karen called up to me.

"Fine. Baxter's checking to see if the man is still alive," I answered. "We'll come down soon. Please just keep Palov with you."

Baxter made his way back up to Flint and me. "He's dead. I'm going to stand guard. You and Karen need to get the police up here. Bring the dogs back to town with you."

He helped me to my feet.

"Are you steady enough to walk?" he asked.

I avoided his gaze. I needed to just keep going. Block my feelings. Get help. "I'm fine." I started to trudge down toward Karen.

"Allie," Baxter said. "It's John's pocket. Sam's holding John's pocket. But he wouldn't have done this. I don't see any footprints near Sam, but the killer could have covered them up, after planting John's shirt pocket. Somebody must have framed John."

I managed a feeble nod. I led Flint to rejoin Karen and Pavlov.

"Are you okay?" she asked.

I nodded.

"Does *your* cell phone have any coverage?" she asked.

I pulled it out of my pocket and glanced at it. "No signal bars," I said. "We need to head toward town until we can get a signal."

We began to walk side by side. She studied my features. "It's someone we know, isn't it?"

"Yes. It's Sam Geller."

She hesitated for a moment, then continued to trudge beside me. The dogs were flanking us, silent now, no longer tugging on their leashes.

"Allie...this is all just.... It's not right. None of this is right. This theater has been producing plays every summer for more than fifty years. We're just doing an amusing little play about a dog wanting to reunite his owners."

"I know. I was thinking the same thing."

After a heavy silence, she asked, "Would John have killed Sam over their dispute with his play?"

"I don't know. I hope not." *But that's sure how it looked.* "Baxter thinks the killer was trying to frame John."

"Maybe it was an accident?" she said as if asking a hopeful question.

I gave no reply. I couldn't envision John and Sam walking along the rim, arguing, then Sam clutching John's pocket as he fell. If that had happened, he would have called the police, and they'd be here.

Was the bloody rock the killer's bludgeon? Why was it so far from the rim? The ground didn't look as if Sam's body had been dragged to the edge of the pit—after he'd been knocked unconscious. Could he have hit his head, then staggered up the incline, and fallen into the rocky pit? After having grabbed John's shirt pocket earlier?

"If it's a frame-up, that's maybe even worse news," Karen said. "It's got to be someone we know, who had it out for both of them."

Karen and I trotted down the path in a dark silence. We kept checking the bars on our phones to see if we were within signal range. We had probably only gone a couple hundred yards or so before we got a strong enough signal to place a 911 call, which I made. I gave the dispatcher my name and said that Baxter McClelland had found the body of Sam Geller when we were hiking on a trail to Inspiration Point.

"No, we left the trail to Inspiration Point," Karen corrected. "We're in North Creede."

"Sorry. My friend Karen says we're in North Creede. We found Sam's body in an open mining pit."

"Can you tell me precisely where you found the body?"

My heart was pounding and I was starting to lose my temper. I wanted to scream at her that there couldn't be all that many open mining pits near North Creede.

"Can you talk to the dispatcher?" I asked Karen and thrust my phone at her. "She needs you to describe Sam's precise location."

Karen answered questions for a minute or two, then asked, "Can you hear me?" three times, before hanging up. "We lost the signal," Karen told me.

"Let's go rejoin Baxter and wait for the police."

We walked in silence and spotted Baxter standing guard at the rim. He turned to face us when Pavlov gave him a little yip in greeting.

"We got through to nine-one-one," Karen told him. "The sheriff will be here soon."

Pavlov whined again, and I released her from her heel and let go of her leash. She promptly went over to Baxter's side and leaned against him. I probably should have done the same thing. Instead I stayed put, feeling miserable about myself and the horror of a human being lying dead just below my vision. I wanted to be whisked back in time to yesterday morning, so that I could decide not to come to Creede after all.

A pair of officers arrived within fifteen minutes. Sergeant Caulfield explained that they'd parked at the trailhead. A second group arrived, none of them in uniform. After we explained that we'd gone on a hike and discovered the body, the sergeant said he'd drive us into town and take our statements at the station house and would then return us to the theater. The three of us and the two dogs weren't going to fit easily into one car. Baxter quickly said he and Pavlov could wait and ride down later, while Karen, Flint, and I went down in another vehicle.

Karen started crying in the police car. "You okay, miss?" the officer asked.

She shook her head. "I just can't believe this is happening. Sam was just... one of those people you see every day and ignore. He's the guy that's always one step away from being a drunken homeless guy. All he needed was a break." She looked at me. "We were only just now talking about him. I feel terrible."

"Because you didn't like him?" the officer asked.

"Because I didn't think highly enough of him to get to know him. He wasn't an actor, or writer, or designer. Not anybody who fit into my circle of friends. It's like I'd already decided he wasn't important enough to befriend."

"Apparently somebody figured he deserved to be killed. Looks like he tore someone's pocket off before he fell. Did either of you recognize the cloth in his grasp?" the officer asked.

Karen and I exchanged glances. "I'm pretty sure it was a pocket ripped off the shirt that John Morris was wearing," I said, realizing even as I spoke that I was fudging. It *was* John's shirt pocket.

I felt like crying myself. I was being a terrible girlfriend. Baxter was reeling at the enormity of what we'd just discovered. As bad as it was for Karen and me, it had to be twice as painful for Baxter, knowing John was so likely to be the prime suspect. Yet I'd left him to wait up there to ride down by himself. Still, at least he had Pavlov with him. She would be his loyal companion no matter what transpired.

Karen got through her individual interview much faster than Baxter or I did. She volunteered to take Flint with her to the theater, assuming there was still going to be a performance that night. I refused to let Flint leave my side, however. I was unwilling to risk John giving him yet another tranquilizer.

It was after six p.m. by the time we arrived at the theater. The lobby was empty. The ticket taker said to us, "The staff is in the auditorium. We've had terrible news tonight."

I merely nodded. Baxter thanked her and opened the door for me. Flint maintained a heel position.

The first person I saw as we walked down the aisle was John. He was sitting on the edge of the stage. His eyes were huge. He looked like a frightened little boy. Sally sat beside him, rubbing his back. He was now wearing a preppy-looking black, short-sleeved golf shirt. Beside me, Flint's tail was wagging at the sight of his owner, but he stayed put. I could see the backs of heads of the three other actors, seated in the front row. Felicity, too, was sitting beside them. Valerie was pacing in the space between the stage and the front row, speaking quietly into her cell phone. As she neared the far wall and turned to face us, she nodded at us and gave us both a sympathetic-looking smile.

Baxter and I stopped at the foot of the aisle, and both dogs sat down beside us.

John looked at me. "Is it true that Sam had the pocket he tore off my shirt in his hand?"

"How did you hear that?" I asked.

"The wife of a rescue volunteer told Valerie," Sally answered on his behalf. She rose and hoisted herself up to sit beside him on the stage.

John sighed. He swiped at his brow. He looked as if he was having a panic attack. "Obviously it *is* true. I didn't kill him. I went to apologize to him. He said he was meeting someone up in North Creede, which is as big as a nickel-and-dime store, so I drove up there. I figured it'd be best if we talked things through in private, right away, rather than let things fester. It looked like he was waiting for someone...up by the 'Keep Off' sign near the strip mine. He started shouting at me right away to get the hell away from him. I grabbed his shoulder just to get him to stay put and listen. He yelled, "Let go of me," and ripped my pocket off. He threw it down and marched off. I left it there and headed back to my car. That's the truth. The whole truth. Swear to God."

"The investigators will be able to find evidence at the site," Baxter said. "Footprints. DNA."

John was staring at the floor, shaking his head the whole time Baxter was speaking. "I'm going to be arrested. I know it. I've hired a lawyer, and we're going to go to the sheriff station and tell them what really happened."

"That sounds wise," I said, thinking that he had ample reason to worry that the police would consider him a prime suspect.

He looked at Baxter for the first time. "Bax, will you come with me? Just to be there? I could use a little support."

Baxter looked at me without answering.

Just then, Valerie ended her phone conversation with a "Yep," and turned it off. "Under the circumstances, John," she said gently, "wouldn't it be best if Allie and Baxter were both here to help out at tonight's performance? Allie will be able to give Flint his cues as we'd already planned. Baxter can handle any interruptions."

"Interruptions?" John repeated.

"If the sheriff needs more information during the performance from the four of you who were...in Sam's vicinity."

John pushed himself off the stage and stood next to Valerie. "I don't want Flint to perform when I'm not here, Valerie. I want to use Pavlov. We'll be better off that way."

"*How* will we be better off?" I asked. "I want to complete what I came here to do, John. Flint is ready, and if you're right that *Sam* was behind the problems on stage, he'll do perfectly well tonight."

"Yeah, but...when Flint acts perfectly, it'll look like *I'm* all the more guilty," John said. "As if I killed him for poisoning me and screwing up my dog's performances." He looked almost wild with fright, and he was raising his voice. "He's my dog and I forbid him to go on tonight. I'm taking him with me to the police station."

"That's your prerogative," I said, though he would be dooming the play to a subpar performance.

"Don't be foolish, John," Valerie stated. "Leave Flint here. Let him perform. Let your dog prove that he can perform the play perfectly as written, without distractions."

John hesitated. He was shaking so badly you could see him tremble even at a distance. "Hell. I've hit rock bottom. I've got nothing to lose. Just...take Flint. Go ahead and put him on stage. No point in taking Flint down with me."

"John. You haven't been accused of anything," Baxter said. "You've hired a lawyer. Just do whatever he or she tells you to do. You'll be all right."

He snorted. "We'll pretend I believe that."

Sally was still sitting on the edge of the stage, her arms wrapped around herself, looking utterly miserable.

John walked up to her and patted her knee. "Break a leg tonight."

She grimaced and nodded.

"Everyone," John said using his theatrical voice, "I want you all to give the performance of your lives tonight. For all we know, this could be our last time. The sheriff might decide to shut down the production." He looked at me. "Allie, I want you to go for the penultimate scene, when Flint shuts Sally out of the house, and Karen comes to Hammond's rescue." He forced a smile. "Thanks for all the hard work you've put in to date. You've been a dream cast and crew. I thank you from the bottom of my heart."

He marched up the aisle and left. Nobody said a word. I couldn't help but wonder if that was part of the Tony-award speech he'd been envisioning delivering in another year or two.

Valerie trotted up the steps and strode onto the center of the stage. "Let's live up to John's words, here, people. Time to get into costumes and makeup. Showtime in less than ninety minutes."

Hammond rose from his seat in the front row. "Let's win this one for the Geller," he said, shaking his fist. "As well as for our beleaguered director," he added.

Sally shot daggers at him, then got to her feet and left the stage in a huff. Felicity and the other crew members, Karen, and Greg filed out of the seats. Pippa, too, had been sitting in a seat. She hopped down and started barking at Pavlov and Flint, then dutifully turned and trotted after Felicity. She must have decided the faux fur cape and hat were too hot for Pippa; she was now wearing what looked like a Brownie Uniform with a vest and cap.

Karen gave me a sad smile. "The show must go on," she said.

"Must it?" I asked. "Are you all going to remember your lines, and everything?"

She nodded. "Pretending to be someone else tonight is going to be the easy part." She went up the steps to the stage, heading to the dressing room, I assumed. She already had her water bottle, I saw.

I took a seat and started petting both of the dogs, more to steady my own nerves than anything else. Baxter took the seat beside me and gave me a hug. "We have to give John plenty of slack. Assuming he truly is innocent, which I honestly believe he is, he's put himself in a terrifying situation."

"Yeah. He sure has." I looked into Baxter's dark brown eyes. "Are you confident he didn't just...lose his temper and act out of blind rage?"

"Not really. I'd like to think he is innocent. I mean, we used to talk for hours. Hell, he was one of the few people I talked to about you. How you were dating this other guy and I knew I should back off. He was the one who told me to go with my gut. Try to let you know that you were special to me and I was willing to move heaven and earth for you."

"Really?"

"Really, Allie. I owe him. He was so happy when I told him you and I were together. And I was so proud to be able to show you off to him."

"That makes me feel all the worse about the mess he's in. But I'm glad you told me. I understand a little better now how he wound up being your friend, despite his faults."

"Right. He gave me great advice. Even though he's turned out to be a pretty big jerk."

"You took the words out of my mouth," I replied, looking down at Flint, who was lying by my feet at the end of the aisle.

A minute or two ago, John had walked right past his dog, without any acknowledgement, let alone the slightest sign of affection.

Chapter 14

"While the actors are getting ready, how about we do a sound check on your headset and Blue's speaker?" Baxter suggested.

"Can we wait half an hour or so?" I asked. "I want to just goof around with Flint for a while."

"Sure thing. Actually, I'll just test it with Pavlov, then I'll take her back to the hotel. It's probably best for Flint to be the only dog in sight during his performance."

"Thanks, honey. I love you forever."

"Love you forever, too," he replied. It was our special phrase. I believed it with my whole heart. Today, Sam Geller's "forever" had come to an abrupt end. Did *he* have a lover somewhere—current or former?

I had a pang as I remembered my former boyfriend, Russell, and how that had all come undone. As good as Baxter and I had proven to be ever since we started dating a year ago, I hated that I'd hurt Russell so badly. A huge part of what was wrong between us was that he'd harbored a deep-seated fear of dogs. He'd moved to Seattle. I truly hoped he'd met a cat-lover there, and that they were living happily ever after.

I shook my head, trying to dispel all thoughts other than my work with Flint. The most important thing I could do to help Flint perform was to use this time building his trust and confidence in his working with me. That's one of the first tips I give to new owners of an untrained dog. After having provided a safe haven, where the dog was unable to bolt out the door, jump the fence, or ingest anything harmful, for the first couple of days, no thought should be given to training, but rather to getting to know each other. Spend quality time together. Roll a ball across the floor. Squeeze the dog's squeaker toy. Even a rescued dog that is so shy and skittish that he needs initially to remain in his crate will assimilate the best by having his owner sit on the floor next to the crate and talk to him. Even if the "talking" consists of a newspaper read aloud.

I led Flint across the stage and into the back hallway. Valerie was leaning against a wall near the rear stage door. She looked worried. I walked up to her. "Are you okay?"

"Depends on your definition of 'okay.' I just—" She shut her eyes and let out a deep breath. She opened them and looked at me. "A man is dead who used to work for me. Nobody seems to think it was an accident. I was told he died from a steep fall."

I nodded. I didn't want to muddy the investigation and explain that the bloodied rock on top of the ledge meant he was likely bludgeoned prior to his landing in the bottom of the pit. "It's really hard to conceive all the calamities that have occurred in the last couple of days. It's been staggering."

"Are you going to be able to step in for John again?" she asked, her eyes searching mine as if she was trying to assess my truthfulness. "Is Flint truly ready for this?"

"I think so. Flint's a remarkable dog. He would probably do fine with anybody reading the cues to him."

"All right then. We'll go ahead and bet the farm on the dog." She smiled at Flint and gave him a pat. "You be a good Blue tonight."

He wagged his tail in response.

"Bet the farm on the dog?" I repeated. "The show's entire run has sold out. Am I missing something here?"

She furrowed her brow. "If the sheriff decides to shut us down for the next five weeks, they might as well hand us an eviction notice. We won't be able to keep our heads above water, financially."

"Why would they do that?" I asked. "A theater is a small business. The sheriff wouldn't close down a business because one of its employees was killed."

She squared her shoulders and said, "Well, sure," as if that was a definitive statement that answered my question. "I'm going to check in with the actors." She marched off.

Preferring Flint's company to hers anyway, I patted his shoulder. I remembered only then that Flint hadn't been fed yet. The sheriff had brought us all here instead of our hotel. We would have to feed him from Pippa's stash—being careful to give him nothing but kibble.

"Let's get you some dinner." He wagged his tail. I loved that. Waggy-tailed dogs never failed to cheer me. It's such a compliment when dogs wagged their tails as you neared them—provided of course they aren't growling as well. To me, tails represented the purity of a dog's emotions.

Flint and I trotted up the stairs. I dumped out and then refilled the water bowl, then scooped a cup of kibble into the food bowl. After checking carefully for chocolate masquerading as kibble, I mixed warm water into it—stirring it only because the appearance of gravy appealed to my esthetics; I'd yet to meet a dog that objected to unstirred food.

Felicity and Pippa entered the room just then, Pippa barking at Flint for happening to be eating his dinner in her bowl, just when she was expecting to be eating hers.

"Whoops," Felicity said. "Bad timing."

"My fault," I said. "I should have checked with you first. I didn't get the chance to feed Flint his dinner. The police brought us straight here."

"No, it's okay. I'm a full hour late feeding Pippa tonight, too. It's just been...such a crappy day."

"Sure has," I said. Her eyes were puffy. "Did you know Sam well?"

She shook her head. "He kept to himself. He told me once that John had told him to mind his own business and do his job. Now John's persistence at being the boss of everyone in his life has made him a murder suspect."

"He says he's innocent." I was repeating something she already knew, but I hoped she'd proffer her opinion.

"He probably *is*," Felicity said. "He has a bad temper and he's always making impetuous decisions. Always looking out for Number One.

But not too long ago, I loved him dearly. I'd hate to think I could be so wrong about the man."

Pippa was still barking at Flint, but less frequently.

"I know what you mean. *I* don't want Baxter to be thinking how a friend of his turned out to be a murderer. I'd like the police to discover it was someone from Sam's past that did this. Someone entirely unconnected to the theater."

"You and me both," Felicity said.

Greg entered the room and strode toward Flint. "How's our doggie star doing?" he said and leaned down to pat Flint on the head.

"Wait!" I cried, a moment too late.

Flint growled and snapped at Greg.

"Hey! What the hell!" Greg exclaimed, jerking his hand back.

"You startled him while he's eating," I explained. "A high percentage of dogs will snap if their meals are suddenly interrupted by someone they don't know well."

"He's never been vicious until now," Greg said, seemingly oblivious to my explanation. "He's too keyed up, is what's happening. He found a dead, bloody body just a few hours ago. Sorry, but I am *not* going to let myself get bit by a dog on stage."

"You're overreacting," Felicity said. "He simply snapped in the air. That doesn't mean he would have bitten you. It is an instinctive warning, dating back to his wolf ancestors."

"Right. Flint's merely saying to you, 'Hey! I'm eating here! This is mine!'"

Unfortunately, Valerie rushed into the room. "What's going on?" She peered at Greg. "Did Flint bite you?"

"No, but he tried to," he replied.

"Greg just should have been more careful with running up to Flint and reaching toward his dog bowl," Felicity said.

"Cripes!" Valerie said, putting her hands on her hips and glaring at Flint. "Maybe we'd be wise to cancel tonight's performance."

"You can't be serious," Felicity countered.

"A man has been murdered because of this show," she said. "The theater could be bankrupted by a wrongful death lawsuit."

"And *I* don't want to get my face ripped off by a frightened dog!" Greg said.

"Have you looked at the number of calls for cancelation tickets we've been getting?" Felicity asked. "Did you realize we have calls from ticket distributors? That we're booked solid for every seat, and being asked to add performances?"

"Of course I know that! It's my job to know our ticket sales! But it's the there's-no-such-thing-as-bad-publicity factor. All of that becomes moot if anyone gets injured on this play. I'm trying to look at the big picture. That's my job. If we continue to put this play on with business as usual, even while knowing that the police are investigating all of us as murder suspects, it would be irresponsible of me. I discussed it with my lawyer."

"Did you ask him what happens if my career is ruined by a dog biting my face?" Greg asked. "I'm the guy who sticks my face at him in Act Two and says, 'Coochie Coo!'"

"Did you discuss the theater's predicament with a *CPA*?" Felicity retorted, ignoring Greg. "Did you ask what kind of financial liability we'd be to have to refund tickets?"

Valerie sank her head into her hands. "Damn it! This is a nightmare!"

"Yes, it is," Felicity replied. "But the best and fastest way out of this nightmare is for every one of to concentrate on doing our jobs."

Valerie stood motionless for a moment, then turned to face Greg and Felicity. "Both of you, please go downstairs."

"I need to feed Pippa," Felicity said.

"I'll feed...the little Brownie," Valerie said, apparently just now noticing Pippa's outfit. "I need to talk to Allie in private."

"She gets half a cup," Felicity said.

"I know, I know. And no Reese's Pieces."

Felicity rolled her eyes, but she and Greg left, and Valerie dumped half a cup of kibble into the bowl. Pippa had started to follow Valerie, but promptly changed directions at the sound of dog food.

"God almighty," Valerie grumbled as she set the food bowl down and watched Pippa scarf down her food. "I love dogs! Now they're going to be the death of me!" She winced as if realizing how ill-timed her last statement was. She grabbed my arm. "Allida. My neck is on the line. Can you promise me that Flint isn't going to bite someone tonight?"

I felt my cheeks growing warm, knowing I could not make such a promise for any dog. Not even my beloved Pavlov was incapable of biting someone under extreme circumstances. "I can promise you that I'm extremely confident he won't bite anyone on stage. And that he won't bite anyone backstage unless he has good reason to feel like he needs to protect himself or his meal."

"Ugh. That's not good enough!" She stamped her foot. "I should never have agreed to put on John's play! I knew from the start that it was a financial risk."

"Yet it's been a huge money earner."

"And our stagehand is *dead*, while the writer director is the *prime suspect*."

"With all due respect, Valerie, that is not the fault of the play itself. Or the dog."

"No, but it's *mine*." Her shoulders sagged. "*I'm* the fool who ignored a clause about needing to put a rider on our insurance policy. If the canine on stage gets too upset and injures someone, we're sunk."

"Is *that* why John gave Flynn a sedative on Sunday?" I asked. "Because he wanted to ensure Flynn wouldn't nip one of the members of the cast?"

She nodded. "I...put it all on him. We had a big fight. He wanted me to hire you. I made the condition that if Flint was to bite anybody on the set, I'd see to it that the theater would sue *him*. And then Flint got so flipped out at the falling lights. That would have been the end of everything right there."

She hugged herself and leaned back against the wall. "I'm just here on a temporary basis. All I needed to do was *not* bankrupt the theater. I can't sleep. I'm counting the performances, waiting until I'm out of the woods. Eighteen to go. I'm never going to survive eighteen more performances."

"On the plus side, you have a hit show on your hands."

"And a murder on my conscience." Once again, she stood stock still for a full minute, then closed her eyes and said, "What is the expression? In for a penny, in for a pound?" She looked at her watch. "Cripes. It's just too late now. The audience will start a riot if I go out there and cancel the play at this point. Let's just freaking do it. *I'll* take the anti-anxiety meds instead of the poor dog." She grabbed my arm once again. "But you have to stay, Allie. Please. You have to help with keeping the dog from flipping out if John should get stuck in jail, unable to meet his bail."

"Baxter and I are determined to stay until things get resolved for John."

"Good. So we're both going to hope that means they find out whoever did this and put the person in jail right away. And that John's innocent. Because *you're* the closest thing we've got to John's understudy."

Chapter 15

The curtain opened at 7:35. I had decided I was too nervous to eat and had simply played with Flint behind the theater, taking care not to get anywhere near the river that formed the border of the theater's property. Although it wasn't a strong current, I'd had visions of bringing a soaking wet dog onto the stage, which would have been difficult to explain away, not to mention that we would have to blow dry his fur between scenes to explain why Blue was still wet two days later.

Baxter returned with twenty minutes to spare. We attached the dime-sized speaker to Flint once again. Even though Baxter had already assured me that the equipment was working, I gave it another test. Flint could hear me perfectly. From the dog's body English, even during his initial entrance onto the stage, it was quite clear to me that he was already aware of his blocking assignments before I could even relay them through my headset.

The play went off without a hitch. To my eye, at least, the performance was flawless from start to finish. None of the actors flubbed a single line. There were no costume malfunctions. No falling lights. Flint was every bit as good on stage as he was in the rehearsals. Even though he perked up his ears and looked at the audience a handful of times, the audience oohed and aahed, appreciating how cute he was.

Best of all, the new scene with Blue alone on the stage as he dialed a cordless phone was nothing short of a triumph. Following his scene, the audience gave him such a thunderous ovation that Karen had to stall by pretending she couldn't catch her breath when she burst through the front door in answer to Blue's phone call.

Even so, numerous times during the performance, I suspected a dog whistle was being blown. Flint's responses were subtle—perking up his ears and looking briefly at the audience. Baxter was once again scanning the audience surreptitiously, but when I glanced up at him after each act, he shook his head. He'd failed to spot any telltale actions in the audience.

My emotions were in a jumble as the play ended. At once I wanted to feel elated, and yet the audience's laughter and cheers felt macabre and inappropriate on this day. Yet I also felt proud of all of us for persevering despite such a hideous, heinous act. I tried to put all of that out of my head and rose with the audience and clapped as the actors took their bows.

On the opposite wing of the stage from me, Baxter gave Flint two long-stemmed roses to carry. Although we'd muffed Pavlov's curtain call on Sunday night, Blue's behavior was fully choreographed. The four actors faced him and called simultaneously, "Come, Blue!" He trotted onto center stage, holding the roses in his mouth. The final twenty-or-so audience members who weren't already giving the actors a standing ovation now rose. The applause was all but deafening.

I grinned, so proud of Flint that my eyes teared up as I awaited the huge, "Aww" he would get from the packed house. He was trained to drop both roses at Karen's feet, then to pick one up and head toward Sally, but stop, turn around, and drop a rose Hammond's feet—Blue's beloved original owners in the play. It was all but guaranteed to get a huge laugh.

Flint, however, dropped both roses before he reached Karen at his "marker two," which was when I was supposed to give him a "Drop it," command. He backed away from the roses and shook his head. Baxter and I exchanged surprised glances as the audience laughed and cheered. I gestured at Baxter to join me on the other side of the stage, and he came right over.

"Flint's still pawing at his tongue," I told him, pointing.

"It looks like the stems must have tasted bad. But Pavlov had no problem with yesterday's roses. Not with holding them in her mouth, I mean."

"Maybe they were coated in something that tastes bad." Baxter immediately sniffed at his own hand that had handled the roses immediately prior to Flint. He grimaced and touched his tongue to his finger tip. "Hot sauce," he said.

I cursed under my breath. Someone had *still* managed to muck with Flint's performance! At least whoever did it hadn't put anything horribly toxic on the stems. Meanwhile, on stage, Hammond fetched the flowers where Flint had dropped them, and gave one to Sally and one to Karen, kissing each of them and almost sweeping them off their feet in the process.

Only then did I realize that John was standing backstage in a darkened corner on the opposite wing. Our gazes met. His expression had gone from a glare to a smile. He mimed applauding for me. I gave him a thumbs-up. Even so, I didn't know what had caused his glare. Probably he, too, recognized someone had tampered with the roses. I hoped, though, that he wasn't jealous that the play had gone so well without him at Flint's audio controls.

"When did John get here?" I asked Baxter.

"He's here?"

"He was standing in the far corner just now."

Baxter looked, but John had left. "I'm surprised I didn't see him when I came down."

I signaled for Flint to come, and he trotted off the stage. I gave him a couple of treats that I had stashed in my pocket. My experience, at least, with hot sauce was a grain-based bite of something was more effective for easing the burn than drinking water.

John rounded the back of the stage and joined us. "What happened to the roses?"

"Hot sauce," Baxter said. "The roses were sitting back stage on the prop table for the whole play, per usual."

"Any idea who tampered with them?" John asked.

"'Fraid not."

"So the police didn't arrest you," I said to John. "That's got to be a huge relief."

"If only," he grumbled. "I *am* being charged. My lawyer got the D.A. to concede that, since this was supposed to be strictly an interview, not an arrest, and I had come to the station voluntarily, they'd let me go home and find a caregiver tonight for Flint. While *I* spend the night in jail. If not longer. I have to hope that the judge will allow me to post bail."

"Geez," Baxter said. "Sorry, bro. That really sucks. And it's...so premature."

"They're going to arrest you when you return?" I asked, stunned.

"Right. They'll have my bail hearing in the morning. Or the probable-cause hearing, or whatever it's called. At least it gives me the chance to talk with Sally before I'm placed under arrest. And to make arrangements for Flint's care."

"But surely you'll be able to get out on bail. Plus, their evidence is just circumstantial."

He shrugged. "They didn't believe me about the torn pocket. I didn't have any witnesses. And Sam's story about meeting the guy who was going to donate lumber doesn't seem to pan out."

"Doesn't Valerie know about the donor?"

"Yeah, and so did I, and a handful of other people. But the donor was at work all day. Sam was supposed to meet with him on Saturday. So the sheriff thinks *I* set him up to go to a place that was typically deserted, where I could make his murder look like an accident."

Sally noticed John as she along with the three actors finally came off the stage. Her coolness toward him as compared to two days ago was difficult to miss.

"Hi, Babe," he said. He tried to kiss her on the lips but she turned her cheek to him. She grabbed his arm. "Are you being arrested tonight?" she asked.

He nodded. His eyes filled with tears.

"We can watch Flint again," Baxter offered. "He and Pavlov are getting to be good buds."

"Thanks."

"I'll come to your hearing," Sally said.

"I didn't do this, Allie, Sally. I didn't kill Sam. I'm being framed."

"Do you have any idea who *did* kill him?" Baxter asked.

"Maybe the same person who planted tongue-burning hot sauce on the roses. Maybe it's someone who wants this play to fail. Even if it takes someone's murder to wreck my work."

Baxter shook his head as if with disgust. He let out a low whistle for Flint, and they both left the room. Once again, John had ignored his dog.

Sally's three fellow actors had been standing nearby, chatting, but were now blatantly listening in on our conversation. Greg took a couple of steps toward us. "At least the performance tonight went perfectly," Greg said. He looked at me. "I'm sorry I didn't trust you that Flint wasn't going to bite me. Maybe the troubles with the dog are over once and for all."

"That's a batch of baloney," John said. "Just a few minutes ago, someone dowsed the roses' stems in hot sauce. Sunday night, it was dark chocolate. And overhead lights crashing. Tomorrow night it could be a lethal toxin." He raked his fingers through his hair. "Allie, you and Baxter are going to have to protect Flint's life. I'm not going to be able to protect him myself from my jail cell."

"We'll guard him just like we would our own dogs," I said honestly.

"Whoever's doing this must know by now that we have a competent understudy," Greg said. "If someone's truly out to destroy the play, Pavlov's in just as much danger as Flint is."

"Now *there's* a reassuring statement," I grumbled.

Hammond said, "Maybe someone was eating a taco at the table and spilled some sauce without realizing it."

"None of us benefit from the show being shut down," Sally said. "We'd all be out of jobs. And it would crater the entire season for the theater."

Felicity was also approaching and overheard. "Are you talking about what would happen if we had to close *Good Dog, Blue!* this week?" she asked.

Sally nodded.

"Oh, that would crater more than just the season," Felicity exclaimed. "It would effectively bankrupt us."

"Right," John said. He now looked more angry than depressed, at least. "Nobody with a stake in this theater's future would be pulling this kind of crap. Which means I have no motive, damn it all! That hick of a sheriff we've got has his head up his ass."

"Unless the murderer was a hothead, who tends to do and say things without thinking them through," Felicity growled, glaring at John the entire time.

John balled his fists. "For the last time, I did nothing wrong, Felicity! And you're every bit as big of a hothead as I am!"

"Tell that to the judge in your bail trial," she snapped. "I'm sure she or he will be thoroughly impressed."

"On that note," I said, "it's time for me to call it a night. Do you want Baxter and me to take Flint with us to the hotel?"

John grimaced, then nodded. "You'd better. I still have to pack a bag before I turn myself in to be arrested. They agreed to let me wear my own clothes tonight. A small town courtesy from our hick sheriff."

"Chin up, Captain," Hammond said. "You'll be out on bail in the morning, and you'll be able to write with authority on what it feels like to be thrown in the slammer."

John gaped at him. "Are *you* trying to help me experience punching my lead actor in the nose?"

"No, sir." He took a step back. "I hope things go smoothly, and you're exonerated quickly."

John mumbled his thanks.

I left and located Baxter, who was outside with Flint, and told them both that Flint was coming to the hotel with us for the night. Baxter said he wanted a private word with John, so I said I'd meet him at the hotel and took control of Flint's leash.

It was a beautiful night, and a pure pleasure to breathe in the crisp night air and walk the couple of blocks to the hotel. Behind me, there was still a hint of a reddish glow tinging the craggy mountain tops from the setting sun. The world continued to go on its course, despite the out of control behavior of its inhabitants. Sunsets, mountains, love, dogs. There were many wonderful things to balance out the bad.

I spotted the car in the parking lot, curious to see that someone had stuck a piece of paper under the windshield wiper; no other car windshields had one, so it was unlikely to be an ad. I pulled it free.

In block printing from a Sharpie, the note read: *Leave now or else you're next!*

Chapter 16

The sheriff had little to say when Baxter and I gave him the threatening note. I had gotten Flint settled in our room with Pavlov and waited for Baxter by the car, showed him the note, and we'd driven here together. "It's most likely a prank," Sheriff Caulfield said. "Folks around here would know by your license plates that you're from out of town. It's a cheap way to get a laugh from some drunkard's buddies. Though I can see why it upset you."

"No kidding," Baxter said. "Do you suppose anyone with half a brain *wouldn't* be upset by a death threat?"

"Like I said. It's upsetting, and we'll do our best to try and track down the jerk who wrote it. If we do, he or she will get their due punishment. But you said yourself just this afternoon that your connection to Sam Geller is all but nonexistent. That you're helping to improve upon the training of a dog that his late brother once owned." He spread his fingers as if to emphasize his words. "For this to be a *serious* threat from the killer, you'd have to be doing something to tick off his killer something fierce."

"Maybe I *am*, and I just don't realize it. Maybe I'm unknowingly interfering with the killer's master plan," I said.

"Okay," Sheriff Caulfield said. "Let's go with that theory. So you tell me. *How* could you have put yourself in the perp's way? You found the body, of course. But what else have you done since you arrived Sunday afternoon?"

"I don't know. None of this makes any sense. All I've done is work with Flint, and had my dog be his understudy in one performance."

"We're also taking care of John Morris's dog," Baxter added. "John's being held in custody until the bail hearing."

"And?" the sheriff asked.

Baxter looked at me, his face blank.

"And...maybe that prevented someone from snatching Flint?" I said. That was such a weak motive, I phrased it like a question. "Or maybe I saw something that identified the killer, and I just haven't put the clues together yet. Or maybe the killer simply *thinks* I might be able to identify him or her, and wants me out of town."

"From what I heard tell, John Morris was at the theater tonight, hiding in the shadows," the sheriff said.

Again, Baxter and I exchanged glances. "Well, I wouldn't say he was deliberately hiding, necessarily. He was simply standing in an unlit corner."

"How many people besides Mr. Morris would be able to pick out your car in a hotel parking lot?"

That was a good question, and Baxter and I looked at each other in silence.

"It's hard to say," Baxter replied. There actually *wasn't* anyone we could say for certain knew what our car looked like.

Sheriff Caulfield leaned back in his chair and eyed us both. "When were you planning on heading back home?"

"Sunday morning," Baxter replied.

"The hotels are all booked solid. Maybe someone tried to scare us into leaving just because he really, *really* wants our room." Getting punchy with exhaustion, I chuckled at my lame sarcasm.

"It does get a mite crowded here during theater season," the sheriff said with a grin.

"Why are you making jokes about this, Allie?" Baxter snapped. "What if the killer is serious? He or she could be some nutcase who's hearing voices to kill anyone who comes into contact with the dog starring in *Good Dog, Blue!*"

"Frankly, I'd prefer *not* have to take this seriously."

"The Subaru is actually *your* vehicle, isn't it, Mr. McClelland?" the sheriff asked Baxter. "Maybe the note was meant for you."

"Allie and I discussed that possibility during our drive here," Baxter replied. "But it makes even *less* sense for someone to target me. I'm just here as Allie's assistant."

"But you're also Mr. Morris's friend, aren't you?"

Baxter grimaced. "Our friendship's taken a bit of a beating this weekend, but, yeah."

"Did you know anyone else at the theater? Sam Geller? Anyone?"

He shook his head. "I've met Felicity a couple of times, briefly, back when they were dating, but that's it."

The sheriff nodded. After a long silence among the three of us, he said, "You *do* realize you can leave town anytime, don't you? We have evidence that shows we've got the right guy in custody. I'm not trying to kick you out of town, but there's nothing holding you here if you want to play it safe."

"Nothing except Flint," I replied. "I want to make sure he's going to wind up in a safe, loving place when this all shakes out."

"And I want to see things through with John," Baxter said. "As long as Allie isn't risking her neck. Which is now a concern."

"That's something I'd want to take into consideration, if I was in your shoes," the sheriff said. "We do know how to reach you at your home, where you'd be safe and sound."

"Maybe you'll be able to identify someone's fingerprints on the piece of paper," I said.

"Maybe." The sheriff rose. "If Mr. Morris's prints are on it, that could help us get a confession."

"*If* he's guilty," Baxter grumbled. They'd taken my prints when we arrived on the theory that they needed to exclude my prints; Baxter had not touched the note.

***

The next day was Wednesday, and the Main Stage was dark, while the Ruth Theater, their second, newer-but-smaller venue a block away was putting on a play called *The Time Post*, which all I knew about was that it required next to no scenery. That performance would be followed by

Boomtown, their improvisational show. Originally, we had discussed taking the dogs on a long hike with John, thinking that would do wonders for Flint in terms of ridding him of his stress, which, sight unseen, had seemed a necessary step to helping Flint overcome his difficulties. After Flint's stellar performance last night, however, and John's arrest, helping to train Pippa as an understudy was a bigger priority.

Valerie arrived at the theater the same time we did. As we chatted in the lobby, Felicity emerged, hauling an armload of clothing toward the door. Pippa was following closely behind her, wearing what looked at first glance like a Yankees striped shirt.

"Something's wrong with our machine," Felicity explained. "The repairman is here now. I've got to run the costumes down to the nearest cleaners."

"If he's here now, why can't you wait until it's fixed?" Valerie asked. "We're not staging *Good Dog, Blue!* again until tomorrow."

"He isn't certain that he's got the right parts for the job. If all of the costumes for two productions need to be cleaned tonight, we'll have a disaster on our hands."

"True," Valerie said and started heading toward her office. "Heaven knows Murphy's Law has been having a field day with us."

Pippa had come downstairs with Felicity and was now tugging at the laces of her sneakers. "Not now, Pippa," she said. She looked at me. "I need someone to watch Pippa until I get back."

"I can do that," I said. I picked her up. She scrambled to get out of my arms and into

Felicity's. I wanted to talk about my training Pippa, but not while said dog was scrambling to get away from me.

"Let me take her," Baxter said.

I took him up on his offer. Pippa struggled to get out of his arms, too, as Felicity brushed past us.

"Let me get the door for you," I said, striding toward the door ahead of her.

"Thanks, Allida," she said a bit brusquely.

A piece of light-brown-plaid fabric amid her armload of clothing caught my eye.

"Wait." I grabbed at the shirt. "Is that John's shirt? With the torn-off pocket?"

A look of alarm flashed across her features. "No," she said, just as I could see for myself that this was some miniature shirt that was likely tailored to fit Pippa. "I made John that shirt for use in the play. He decided it was too casual for the character, but he liked it and wanted to keep it."

"You make duplicates of your costumes, tailored for the understudies, right? Was John's shirt with the ripped pocket the only one you made?"

"Yeah. This was back before Hammond took the role. I make Pippa's costumes with my left-over fabric."

"Was the pocket on his shirt just basted in place?"

"Probably, since it was supposed to be strictly a costume." She turned and continued walking. "I've got to keep going. This is starting to get heavy."

I wondered why she was taking Pippa's shirt—which, unlike John's, had not been worn since I'd arrived—with the costumes from last night's laundry fiasco. Maybe I was being unduly suspicious, but the only answer that came to me was, now that this particular fabric had become evidence in a crime scene, she wanted to take this opportunity to remove it from the premises.

I trotted after her. "Let me get the car door for you, too."

"Thanks," she said again, this time almost surly. She gave me a frosty, "Excuse me," and rounded the car to get behind the wheel.

Hoping to learn that John was innocent, I wanted to get to know Felicity better. For that matter, if John was guilty, I sure as hell didn't want him to go free and keep the wonderful dog that he'd essentially stolen from his murder victim. "Felicity, I'd like to work with you and Pippa on training her how to fill the role of Blue in John's play."

She stopped and looked at me, clearly delighted at the notion. "You'd be willing to do that?"

"Absolutely."

"That would be wonderful! I'm barely making ends meet, but I'd be happy to make a nice outfit for Pavlov in return."

I managed not to grimace at the notion of putting a costume on my German Shepherd. Not to be a dog snob, but I was not into dressing dogs in people clothes. Especially not large dogs who'd been bred as working dogs. German Shepherds frequently worked in canine crime units, for heaven sakes!

"Thanks, but I'm not entitled to any payment from you. Valerie already considers training Blue's understudy as part of my job here."

"Even so, I'd prefer to consider this a friendly exchange of our skills, okay?"

"Sounds like a win-win," I said. "We can get together as soon as you're back from the cleaners, or tomorrow morning."

"Now's good for me. It will only take me twenty minutes to drop the clothes off at the laundromat."

"Great." In my mind's eye, I was imagining my noble Pavlov wearing a multicolored clown costume. She would never forgive me. And Baxter would be teasing me to no end.

"I'll see you soon."

Chapter 17

When Felicity returned, Baxter told me he had some work to do and would return in a couple of hours with Pavlov and Flint.

Once again using the large room upstairs to practice in, Felicity and I grabbed a pair of foot stools from the prop room to use as pedestals for Pippa. We placed them on opposite sides of the room. We also found some rubber placemats to serve as Pippa's first, second, and third targets. Felicity joked that we should put the placemats in a diamond shape and call them "bases" in honor of her uniform, so I was right about the Yankees stripes. Maybe she'd make a Colorado Rockies shirt for Pavlov.

Truth be told, Felicity was number one on my list of suspects. She had every right to be vindictive toward John for his treatment of her and had the most to gain by setting up John to take the rap for a murder that she had committed. Surprisingly though, I found myself really enjoying Felicity's company. Most of our affinity was due to Pippa's delightful company rubbing off on us. Pippa was truly a hoot. During a sit-stay command, she did a hilarious inching of her butt toward us whenever we looked away; if this actually *was* baseball, she'd be great at stealing bases.

The adage *you can't teach an old dog new tricks* is patently false. What *is* true is that, unless you change a dog's owner, you cannot change an old dog's disposition. Pugs are adventurous, happy animals. I helped Felicity to refine a "dance" command, in which she raised up and turned in circles on her hind legs. It was adorable, if impractical. "Blue" had no scenes in which he or she turned in circles. For Pippa to become a suitable Blue stand-in, she had to learn how to go from Point A to Point B on command, which was best accomplished with pedestal-to-target training. Putting the dog on a small pedestal cuts down on her distractions so that she focuses solely on her trainer's command—and the treat that obeying the command will earn her. Pedestal training is especially valuable with a less food-motivated dog that often prefers to wander off and do her own thing, despite the promise of a biscuit; the pedestal makes those dogs think twice before walking away. Pippa *was* food-motivated, and we made quick progress with her.

After an hour or so, we decided to take a coffee break, and we chatted about how smart and amiable Pippa was. "She's doing great with the targets, Allie. I'm really impressed. We can't put the placemats on our stage, though," Felicity said. "What did you use for Pavlov on Sunday night?"

"I put an X of masking tape on each of Blue's three targets. They were subtle enough that the audience wouldn't see them, but Pavlov could both see and smell the tape."

"Wow. Good idea."

I shrugged. "It was a short-cut. We didn't have time to train Pavlov to memorize an unmarked target on stage."

"Exactly. I wish we'd consulted with you for training Pippa. Almost all of the rehearsal time went to Flint, of course, so when we threw Pippa into the role that second night, we had the actors surreptitiously drop treats where they needed her to be."

"At which time the audience saw her gobble them down, and then she would sniff and bark at their hands."

"Well, sure, that's exactly what she did. But again, the audience loved her. She was hilarious."

"It must have been hard on the actors, though. They would have to stay in character and deliver their lines while attempting to lure a dog this way and that. And not to beg for more treats the whole time."

"That's what John said. Or rather what he yelled at me."

"Why didn't he use a more suitable dog as the understudy? There are several ranches within a fifty-mile radius. There must be dozens of herder-breed dogs."

She crinkled her nose. "Well, that's kind of my fault. John felt guilty for dumping me and for stealing my idea for the play. He had plied me with the idea of having Pippa as Blue's Underdog."

"It doesn't sound like that idea lasted long."

"Yeah. Pippa's a little scamp. She was never going to act like a herder."

"Oh, I don't know. *All* dogs try to herd to some extent. They want their packs to stay together, and they don't want non-pack members to usurp them or impede on their packs."

"I guess that's true." She smiled at me. "We should get back to work."

By the end of our session, we successfully used our audio equipment on Pippa; we clipped the earbud onto her collar. She was able to go to the correct target on command, albeit waiting there eagerly for a treat. It was an excellent start. I also got her to growl on cue, when I made the growling sound—rolling my tongue.

"How long do you think it'll take me to train her to hit her targets?"

"If you work with the footstools and placemats every day for at least fifteen to twenty minutes, I'd say a week. Maybe you could even get her to strictly use masking-tape targets by then." I paused. "You'd have to work with the script and all of the other tricks that Blue does, though. You have another fifteen tricks to teach her. Even *I'm* starting to learn the script."

"Me, too. Though that shouldn't be hard, considering I wrote almost half of them."

I was surprised, and a little alarmed. "Are you serious? You *wrote* half the script?"

"I told you that before."

I shook my head. "You told us that John purchased the first draft, and that you'd written it with Blue barking so loud, she drowned out Sally's lines."

Felicity furrowed her brow. "I guess it's fair to say I wrote forty percent of the play. After John bought it, he'd constantly get me to run lines with him and make suggestions. I came up with a lot of the lines for him."

I studied her features. On a scale of one to ten, I'd give her only a three in terms of her anger toward John, which seemed off to me. "Didn't that make you furious that he took full credit?"

"Well, the thing is, he contrived a method for me to profit from the play, too, if it's successful and is picked up by lots of theaters. He wrote up a contract for me. Just like he did for Sam. If a theater hires me for costumes, they get an excellent price and simply have to provide the actors' measurements. I can make their costumes remotely and continue working here at the Creede Playhouse."

"Is that common knowledge? Does Valerie know about your contract?"

"No, we agreed to keep it quiet, just in case Valerie had any objections, which is unlikely. *Now* the issue is whether my contract is worth the paper it's written on."

I didn't know how to respond and remained silent.

Felicity snorted. "Boy, I'll tell you what, though. John's private funders must be loving this. They'll get their money back and then some."

"Because the show is sold out?" I asked.

"Not only is it sold out, Valerie extended the season."

"You mean the additional week she tacked on?"

"Not just that. She created a whole new late-fall, weekends-only season at the theater. Part of the ticket costs for the weekend performances are considered donations to the theater. None of this cast will be featured, though, not even Flint. We held a fundraiser the week before the show opened in which donors paid to have their dog trained for a week and then perform as Blue."

"Who were they planning would train the donors' dogs? Sam?"

"Yes. So I guess they'll have to hire someone now. John had no problem training Flint, but the next Blue is going to be a poodle."

"That could be a challenge. Poodles are typically not especially food-motivated."

"We'll have to muddle through with our regulars. Humorous adlibbing has always worked really well for us. I'm sure you'll enjoy the *Boomtown* performance tonight, if you get the chance to see it."

"We're planning on it."

"Good. I've got the okay to add more improvisational shows, once Valerie moves on, and I take control of the theater."

"Valerie's leaving?"

"After next year. The owners thought I should have an experienced theater manager to mentor me this year, so they brought in Valerie. Then next year, I'll hire someone to take my place as head costume designer. But this year, I'm shadowing Valerie, as much as she'll let me."

"That means you'll be able to choose the shows you want to stage. You would have been able to select *Good Dog, Blue!*, even if Valerie had turned it down this season."

She averted her gaze. "Yeah, I kind of lost out on earning some money from a sure thing."

"To be honest, Felicity, if I were in your shoes right now, I'd have been vindictive as all hell."

She gave me a sly grin. "Oh, I had my share of vindictive behavior. Karen was supposed to be the other woman. John switched Karen and Sally's roles once Sally and he became a thing."

"Why?"

"Probably because Sally asked him to. Though it is possible that he could see Sally was truly better in the bigger, showier role."

That had to have been painful for Karen. "How long were they playing each other's roles?"

"Just a little over a week. Only in the rehearsals, of course."

"Was that confusing for Flint when they switched parts?"

She shrugged and averted her eyes. "A little."

I waited. When she didn't say anything, I asked, "Is this where the 'vindictive' part kicks in?"

"Sort of. But keep in mind that, again, Flint was just being used in rehearsals, and this was long resolved by the time you came into the picture. It had nothing to do with Flint's problems with his performances and was utterly unrelated to John's poisoning and Sam's death."

"Go on," I said, already assuming she was scenting the costumes to confuse Flint.

"Karen and I wore the same size. So I'd make the costumes and wear them when I was home alone. I'd even...rub them on Flint. Which was highly inappropriate, back when she was playing the other woman. I'd put John's scent on articles of Hammie's costumes from some personal items of John's. *I'm* the costumer, and it was common sense to further encourage Flint to cozy up to costumes worn by his stage parents."

"Except you scented the other-woman's clothes," I said.

"Right. Once they switched roles, I started rubbing Sally's costumes on Flint and me. I did that in their rehearsals, and I laundered them before the premier."

"Border Collies are smart enough to identify people in more ways than their scents. Flint would know he was always supposed to herd Greg and Karen away from his humans and toward each other."

"Right. So my trickery only indirectly led to the troubles on stage. The week before the season began, Sam caught me rubbing one of Sally's skirts on my legs. He got a kick out of it. He told me he was Flint's rightful owner, and that he hoped one day to convince John to let him train another dog for the role and keep Flint for himself."

"Uh, oh. Are you saying *you* were behind wrecking Flint's stage performances?"

She grimaced. "Partly. Sam and I joined forces."

I stared at her, stunned. Maybe she had put Sam up to ruining John's play and poisoning him.

Chapter 18

My thoughts raced. Perhaps I should have been angry on John's behalf, but prank-playing was so trivial compared to murder. Felicity was playing patty-paws with Pippa; the Pug was wriggling on her back, making cute little grunty noises. Her dandling with her dog allowed her to keep her eyes averted. She was blushing.

"Did you tell the police that?"

"Yes. But...only after Sam was murdered. I was afraid to tell the sheriff the truth when he interviewed me about the poisoning. I was scared it would incriminate *me*. I mean, here it was, a poisoned sharp tack sewn into an alteration that I made just an hour before John went on stage. I explained that to Sheriff Caulfield once Sam was killed. I'm probably *still* the top suspect for the attempted murder. I didn't do it, yet they can always press charges. John's probably trying to convince them I'm guilty. His motives are lessened if he convinces the police he didn't think Sam was the one who tried to kill him."

"*Did* Sam try to poison him?"

She grimaced a little. "He told me he didn't."

"Did you believe him?"

"Not really." She rubbed her forehead. "But like I said, Allie, I just wanted to mess with John's head. I never would have teamed up with Sam if I'd known that Sam wanted to poison John."

"We'll probably never know either way," I said. Now that Sam was dead, if someone else was behind the poisoning, he or she would keep their mouth shut. I wasn't even sure how seriously the authorities would be motivated to investigate other suspects beside Sam, now that the victim was under arrest for his murder.

"My point is, though," Felicity said, "now that someone killed Sam, I knew I had to come clean immediately. I told the sheriff all about the arrangement we had."

"Was Sam using a dog whistle?"

"Sort of. It was a squeaker toy he tucked inside the hem of his sock. All he had to do was squeeze his ankles together as he was standing to make it whistle."

"Huh. It looked to me like the sound was coming from the audience, not from backstage."

"Yeah. He moved it after the second performance...when Pippa was starring. Though I have to say, I doubt he ever used it with Pippa on stage. She was already struggling. Sam didn't want John to get wise to him. Then I saw Sam repairing a cushioned seat in the auditorium. At least that's what he *told* me he was doing. After Flint's *second* bad performance, I told him flat out that he either stop with *all* the dog whistles, or I was blaming everything on him."

"I see." I wondered if I was being played. It wasn't as if Sam could speak for himself. Maybe the squeaker toy had been entirely her doing all along. Furthermore, I was fairly confident that Pavlov and Flint had been annoyed by the dog whistle during the two performances to date in which I'd been cuing Blue.

Felicity glanced at her watch, then rose. "I have to go pick up the costumes from the laundromat and check with the repair man. Hopefully our machines will be up and running."

The moment she left, this time choosing to take Pippa with her, I called Baxter and told him what Felicity had said about a squeaky toy being hidden in a seat's upholstery. He rushed over. After getting Valerie's permission, he began to search the seats one at a time, from front to back rows.

He was in the fifth row when he cried, "You were right, Allie." He headed toward me with a plastic toy not much larger than a golf ball. "Look what Flint, Pavlov, and I found in the cushioning of one of the theater seats."

"A squeaker toy!" I said.

"He'd removed a small section of the seat's foam padding, and filled it with the toy. It was somewhat to one side, so it would squeak when the person in that seat shifted their position."

"I'm glad we finally managed to get that issue resolved."

"It makes me wonder if Sam died because of his own stupid prank."

My thoughts returned to my first conversation with Greg, while he was sitting on the steps of the back exit. "I can't help but wonder if the dog whistle was all that there was to Flint's troubles. What if it was John, sabotaging his own play?"

"Why would he do that?" Baxter asked, a hint of annoyance in his voice.

"To get publicity, maybe?"

He spread his arms. "By having the star of his play act up?"

"It's possible, Baxter. Everyone we've talked to so far says they liked the play better with the dog as something of a straight-man for punch lines."

"We've only heard that from a couple of people, though. And John was fairly convincing about not wanting Blue's hijinks to steal his thunder."

"But *Sam* was originally planning to train herding dogs as his career. He was getting a cut out of what the script earned in royalties. He was saying they could do this show in high schools all throughout Colorado. All of which would work nicely with the seemingly adlibbed lines. That way, they'd appeal all the more to dog lovers. It might not have been a bad gig for Sam at all, whereas it might have taken a big chunk out of *John's* profits."

"But if that was John's intention, why hire *you* to fix the dog's training?" Baxter asked.

"We don't actually know when he would have revealed his ruse. Maybe he planned to wait until partway through the show or the end of the week, even, so I'd be the hero and nobody suspected John had contrived the whole thing. The theater is picking up our tab, not John."

Baxter stayed silent for a long time. "I see your point. It might generate early publicity, like you say. I'd like to think John isn't that underhanded."

Not to mention that he very well might have murdered someone.

***

We went on an abbreviated hike/picnic lunch with the dogs, enjoying even a brief break from the terrible murder and all its ramifications. I could tell from Flint's body language, though, that he was hoping for his master to return. Flint was looking for John at every bend in our path. I tried to push away how sad that made me. Baxter told me that John had simply sent him a text that read: *Made bail. I need some ME time. See you Thursday.* My fear that he was planning on going on the lam was so intense that I made the decision not to burden Baxter with it. We would either see John tomorrow, or we would reevaluate if he didn't show, dealing then with the reality that John Morris had murdered Sam Geller.

We returned to town in the evening and decided to grab a pre-dinner beer. We chose an establishment with a large informal patio, where the management and patrons didn't look twice at customers bringing two dogs with them to their rustic picnic table. We sat close together on a shaded bench and chatted about Baxter's business and our slow transition toward eventually establishing a kennel on our property in Dacona.

"Hey, that's '*Good Dog, Blue!*'" a burly man with tattoo sleeves at an adjacent table announced, pointing at Flint. He shifted his gaze to Baxter and me. "I saw the play last night. For the second time."

"We both loved it," the equally tattooed—and equally burly—woman beside him declared. "It's a real hoot. Are you Blue's actual owner?"

"No, we're not," I answered. "We're just dog-sitting. His real name is Flint."

The woman nodded. "Yeah, like my husband said, last night was actually our second time. We went to the opening of the show, too. That was kind of nuts. Blue was all over the place."

"So I heard."

"This is Allie Babcock," Baxter interjected. "She's a dog therapist. She's been working with Flint since right after the opening-night fiasco."

"Well, you certainly did wonders with his training," the woman said. "But it's kind of too bad. It was a riot when he was just having random interactions with the actors. A friend said the same thing about the Pug that played the role the second night. And *another* friend said she saw it with a German Shepherd as Blue. Is this him?"

"Her. And she actually *is* our dog."

"Yeah. My friend said he wasn't all that funny. *She* wasn't, I mean. Blue is a he, isn't he?"

"Not when he's played by a female dog."

"You should have used jokes about him being a bitch, then," the man said. "That would have livened the thing up."

"I'm glad you enjoyed the performance." I modulated my voice to make it clear that I intended my remark to serve as the end our conversation.

"From what I hear, the playwright is in jail for killing the stage manager."

"He was just a stagehand," the man next to her corrected.

"Stagehand. So you must know them, right?" she asked.

Baxter said nothing. The woman kept shifting her gaze between Baxter and me, so apparently that was a plural "you." "A little," I replied.

"That's kind of nuts. Considering that one actor who had a nervous breakdown or whatever and tried to run over his girlfriend. Who was that?" She elbowed her husband. "The actor playing the role of Blue's owner's new love interest. The guy's name starts with a G. George something?"

"Greg?" I asked.

"Yeah. My parents moved out here when they retired, just as all of that was coming down. When was that, Hon? Maybe fifteen years ago?"

"I don't remember," he said with a shrug. "They're *your* parents."

"It was one of those dumb things when he caught his girlfriend cheating on him and tried to run her over with a car when he was totally wasted. He was here for the summer intern program at the theater or something, and he spotted his girlfriend and his rival on the sidewalk. He kept crashing his truck into the store fronts along the street, and the other guy kept dodging him, but I guess his girlfriend wasn't so lucky. Engine finally stalled or overheated, and he passed out. I guess they sent him away for a long time."

"Yikes," I said, trying to picture Greg in that role. It was a difficult fit—and far worse than "one of those dumb things" that people do.

"Yeah, so, you know, here we are with that same looney-tunes actor trying to make a comeback, but this muscle-bound stage manager winds up dead. Or stagehand. In any case, the guy was a dead ringer for the guy he tried to run over that stole his girl."

"Really?" I asked, now intensely curious. "He wasn't the victim's brother, was he? Sam Geller's brother?"

"Lucy's wrong," the tattooed husband said. "This Greg Gulliver that you're talking about was just a teenager back then. Went to Alamaso High, an hour or so from here. So did his girlfriend, *plus* the guy she'd been cheating with. He was a black kid." He glared at his wife. "How the hell do you call a black teenager a dead ringer for a forty-three year old white guy?"

"Well, they're the same basic body type—five-nine or so, athletic, muscular. If the actor was looney-tunes, he might have had a flashback and killed him accidentally, thinking he was the other guy that stole his girl."

"I'm sure the sheriff would be on top of that," he retorted. "It's not like he'd suddenly forget about an incident like that. They keep records of police arrests and everything."

"Well, sure. But that doesn't mean they couldn't have made a mistake. Arrested the wrong guy. I mean, the play was so fun-loving. Silly, even. You're not going to see someone write a happy play and then crack someone's skull with a rock and push him into a pit."

"Maybe he *would*. We don't even know the guy who wrote the play."

"*I* do! I've seen him around town plenty!"

"Not enough to recognize he was Flint's owner," her husband said with a "gotcha" sneer.

"I did, too. I was just trying to be friendly. I didn't want to invade their space and ask, 'What are you doing with John Morris's dog? Are you watching him while he's in jail?' That would have been super rude."

"Um, Allida," Baxter said, "maybe we should go get something to eat."

"Oh, they have great brats or burgers here," Lucy said.

"I'm a vegetarian," Baxter replied, lying.

Lucy snorted and slapped her knee. "Oh, of *course* you are. You're from Boulder. Well, in that case, you'll want to go to Arp's. They're the only vegetarian-friendly restaurant in town."

"So does that mean the other restaurants are *hostile* to vegetarians?" I teased.

"Just that we're mostly meat-lovers," she replied.

"It's not like they'd kill you, grill you, and serve you to us carnivores," her husband added, laughing heartily.

On that note, I decided to guzzle the rest of my beer. I was beginning to get the idea that the man enjoyed disagreeing with his wife—and our relaxed mood had been spoiled.

"We're actually from Dacona, well outside Boulder's city limits." Baxter stood up. "We'd probably be harder to chew than your average Boulderite."

"Thanks for the tip about Arp's," I said, rising. "Have a great evening."

"You, too."

We left. Baxter grimaced at me as we walked down the sidewalk. "I kind of stuck my foot in my mouth. I just wanted out of the conversation, then I realized in a town this size we could keep running into that couple, and I didn't want to be limiting my diet."

"Actually, we *should* stop eating red meat. It's bad for the earth's ecology. To say nothing of the inhumane treatment of animals."

Baxter sighed, and I chastised myself. We were under enough stress without undertaking a self-improvement project. I looked at Flint, who perked up at the sight of a couple of men turning the corner. He sagged again when they continued on their way, and Flint realized that neither of them was his owner.

Chapter 19

Several hours later, Baxter and I left the dogs in our hotel room and kept our plan to watch a special Wednesday-night showing of *Boomtown*—Creede's comedic improvisation show. The show was staged right after the *avant garde* play at the Ruth Theater, which was a short walk from our hotel.

We both pretended we were going there merely to kick back and be entertained, but I think Baxter was every bit as curious as I was to see the full troupe of repertory actors here. To our surprise, as Valerie introduced the show, she announced they were going to be joined by a four-legged cast member, Pippa. Ironically, now that Pippa was on stage, she was not in costume. "I wonder if they're going to try Pippa's 'dance' trick," I whispered to Baxter. "She can turn in circles on her hind legs."

"That could be cute. Maybe they can do some break dancing numbers," Baxter replied. "I read in the program that one of the actors in the avant-garde play is quite good at hip-hop. He can spin on his shoulder while Pippa's spinning on her back paws."

A pair of young, enthusiastic actors in the group asked the audience to shout out some nouns and verbs that would allow them to formulate ideas for the show. They settled on *grandma, pig,* and *kindergarten* for nouns, and *teach, curling,* and *smelting* for verbs. They started the routine, and the actors did indeed use Pippa as their foil, pretending that their blind grandma had won her by coming in third at a Canadian curling contest, believing that Pippa was a pig, rather than a dog. They had brought "the dog that was not a pig" with them to their Kindergarten class to teach their class how to smelt—which became more of a play on words than the actual process of getting metal from ore. Pippa would respond to the actors' hand signals to lie down and roll over. Pippa also did a wonderful job executing a walk-backward hand signal that led to an actor pulling off a pratfall when the dog and he were both walking backwards and the actor tripped over her.

"Pippa's surprisingly well-trained," I said quietly to Baxter afterwards, as the actors were taking their bows.

"That just what I was thinking. Did you work with her on any of the tricks today?"

"On the dancing, at least, but I don't really deserve any credit for her acting today. She's clearly been doing stage work since she was a puppy. It's almost as surprising that Pippa bombed at playing *Blue* as that *Flint* bombed."

"Which probably just means that they both got rattled by the whistle."

I held my tongue, rather than point out that the dog whistle had been lodged in that seat last night, when Flint had managed to ignore it, as well as on Sunday night, when Pavlov had managed the same feat. The only possible explanation to my mind was that John was giving both dogs the wrong cues. And that Baxter was in a denial about his friend's true character.

For the second skit, a pair of cast members brought handheld microphones into the seats and would ask audience members questions about their lives. From the answers, they created a composite biographical story of two people's lives, and how a Pug named Pippa brought them together.

Sally, Karen, and Hammond were taking part in the proceedings, but Greg was not. Even those three were clearly taking a backseat to the other seven or eight actors. In the first skit that they performed, she and another young man appeared to be the ringleaders, figuring out when they needed to shift the direction of the skit and call in different characters. The one time Sally was in a comedic scene, she once again shone.

Hammond, Karen, and Sally were never interacting on the stage at the same time. That was surely by design. Although they had some truly funny, enjoyable moments, I failed at shutting out my negative thoughts. After seeing that Pippa could hold her own well on stage, I was all the more certain I'd been set up by John. At intermission, I told Baxter that I'd like to leave, and he said he did too.

Surprisingly, the trio of actors from John's play were also leaving the theater, albeit through the back exit. It was mildly embarrassing to bump into them. Hammond immediately blurted out, "Fancy meeting you here."

"You're not performing in the second half of the show?" I asked.

"No, it's actually not a contractual obligation," Sally said. "We just all volunteered because we enjoy it. We're essentially guest performers."

"Greg doesn't enjoy it?"

Hammond snorted, but made no comment.

"He follows the beat of a different drummer," Karen said.

"Because the guy's mentally ill," Hammond grumbled.

"Hammie," Sally snarled, "that's untrue and unkind."

"I guess *you* would know," Hammond replied under his breath.

"What's *that* supposed to mean?" she asked.

Hammond turned his attention to Baxter and me. "If you ever want to spend an hour or two listening to someone prattle endlessly about ghosts, ask Greg Gulliver about Annabelle Dancer."

"Who?" Baxter asked.

"That's Greg's name for the ghost that haunts the theater," Karen explained, "and also the restaurant next door." She touched Hammond's arm. "Greg's hardly the only one who's encountered the ghost. The entire staff at the restaurant has seen her."

"Which just means they're doing drugs in the kitchen," Hammond retorted. "Have a good night," he then said, flashing a toothy smile at Baxter and me. "I'm going to quit thinking about the dead, and turn my thoughts to merry diversions. Such as booze and loose women."

The three of them headed across the street toward the theater's housing. I grabbed Baxter's arm as we continued toward our hotel room. "I'm suddenly thinking I could use a nightcap."

He chuckled. "You mean at the restaurant next to the main stage? To see if Annabelle Dancer has ever been known to tamper with actors' costumes? Or to distract the dogs on the stage next door?"

Only half joking, I gave his hand a squeeze. "Maybe it was the combination of a squeaker toy and Annabelle Dancer's ghost." We reversed our direction. We were now heading toward the restaurant and inn next to the main theater.

"Flint did great yesterday," Baxter replied. "The only problem was when the actors were taking their bows. And Flint his bow wow."

"You've been listening to the puns in John's play for too long."

"And *you've* been letting all of this theatrical havoc get to you. A *ghost*? Seriously?"

"You never know, Baxter. Dogs are more perceptive than us mere humans. And besides, I'm a fan of ghost stories. They're fun. Don't you think?"

"Not compared to booze and loose women."

"In that case, it's your lucky night! You're about to hear a ghost story from a waiter serving you booze, as you sit next to your own personal loose woman."

"*Now* you're talking," Baxter said.

***

I ordered a glass of port. Baxter ordered a Guinness ale. We were the only customers, although the crowd at the Ruth Theater would likely bring them more customers in another hour or so when *Boomtown* ended. The waitress asked if she could bring us anything else.

"No, thanks," I answered. "I was just hearing from a couple of the actors that the theater is haunted. Is that true?"

"Totally," she said with no trace of deceit.

"Was it a woman named Annabelle Dancer?" Baxter asked.

She smiled a little. She was in her late thirties or so, with her long black hair in a braid on one shoulder, wearing a flowery-pattern dress that was shabby-chic. "Some say they've seen Annabelle do a pirouette, so that's probably where the last name came from. She's been here for ten years or so. Although, there are also those who say her name is Suzette, and she's been haunting the building for more like forty years."

"Is there an older ghost and a younger ghost, then?" I asked.

The waitress shook her head. "They're both former actresses who died in Creede," she said, "but they've never been seen together, so it's impossible to say which spirit is still here."

"Can't you tell by her clothing?" Baxter asked.

She studied his face for a moment, as if hesitating to see if he was just playing along. "It's not a solid apparition. At least not for me. I see her outline sometimes. Mostly it's just like...a temperature shift. And she rattles and bangs things in the kitchen sometimes."

Baxter chuckled a little.

"I'm serious. I close down the place most nights, and at least a third of the time, I hear her making noise in the empty kitchen."

"Could be rats," Baxter said. "Or a feral cat, chasing mice."

The waitress arched an eyebrow. "I once saw her stirring a pot. The spoon was floating in air."

Baxter said nothing and took a swig of his ale.

"I've been hired to help train the canine actor playing Blue," I said. "I've been thinking that it's not out of the range of possibility that lingering spirits in the building are throwing him off track."

"If you ask me, I'm *positive* the ghost has been throwing off the dog's performance. They're more sensitive to the spirits from the other world than we people are."

I nudged Baxter's leg with my foot. "See?" I gave him a triumphant smile. "That's exactly what I've been telling Baxter, here."

"You're a believer," she said with a nod.

"Sort of. I'm not a believer when it comes to ghosts that haunt places and throw things and try to scare people. But I do believe we have souls that can be separated from our corporal bodies after we die. And I think if the majority of a collective consciousness of a community believes there is a ghost in the theater that inhabits this whole building, it *does* exist."

"Could be," she said with a shrug. "Would you like me to bring—"

She broke off, and just then, I felt ice cold for just a couple of seconds. I looked at Baxter and he, too, crossed his arms as if to warm himself.

"Hah! There you go," the waitress said. "See what I mean?"

Baxter and I both looked at each other in bewilderment. Then we had to grin. There was no chance that a chill breeze had just happened by;

it hadn't been moving air, but rather an enveloping sense of coldness.

Baxter looked at the ceiling, no doubt searching for a swamp-cooler vent. I followed his gaze. The ceiling was solid. "I'm impressed," Baxter said, returning his gaze to mine.

"And *I'm* convinced."

"The ghost is a dog lover," the waitress said. "My Alfie gets along great with her. Can I get you anything else?"

"Just the check," Baxter said.

We downed our drinks, left cash on the table, and started to head back to the hotel. We almost literally bumped into Greg Gulliver on the sidewalk. He gave us an odd smile and said, "Oh, hey! How's it going? You're not still working, are you?"

"No, we were just enjoying a night out," I said. He shot a nervous glance over our shoulders. I turned to see if someone was right behind us, but the sidewalk was empty. I realized he was probably wondering about Flint and Pavlov. "We left the dogs to fend for themselves."

"Their such good dogs, I'm sure they do a great job of...self-fending." His voice faded. He was acting surprisingly uncomfortable, which made me feel a little awkward as well.

"Do you have a dog?" I asked.

"I wish. I travel too often. I doubt I could even give a goldfish enough attention."

"You're a full-time actor, then?" *And living alone*, I assumed.

"I'm a temporary full-time actor. I sometimes teach, sometimes wait tables. This play, though, has been giving me some ideas for finding another part-time job. Since I work nights and am off during the day, I could be a dog walker in Denver."

"Hey, I've got a friend in Boulder who's got a dog-walking business," Baxter said. "I can get you his card."

"You don't think it'd count against me that I have a spotty employment record, do you?" Greg asked him.

"I'm not sure, but my guess is the fact that you're an actor would immediately explain gaps in your work history. I think they'd just want to know you're dependable and can be trusted with the keys to clients homes and so forth. "

It was too dark to tell for sure, but he appeared to wince. He might have been worried that his record of vehicular homicide would be a deal breaker.

"Here," Baxter said, grabbing his phone. "I'll just forward you a couple of contacts on my—"

"That's okay. Let me knock the idea around in my head for a while first."

"Are you heading to the theater?" I asked.

"No, it's not open. I was going for a walk is all. I'm such a night owl, thanks to my professional schedule. I need to get out and get a little exercise, or I can't ever get to sleep."

"I know what you mean," Baxter said. "Allie and I like to take the dogs out for a walk before we turn in."

"Good talking to you.

Just then, Valerie came out of the front door to the theater. I caught just a glimpse of her before she ducked back in.

"Valerie must be working late," I said.

"I guess so," Greg said.

"Either that, or she really didn't want to see us," Baxter said. "She looked like she'd deliberately changed her mind about leaving the theater when she saw us."

"She wouldn't do that. But something might be wrong. I should probably go check. See you tomorrow." Greg strode toward the theater.

"That was odd," I said quietly as we once again started heading toward the hotel. "I get the impression that Valerie and Gregory have some kind of a date scheduled tonight and don't want to be found out."

Baxter gave no reply.

Just as we'd reached the front door of our hotel, a gunshot resounded.

Chapter 20

"Was that gunshot from the theater?" I asked Baxter.

"Maybe. Or the sound could have been right by the cliffs and just reverberated."

A man—probably Greg but it was too dark to tell—bolted through the theater doors. A woman followed on his heels, and I was guessing that was Valerie. The man stopped on the sidewalk as the woman trotted across the street. "What's going on?" he called down to us—definitely Greg's deep voice. "Did you see anything?"

"No," Baxter called back.

"Something's going on at the theatre housing," Valerie exclaimed. Greg trotted across the street to follow her.

"Wait for me in the hotel room," Baxter said.

"No, I'm going, too."

We quickly traversed the two blocks to the housing units. We arrived in time to hear Valerie shout, "Hammond! What the hell do you think you're doing!"

Hammond lifted his hands, one of which was holding a pistol. "It's just a blank, everybody. I was just goofing around."

"What the hell, Hammond!" Valerie cried again. "What's the matter with you!"

"There was a woodpecker driving me nuts, so I shot at him with a stage bullet."

"You fired at it right over my head," Karen shouted, stamping her foot. "You could have hurt me!"

"Sorry. I didn't see you standing there. I was half asleep and not thinking straight."

"Now you've got all the dogs in town awake and howling," Karen said.

There were indeed many barks and howls in the background.

"But I scared the woodpecker off. It's not a total loss." Hammond gazed at Karen. "What were you doing out here in the pitch black anyway?"

"I was just chatting on my cell phone, trying to get better reception."

"Chatting with whom?"

"My fiancé, not that it's any of your business."

"You have a fiancé?" Greg asked.

"Oh, dear God, Michael," Hammond said to Greg, using his character's name. "You're sweet on her, aren't you! We cannot handle another real-life couple in this production." He was overacting and clowning with exaggerated motions. His antics were doing a wonderful job of lightening the mood, I had to admit.

Valerie, however, stamped her foot again. "Hammond. You've stayed here countless times over the years. This property belongs to the theater, and you know full well guns are strictly prohibited in the apartments."

"So sorry, my dear. Bad judgment."

"You can say *that* again!" Valerie snarled. "I'm supposed to expel you from the premises.

Immediately. Read the accommodations clause in your freaking contract if you don't believe me!"

"I'm sorry, Valerie. Bringing a gun here was a stupid mistake. What with Sam Geller getting killed and everything, I wanted a little extra protection."

"In case of a homicidal woodpecker?!" Karen asked.

"In case I needed to scare someone off the premises. I wanted to protect you and Sally!" He snorted. "Though I should have realized Sally still wasn't going to be around," he said under his breath. "But, folks, like I said, it's just loaded with blanks."

"Which can still be lethal, if you hold it against someone's head," Karen said.

"Here." He thrust the gun at Valerie. "Take it back to the prop room."

"It came from the prop room?" she asked.

"Yeah. I saw it there a couple of days ago. I decided to scare off the woodpecker once and for all. And anyway, you should see what he's doing to your eaves. Since you're trying to protect the property and all."

"You didn't know there was a gun on hand?" I asked Valerie.

"No. We don't stockpile guns, we just acquire them on loan...and keep them locked up in a cabinet...when we happen to be staging a play that calls for a firearm. It shouldn't have been there. *None* of our productions this season call for a gun."

"Maybe John was getting so frustrated with the script he ordered it," Hammond said. "He could brandish it about during rehearsals and threaten to shoot us."

Karen clicked her tongue. "It was probably just unclaimed from one of last year's productions."

"We didn't need a gun last year, either," Valerie said. "And we overhaul the storage room at the end of every season. This gun was *not* in the storage room when we first opened the season. I'm one-hundred-percent certain of that."

Hammond held up his empty palms. "Regardless, Valerie, I have relinquished the pistol and promise to never shoot at an obnoxious woodpecker again."

Valerie sighed. She truly seemed to be in a horrible mood. "Let's all just go home, and we'll deal with this in the morning. I, for one, have better things to be doing than standing in the dark and yammering. Meanwhile, Hammond, you'd better call the police and explain why some moron discharged a firearm in downtown Creede, or we'll be getting late-night visits from the sheriff once again."

Valerie pivoted and marched away. Greg was rocking on his heels. "I was about to take a nighttime stroll. I think I'll go home and have a nightcap instead." He strode toward what I assumed was his apartment. "Anyone care to join me?"

"No thanks, Greg, but sleep well," Karen said. "I'm going straight to bed."

Only Hammond was left outside with Baxter and me.

"I guess Sally must be staying at John's tonight, which means he's not in a jail cell,"

Hammond said in what was a clear annoyance to him. "No accounting for taste." He patted both Baxter's and my shoulder. "Good night, you dog handlers. If only you could morph into *people* handlers, we'd be doing a whole lot better." His breath was so heavy with alcohol, I turned my face away.

Baxter wished him a good night, then he and I walked back to the hotel in silence. We took the dogs out on leashes, waiting with our matching green bags in what we termed Double Poop Patrol Duty.

"Jeez, Allie. I'm starting to think I couldn't have done worse by you than to drag you up here for this fricking assignment."

"On the other hand, there hasn't been a dull moment since we arrived."

"Meanwhile, someone on the staff, cast, or crew brought in a handgun." Apparently he was having nothing of my attempt to cheer him. "Maybe John is still alive only because he got arrested so quickly. Maybe the gun was brought to the theater by the killer because the poison wasn't strong enough."

"If that's true," I said, "wouldn't it *also* be true that Sam would still be alive?"

"John's innocent," he said under his breath.

"I'm losing my confidence in that being true," I said quietly.

"I can see why. I just think we're going in opposite directions."

"Let's have a heart-to-heart discussion with him when John gets home tomorrow. Maybe that will prove enlightening and give us the answers we need."

Baxter snorted. "The way our luck has been going, the closest thing to anything *enlightening* is a *bolt* of lightning that takes us all out."

***

Not fifteen minutes later, someone knocked on our hotel door. I could tell by Flint's wagging tail who it was. I had been searching for reviews on the play and had found one that I was just about to discuss with Baxter, who was about to climb into bed.

"Has to be John," Baxter said as we both headed to the door. He was in his striped pajama bottoms; I was still fully dressed.

As I swept open the door, John was rocking on his heel. "Sorry to drop in on you so late. I saw your lights were on, though." He grinned at Flint and started petting him. It was high time he showed his wonderful dog a little affection.

"Come on in," I said.

We took seats in our tiny living room, Baxter and I on the sofa, John turning one of the two kitchen-table chairs to face us.

"I was granted bail this morning," he said. "You probably got my text. I've been keeping a low profile today. Trying to make a plan." His brief smile for Flint was gone. He looked utterly disheartened. "My lawyer says I have a couple of months until the trial comes up. I don't know what to do. I can hire a private investigator to help find evidence to prove my innocence. It just...really looks bad, though."

"Yes, it does," I said.

"Hang in there, John," Baxter said, giving me the briefest of sharp looks.

Despite Baxter's disapproval, I couldn't simply ignore my suspicions. "I have to ask...did you scramble with Flint's training yourself?"

"Of course not. Why would I want to do a stupid thing like that? Screw up my own play?"

"I was searching for reviews of *Good Dog, Blue!* a few minutes ago. I found an article in the Post. It had an interview with you talking about how much the audience loved the dog's miscues and how well-rehearsed the actors are at responding to the dog's antics."

He furrowed his brow and hesitated. "Right. They called me out of nowhere, and I had to talk up my work. What I was supposed to do? Admit that the play was a disaster?"

"Actually, she mentioned in the piece that you had contacted *her* initially."

John shook his head. "That's misleading. After I'd heard it was going to be written up, I went on the offense to help control the story."

I held his gaze, and he could see I wasn't buying it.

"Damn it all. Okay, yes, Allie. But it wasn't my idea. Not entirely. I was following Valerie's orders."

"When I ask Valerie about this tomorrow, she'll tell me was upon her orders?"

He grimaced a little and shifted his gaze to Baxter, whose arms were crossed. His expression hinted that he was ready to spit nails at John. "We were brainstorming. It was a mutual decision, but considering she's my boss, yeah. It's not like I would've done this without her support.

She likes the SRO sellouts. I like the publicity. *And* I was doing you guys a favor. I figured you'd have a free vacation and lots of publicity to increase your profitability."

"That's bullshit," Baxter said.

"I swear, bro. That's what I was thinking. You guys could come up and work with the dog so nobody would suspect I was...gaming the system a little by getting free publicity."

"And how did Sam Geller figure into the situation?" Baxter asked. "Did you tell him to use a high-pitched squeaky toy to throw off Flint?"

"What are you talking about?" John asked.

Baxter glanced at me, and I shook my head just slightly. I didn't want John to know about Felicity's agreement with Sam.

"I found the toy in a seat cushion in the theater," Baxter said, "with Allie's and Pavlov's help."

"I didn't know anything about that. I swear. How did you know it was Sam who put it there?"

"He'd been repairing the seats," I interjected.

John hesitated, then said, "Look. I figured Sam would catch on that I was giving Flint the wrong cues. So, yeah, that's what we argued about. But I swear to God I didn't go after him." His gaze darted from me to Baxter and back. "You need to see this from my side. I got Sam the job, and I tried to cut him in so that it was in his best interest to keep his mouth shut and do his job. Obviously he couldn't manage. He was sabotaging my play even so."

"Which you were already doing intentionally," I retorted. "So, why hire *us* to make it seem like we'd 'cured' Flint from his antics? Why not let

Sam be your puppet in this whole freaking charade of yours?"

John stared at the floor. He was taking turns massaging one fist and then the other with a free hand. Watching him, I wondered if he was thinking he'd get into a fistfight with Baxter over his sorry tale. "Sam was a loose cannon. I knew from the get-go that he hated me. And making Flint appear to have stage fright was the only way I could have gotten that article about my play in the Denver Post. I planned to have just three or four botched performances. And then give *you* all the credit."

I cursed under my breath.

"I still think Sam jerry-rigged those lights to fall at some point. I wanted to make sure there was no chance he had to perform again until I got the chance to get Sam the hell away from my dog, once and for all."

"So…you insisted that Pavlov be put in mortal danger instead?" I barely managed to refrain from unleashing a torrent of expletives at him.

"Nothing happened," John cried defensively. "It was all fine."

"But you didn't know that at the time," Baxter said.

"I knew that chances were…. Look, I just couldn't risk Flint's life and the collapse of all my dreams in one fell swoop."

"Did *you* remove the bolts from the light?" Baxter asked.

"No! Like I just said, that had to have been *Sam*. That's when I knew he was trying to get back at me for my cheating his brother."

"So you killed him in self-defense?" I phrased it that way to see if I could get a confession out of him. The killer had clobbered him with a rock, and he'd broken his neck in his fall.

"No."

"Was it just an accident?"

"No, Allie. Baxter." John scooted off the chair and let himself drop onto the floor in a heap. He started sobbing. "God. I'm in so much trouble now. Everything I've done has only made things worse."

We let him cry. For my part, I was simply too stunned to know how to react. After a minute or two, he got control of himself and rose to his feet.

"I didn't kill Sam. I'm telling you the truth. I know you don't believe me. How *could* you when I've lied to you all along? I've been a complete shit head. I know that. But honest to God, I *thought* this was going to be the perfect plan that would be great for Creede's theater, great for your business, great for me and Flint. This was my one big chance."

Once again, he dropped into the chair and started sobbing so hard he couldn't continue. To my relief, Flint quickly rushed over to comfort him. If he hadn't acted, I'd have felt obliged to put my arms around him and let him cry on my shoulder.

Baxter's and my eyes met. I was certain he, too, believed his deeply flawed friend.

When he seemed to once again be getting his emotions back under control, I asked, "Have you talked to anybody about this since you were arrested?"

He nodded. "My lawyer. I told him the whole story. He thinks it incriminates me. Which is true. But he also told me I had to come clean before Valerie did." John cleared his throat. "My lawyer went ahead and had me tell the D.A. how I'd been manipulating Geller." He dropped his face into his knees. "I'm going to lose Sally over this. I probably already *have*. She's the best thing that ever happened to me. And I already gave away my chance to stay with Felicity, once it seemed like I'd have Sally. I'm going to be alone. Even if I don't go to prison. For a murder I totally didn't commit."

"The police have to think the killer was a man to have enough strength to hit him that hard with a rock," Baxter said.

"Sam lied about meeting with someone to get lumber," John said. "Or maybe the killer fooled Sam into thinking he'd be meeting the lumber guy there. In any case, *that's* who killed him."

"There's a copse of trees right where he was killed," I said, thinking out loud. The killer could have hidden from view while you and Sam were arguing." I paused, thinking. "A woman could have hidden and slung the rock like a pair of nunchucks by tying it into a shirt or something."

"You're thinking it was Felicity?" John asked, his voice taking on hopeful tones. "She could have washed *her* clothes and a bloody shirt, along with the costumes."

"Or some *other* person could have done the deed," I said.

"The thing is, Sam was bad news," John said. "He didn't just turn bad because of me. The guy with the lumber could have had a grudge against

Sam. He could have been killed for a number of things that have nothing to do with me."

"Maybe a stranger heard you argue and put your torn pocket in his grasp," Baxter said, but without much confidence.

John cursed and rubbed at his eyes with the heels of his hands. "What am I going to do? My lawyer says I could plead self-defense, but I won't do that. I didn't do it, and I didn't see who killed him."

"If the D.A. believes your story is credible," I said, "he'll tell investigators that he needs more evidence. Maybe they'll find something that clears you."

John shut his eyes. After a while, he opened them. "You know, you two should just go back to Boulder. It's my ass that's on the line, and I betrayed your friendship. I'll just have to hope the killer reveals himself and the police...sheriff...whatever...withdraws their charges against me."

Baxter looked at me and I gave him a nod.

"We'll stick around," Baxter said. "Allie was involved in a murder case when she and I first met. She helped the police identify the killer. We can have your back."

He snorted. "Thanks. It's a dirty job but somebody's got to do it."

"You didn't see anyone or hear anyone?" I asked, though I knew the question was pointless.

"No. But it was just a fifteen-minute walk from the theater where we got into the argument. And you can reach that abandoned strip-mine in another ten minutes. Someone could have easily gone there and back during their lunch break."

It all seemed so unlikely, though, I thought. "Who else knew about this donor with the lumber, John?"

"There's Andrew Yates, who builds the sets," John said. "Valerie and Felicity knew about it from the..." He paused and winced. "All of the actors knew, too. I spotted Yates during a rehearsal and asked if he would have plywood. I'd been considering constructing a floor on top of the stage, so we could run wires underneath it. Geller figured out how to rig the chair more easily when Blue is supposed to move it in front of the door."

So much for winnowing down the list of suspects.

Chapter 21

We worked with Flint on his solo scene the next day, with me standing in for Sally, and Baxter calling out Hammond's couple of lines and working the wires that shut the door and moved the chair. He and I made more mistakes than Flint, so I doubted our efforts had any effect on his performance.

That afternoon, we rehearsed the play with Pippa in the role of Blue, omitting Blue's solo scenes, which were out of the question for her. For one thing, to be credible, she would have needed the chair to be on rollers, which would have defeated the illusion that it was blocking the door for Hammond. Overall, though, Pippa was as good in the role as Pavlov, which made me glad for having done at least *some* valuable work for my salary.

Felicity told us she needed to run home for a few minutes prior to the actors arriving, and we agreed to keep an eye on Pippa. Baxter called John, but he didn't answer. None of us knew if he was going to plan on cuing Flint himself, or if I would. With no particular pressing assignments ourselves, Baxter and I played a tame game of fetch with Pippa and Flint. Flint would wait his turn to fetch the tennis ball. Pippa would not, but Flint could outrace her to the ball, so Pippa would trot beside him as he returned the ball, as if she had intended to merely be his supervisor.

Felicity rounded the corner. "Thanks for watching Pippa," she said. "I left Pippa's costume at home. I'm superstitious about what could happen if she is out of costume during a show."

I couldn't help but guffaw. "You think *Good Dog, Blue!* could get even *more* unlucky?"

She chuckled. "Meteor strike, wiping us all out?"

"There is *that*. So are we going to see Pippa in diamond spangles?"

"I'm saving that for tomorrow's performance. Her Friday night glitter." She winked at me and led the dog back up the stairs.

Baxter was having problems with his cell phone and had some business calls to make. He took Flint for a potty break while he searched for a clearer signal. I walked around on the stage, mentally going through Blue's blocking assignments. I stood directly under the now-unlit stage lights that had crashed the evening we'd arrived. None of Flint's targets were within two feet of the lights. Now that I was intimately familiar with the play, I was standing directly on one of Hammond's most-frequent marks. I looked up again at the light fixture, only to find myself getting dizzy. I closed my eyes until the vertigo passed.

"Are you okay, Allie?" I turned and spotted Karen in the wing.

"I'm fine. I have such bad fear of heights that I was getting vertigo just by looking up at the lights."

"I made one of the stagehands promise me he'd check the lights every day to be sure they're bolted tight. So far, so good."

"Did *he* think someone deliberately sabotaged them?" I asked.

"He felt certain four of the five bolts had been removed recently," Karen said. "So, either Sam removed them, or his killer did."

I peered at her. "Isn't that nerve wracking? To keep having to perform on a stage that could be booby-trapped?"

"A little. But it's reassuring that Baxter's up there in the cat-bird's seat every night."

Now that the dog whistle had been discovered and removed, I wasn't sure he'd be watching tonight's performance, but decided not to mention it.

"I need to grab my lemon water and get into costume," Karen said.

"Is drinking lemon water good for your vocal cords?"

"Absolutely. Although I have no idea if there's anything medicinal about it. But regardless, that's what I tell myself, so it's good for my psyche. Are you giving Blue the commands for both shows?"

"As far as I know."

"Good. You're much better at that than John is."

"Thanks," I said. Maybe at some point, I'd tell her that John had been giving Flint bogus commands, but it felt inconsiderate to tell an actor that shortly before a performance.

I went outside and wandered around for a while—taking an outdoors break from my doing nothing indoors. When I returned, Hammond was standing in a dark corner backstage, staring into space. He jumped a little when a floorboard creaked below my feet.

"How's it going?" I said.

He shrugged. "Still alive. That's saying something."

"*Something*, yes. Just not that you're doing *well*."

He shook his head. "I've been asking myself how I got here. It's hard to believe. I almost made it to the big-time. I was given a starring role in *Chicago P.D.* Have you ever seen that show?"

I shook my head.

"This was a few years back. When they created the pilot. The actor who was playing my supposed partner backed out of the role, and the director decided the mix wasn't right. Recast both of us." He snorted. "My agent tells me: 'no worries.' He assured me that cop show wouldn't last a full season...whereas he'd already gotten me placed to be the lead in a sitcom." He cocked his head toward me. "I guarantee, you've never heard of it. The script was crap. The pilot episode was so bad it died in a test-audience screening. Never even aired the thing."

"I'm sorry," I said. "That would be extremely frustrating."

"Yeah. It was. But that's the way it is in this business."

"You're excellent in the play," I told him sincerely.

He plastered one of his toothy, mocking smiles on his face. "Everybody is very excited." His face fell. "That's an old show-business cliché we kick around. The way I see it, John may be right about his show's potential. He thinks he's licked the 'no dogs on stage' salvo of live theater. If so, he could make a decent go of it. If he's *wrong*, he'll wind up like me...telling his amateur cast members how he almost made it to the big leagues."

"You're making a living and doing what you love, though, aren't you? That's more than a lot of people can say."

"True. And that is indeed something to be proud of. That used to be enough for me. It still would be, if I could have won my lady back."

"Sally Johnson?" I asked.

He nodded. "Rumor has it she's already let John know it's over. Hardly matters. She let *me* know the same thing in no uncertain terms."

I was uncomfortable and surprised he'd spilled all of this to me. "I'm sorry to hear that," I said, unable to think of anything better to say.

He nodded. "Yes, well...on with the show." He gave me that signature smile of his, emphasized with jazz hands, then walked away.

As soon as I turned the corner, I saw Sally sitting on the staircase. She was holding Pippa on her lap, while straightening Pippa's gold-Lamé outfit, which, from my vantage point, appeared to be a miniature Star Trek suit.

"Sorry, Allie. I was eavesdropping," she told me as our eyes met. "I just wanted to know how he was doing. I worry about Hammie. I wish him no harm."

I took a seat on the step next to her. Pippa immediately climbed off her lap and onto mine. "Ah, the fickleness of us females," she said, shaking her head at Pippa.

"He certainly made it clear how tough your profession is."

"It's much harder to make it as an actress than as an actor. At least *men* are allowed to age."

Now that I'd sat down, I was frustrated at my lack of conversation starters. Had it not been for the rumor of her breakup, I would have asked if she'd heard anything from John regarding if he was planning on coming to work today. "Are those Spock ears on Pippa's hoodie?" I asked.

She laughed. "I think so."

Another pause. "I'm sorry things didn't work out between you and John. He was clearly infatuated with you."

"Infatuated. Exactly the right word. But I'm grateful I found out about his true nature before I'd gotten even more deeply committed to him than I was."

"So *there* you are," Felicity said, heading down the stairs, looking at Pippa.

"Oh, sorry," Sally told her. She rose and stood at the base of the stairs. "I didn't mean to hijack your sweet little doggie. I just needed to cuddle with someone who wasn't going to hurt me."

"Yeah. I know the feeling, sister."

She gave Sally a big hug. "And, trust me," Felicity said, "when it comes to John, we're both better off."

Chapter 22

With the butterflies in my stomach increasing as time went on, I roamed the hallways, only to discover a sign in the lobby indicating seating for the matinee was a half hour sooner than I'd expected. "Why are the doors opening so soon?" I asked the ticket taker—a volunteer named Joan.

"For the *Good Dog, Blue!* Talk," she answered. "We do it once or twice a season for our featured shows. The director and a couple of cast members sit on stage and have a Q and A with the audience."

"So Flint doesn't need to go on stage early," I said, in a pseudo-question.

"Not so far as I know," she said.

I thanked her and returned to my meandering. Baxter and Flint were in the hallway, roughly half the way between the dressing room and the stage. Baxter was getting a stronger signal now and was texting someone. I smiled at Karen, who'd just then emerged from the dressing room.

"Still anxious?" Baxter asked as he put his phone back into his pocket.

"Yeah. This is going to be my third time cuing Blue, and it's gone well each time, but I *still* can't wait for the play to be over."

Karen gave me a sympathetic smile and came closer. "I feel that way right before I go on stage, every single time. And I've been in hundreds of performances. Then I'm on stage, and there's no place I'd rather be. Every single time."

"Yeah, but I'm never actually *on* the stage," I replied, "although you've cheered me up a little."

"Speaking of eavesdropping, which we weren't," Karen said to me, "I overheard an interesting rumor about you."

"Unless it's complimentary, it's false," Baxter quipped.

"It's neither good nor bad," Karen said affably. "A couple of days ago, my boyfriend and I were having lunch downtown, and the couple at the table next to ours said that the theater's dog trainer was an amateur sleuth. That you've gotten involved in a couple of murder investigations in Boulder."

I nodded. "I have a good friend who's a detective." Unfortunately, she'd spoiled my mood again. It had been my great misfortune to know more than one murder victim, and that was not a subject I liked to discuss.

She sighed softly. "I wish your friend was here. I'm not feeling very safe these days. Another bouquet from that secret admirer was delivered to the theater this morning. This time it's two-dozen long-stemmed red roses." Quietly, she added, "The handwriting looks suspiciously like Greg's, and things have been a little awkward between Valerie and me lately."

"Because Valerie is smitten with Greg?"

She rolled her eyes. "They renewed an old fling, from clear back when they were in high school and interned here over the summers. A fling that nobody was supposed to know about, because it dates back to his getting...crazed behind the wheel, let's say. They've been doing a terrible job at keeping their romance a secret. Word has it that he dumped her."

"I heard about that recently myself," I said.

Baxter, I noted, was getting a glassy look in his eye, which signaled he didn't want to be involved in this conversation.

"All I know is that I truly do not want to find out that *he* is my secret admirer," Karen said. "You'd like to forgive someone for their distant past. Hopefully, we all outgrown the crazy behavior of our teens. But Valerie told me he was so jealous over his first girlfriend that he stalked the poor girl. The thing is, I've been hoping my significant-other back in Denver was having a florist here pen the notes on the bouquets. But he told me he didn't send the wildflowers."

"That's too bad," I said, sincerely sympathetic. If I was getting flowers from a secret admirer, I, too, would hope they were from Baxter. Albeit, considering my personal history with sleuthing, an anonymous sender might have hidden a ticking bomb inside my bouquet.

"Since *he* didn't send them, I just have to hope this isn't tied to the murder. Maybe the poisoner and the killer are the same person, and he or she wanted to implicate me."

"*Or*, maybe the roses really *are* from your boyfriend, now that he knows he has competition in the area."

"Ooh. I like that theory. Let's just go with that, shall we?" She grinned at me, but only for a moment. "Please tell me that there's no such thing as a poison that can be made from rose stems."

"No such thing a rose-stem poison."

"Good. All of which reminds me, I've been meaning to thank you both for sticking it out and helping us on the play. I think if I was in your shoes, I'd have packed up and left town when things started getting so ugly."

"No need to thank me," Baxter said. "Allie's the one who's been doing all the work."

"It's mostly just because of my devotion to dogs. I've wanted to make sure John wasn't abusing Flint or anything." I glanced at Baxter to see if he was offended on his friend's account, but his expression hadn't changed. "And he *isn't*, right?"

"Right." Karen said. "Jeez. I still have to grab my lemon water. We're doing a preshow "Talk" about *Good Dog, Blue,* and I'm filling in for John now."

"I'll come with you," I said. "Flint is panting slightly and can use some water himself."

"I'll get your headset and Flint's earbud ready," Baxter said. "I'll leave it on your chair."

"Okay, thanks, sweetie." I patted my thigh, and Flint fell into step beside me.

"You know, Allie," Karen said quietly as we walked side by side, "I can't stop thinking about this whole tragic mess. It seems to me, someone involved had to either have set up John, or the authorities are right and John did it."

"I came to the same conclusion."

"It makes me realize when I'm on stage, one of these actors might have actually taken another person's life. It's creepy. I've tried to picture each one of them in turn, whacking Sam with a rock and shoving him over the edge. Yet it could only be Greg or Hammie. I don't think Sally's physically capable of it. She's such a skinny little thing. I think that's part of her allure to men. They see her as somebody to protect, as a delicate flower."

"Felicity must have had to make complete duplicate wardrobes for her and her understudy."

Karen chuckled. "Sally's understudy is Felicity herself or Valerie. Felicity told me Sally is petite, it was like making matching mother-daughter costumes."

I emptied the water bowl and refilled it with fresh water. Karen opened the refrigerator, grabbing her lemon water.

I set the bowl down, and Flint started lapping water. It popped into my head that one of the actors could have overheard John giving fake cues to Blue, and maybe that was somehow tied in with Sam's murder. Greg had already told me at the beginning he suspected as much.

"Have you ever been standing beside John, awaiting your entrance, when Flint went off the rails?" I asked.

She paused, considering my question. "I think I've always been on stage with Flint whenever he forgets his training."

"Do you think that's true for all four of you?"

She flipped open her sipper top and took a big swig. Although she managed to swallow first, she made horrible grimace. "Oh, good God!" She coughed a couple of times. "This tastes terrible!"

"Too much lemon juice?" I asked.

"Maybe. If the juice has turned rancid."

She set the bottle down and grabbed a green plastic bottle of lemon juice. Holding it up to the light, she said, "I *did* wind up leaving my lemon juice out yesterday. I always try to mix it up the night before so it's nice and cold when I arrive. It looks okay, though. Usually it gets little lumps in the bottle if it's starting to turn."

"Since lemon water is so tart when it's ripe, does it start to get sweet when it's spoiled?" I teased.

"Not according to the way my water tastes." She started unscrewing the lid. "My tongue even feels weird," she muttered.

I gasped, mostly due to my own cluelessness. Karen started to dump out the water.

"Don't!" I cried.

She straightened the bottle, having only sloshed a little into the sink.

"What's wrong with your tongue?" I asked.

"I don't know. It's a little...tingly. Along with my lips." She eyed her bottle.

"Don't take another sip," I said. "Give it to me."

"You're not thinking it's been poisoned, are you?"

"That's *precisely* what I'm thinking," I said. "Someone could have ground up some leaves and stems. Aconite is really acrid. The flavor could be masked by lemon juice. I don't know how potent it is, but a woman was poisoned not that long ago when she bought what she thought was tea and drank a full cup of infused aconite."

"Oh, crap. I might have ingested poison?"

I nodded. "We need to get your lemon water tested. And you should get yourself tested in the hospital."

"I only took one sip," Karen said. She started running out of the room and called over her shoulder, "I'm going to force myself to puke."

Flint had finished his drink of water and was watching the commotion with interest. I knelt and stroked his fur, saying, "It's all right, boy," although I was really only reassuring myself. I tightened the screw-lid onto her bottle and looked around for something I could hide it in so I could get it out of the building unseen. I found an old, soiled T-shirt under the sink and draped it over Karen's indigo-blue bottle. I then went in search of Baxter, with Flint trotting behind me. Baxter was standing near my pseudo-director's chair, chatting with a couple of stage crew members.

"Got a minute?" I asked him.

"Sure," he said, and excused himself. I put Flint into a sit-stay, and Baxter followed me out the rear entrance.

"Karen's water may have been poisoned," I said in a low voice. "She might need a ride to a hospital. And we've got to get this into Sheriff Caulfield's hands to be tested." I handed him her bottle, and the T-shirt as well.

"Should I wait here or—"

"I'm going to ask her what she wants to do now. I'll let you know."

He nodded. "I'll go get the car and bring it around back. Is Karen okay?"

"I think so. She said her tongue and lips were tingling. I'll meet you at the back exit in a couple of minutes."

Baxter left. I went back inside, entered the women's room, and locked the door behind me. Karen was just leaving the stall. She was dabbing at her brow with a tissue. "Is your tongue still tingling?"

"It's already fading. The sensation I mean." She closed her eyes and took a calming breath. "I'm fine. I'm mad as hell, but I'm fine."

"You should probably go to the hospital just in—"

She was already shaking her head. "I'm going on stage. We need to force whoever did this to show us their hand."

"I just wish we had an identical water bottle," I said. "We could aim a nanny camera at the refrigerator overnight and maybe catch the killer red-handed."

"I bought it at the General Goods store across the street. They had a couple more there."

"Perfect! I gave your bottle to Baxter. He's awaiting my word. We'll have him buy a duplicate bottle. We already have a tiny camera with us. I thought it might come in useful during Flint's training."

"But *then* what? How do we get the person behind this to reveal themselves?"

"You'll make a show out of knocking over your water bottle and needing another chilled bottle. Then we can hope that the guilty person poisons it again."

"Simple enough. During my talk to the audience, I'll knock the bottle over on stage. And I'll tell the cast and crew all about it."

"Perfect. Baxter will buy a duplicate at the store now, and take the poisoned one to the sheriff."

"It's a plan," Karen said. "Tell Baxter that I'm going on stage and pretending to have forgotten my water bottle. I'll ask him to grab it for me. It's an informal chat that we do. It will look like a perfectly casual, harmless exchange."

"And he'll hand you the bottle with a loose lid," I said.

"Precisely."

We spontaneously gave each other a hug. It felt great to have a comrade.

Flint was waiting patiently for me outside the women's restroom. I let him come with me as I filled Baxter in on the plan outside the theater. He was confident he could quickly rig up the camera.

I hugged him, then Flint. "We're going to catch the killer! Just...be sure and tell Sheriff Caulfield about this. Obviously he needs to be the one who arrests the person, once we've got a video of him or her poisoning the water bottle."

***

As nervous as I'd been before and during the performances of the play, my heart felt like it was pounding loud enough for the audience to hear as I watched Karen. Greg and Hammond were flanking her. Baxter appeared beside me, and Karen spotted him and cleared her throat, then asked if he'd "be a dear..." Baxter brought her the safe water bottle a minute or so later. She pulled off a masterful intentional accidental spill of all the contents, mostly in her own lap, followed by her jumping out of the chair in surprise. She asked a stage hand to notify Felicity to see if she could help her dry out her costume, and also notify Valerie, in case the start time needed to be delayed. She apologized to her fellow actors and joked with the audience not to take any of her remarks about the play seriously, because she was "all wet."

Curtain time was indeed five minutes late. The first couple of acts went fine, although I was operating on autopilot, concentrating on my cuing so hard that I was paying attention to nothing else.

After the second intermission, I had settled down and was able to enjoy the show even while working. The final act went so well that it lifted the entire performance. Flint had been perfect throughout. Remarkably, there were no incidents of any kind. Afterward, Baxter congratulated me. He gave me a hug and a kiss.

"Even the roses were delivered perfectly," Baxter said. "No hot sauce on their stems."

"Plus Flint got a huge standing ovation," I added. "I'm surprised John didn't come to watch."

"He called me right before the performance began. He wanted to know which dog was Blue. He wasn't pleased when I told him. He said he wants Flint to be fresh for the five Friday-through-Sunday performances."

I clicked my tongue. "Herding dogs are happy to be on duty ten hours a day, seven days a week."

"Yeah, that's pretty much what I told him."

Baxter was looking over my shoulder and said, “Hi, Valerie.”

“Baxter,” she said with a nod, then shifted her gaze to me. “Good show. You’ve certainly made a big difference in Flint’s behavior in front of audiences. You’d be doing the theater a great service by training Pippa in the part.”

“I already *am*. I’m working with Felicity. Pippa has been responding really well to the training.”

“I’m going to take Flint outside for a couple minutes,” Baxter said. He and Flint left so quickly that I wondered if he was worried that Valerie and I were about to talk about the romantic couples again.

“We’ve been using Pippa periodically in the *Boomtown* show,” Valerie told me, “so I’m not surprised she was a good student.”

“Neither am I.” I paused. Nobody was within earshot. This was the perfect opportunity to check John’s story with Valerie. “I saw Pippa perform last night. She was excellent. In fact, that made it pretty clear to me that she could have done a passable job as Blue. I didn’t realize until then that she was *also* given all the wrong cues when she subbed for Flint.”

For just a moment, Valerie’s features had a flicker of alarm. “Wrong cues?” she repeated.

“Did you truly approve of John’s plan to give the wrong cues to Flint to garner extra publicity?”

She crossed her arms. Our gazes locked. I realized then that she had indeed greenlighted John’s plan. The only question was whether or not she would tell me the truth. “Our idea to garner publicity worked beautifully,” she replied. “I’m sure you’re familiar with the old saw that there's no such thing as bad publicity. This theater's future is always hanging by a thread. The money we make from selling tickets only covers a portion of the annual costs to bring live theatre to our stage."

"You and John set me up with phony bickering when Baxter and I first arrived."

"Yes, because we needed you to work with Flint, so we could explain his transformation. We're giving you a salary that's more than fair."

"It is fair. It's just been wasting the theater's funds, considering my services weren't even needed. At least John's play is bringing in donations, in addition to the dog's supposed hijinks are filling the seats."

Valerie furrowed her brow. "What are you saying?"

"I heard how you auctioned off the right to have a Poodle star as Blue in a performance in October.

"Yes," Valerie said. "That's part of the reason John convinced me to hire a combination dog trainer, stagehand. Sam fit the bill nicely. Or he *would* have, if poisoning John hadn't been an item on his personal agenda. Truth be told, I don't have a whole lot of sympathy for the death of someone who'd recently tried to murder a friend of mine. Seems to me, Sam got what he deserved."

"But you're only *assuming* he was guilty of the attempt on John's life."

She spread her arms. "Who *else* could have done such a thing?"

"Whoever murdered *Sam*," I said, stating the obvious, to my mind.

"Which the police arrested John for!" She paused and stared into my eyes. Her expression grew sad. "I'm sorry, Allie. My mistake," she said. "You're a friend of John's, too. You don't want to admit to yourself that he's guilty."

I held my tongue. An upsetting thought had crept into my head, however. The cast and crew all knew by now that Karen had dumped the lemon water that, presumably, someone believed they had poisoned. But one suspect had been absent, and wouldn't know anything about our setup. John. He had keys to the theater and could easily have done the deed last night.

Chapter 23

Karen emerged from the dressing room, back in her civilian clothes. She gestured with her chin that I should follow her. "That performance went better than I expected," she said as we were passing Valerie's office, "especially compared to my klutziness during the talk."

We entered the women's room, and we checked to make sure they were empty.

"You were right, Allie," Karen told me. "Sheriff Caulfield left a message for me, and I called him back. He said that there was a high dose of aconite in my water, so it's lucky I only had one sip...and threw up immediately afterward. I'm going to go to the stationhouse tonight. After they have me get a blood test."

"Are you still feeling okay?"

"Yeah, I'm fine. Is the camera focused on the refrigerator in the green room?"

"I haven't had the chance to check that yet, but I assume so." I studied her features. She certainly looked fine. "Did the sheriff say anything about your needing to take it easy? You didn't drink enough to have lingering effects or anything, did you?"

"Well, he said I should have gotten a charcoal treatment instead of vomiting. But I would have had to drink six ounces or so to put myself in bad shape. Which is rather chilling. I easily could have swallowed that much water in a few gulps, if I hadn't picked up on its terrible taste. And I don't get why someone would want to poison me. I'm probably the most isolated member of the cast. I'm completely unconnected to John or Sam."

"Maybe we're all in jeopardy. None of us should eat or drink anything that's been left unattended in the refrigerator."

"Which means we're not able to warn all of the *innocent* people until the killer tries to strike again," Karen said.

"We'd better clear out everything in the fridge that isn't sealed, just to be sure. If we don't catch anyone in the act by tomorrow afternoon, we should tell everyone the truth about why you spilled your water today."

"If the sheriff doesn't shut us down by then," Karen said. "It was all I could do to stop him from coming straight here to 'make sure we weren't taking our lives into our own stupid hands' was the way he put it," she added, using air quotes.

Karen left, and I headed to the green room. Baxter was tossing the contents of the refrigerator into a bag, replacing them with new, unopened items. Both Pavlov and Flint were watching him. "We're on the same page, once again," I said.

"Notice how nicely Pavlov fits under the table."

I was certain he was saying this so he could surreptitiously show me the hidden camera. I looked down and immediately spotted the tiny camera that had been fastened onto the black table leg just below the ledge. I knew to look for it, however, and felt confident nobody else would find it unless they happened to drop something underneath the table.

Karen's water was in the bottom shelf in the door, per usual. It would be hard to miss that the refrigerator contents had been changed, which would make the killer suspicious. My spirits sank. I hadn't thought this through. We likely had next to zero chance of recording the poisoner in action.

"Hey, guys," John said, striding into the room just then. "Thanks for taking such good care of Flint for me. Are you sticking around for your full week?"

"Yeah," Baxter answered quickly. "Planning on going back on Monday. So is everything all right? Your lawyer is still keeping in touch with you, and vice versa?"

He plopped into a chair, called Flint over, and started petting him. "For someone who charges two hundred dollars a second, my lawyer's surprisingly willing to chat at length."

I chuckled in spite of myself.

"Anything turning up here?" he asked. "Suspicious activity?"

"Nothing," I replied. "The only thing that caused a bit of problem was that Karen spilled her entire bottle of lemon water on stage, during the talk with the audience."

"Oh, right. Valerie mentioned that. I guess the curtains went up a tad late just so Felicity could dry out her costume. She also mentioned you were asking about the fundraiser with the loaded-couple's Poodle. Are you interested in the gig?"

"No, but thanks," I replied.

He frowned a little but nodded. His forehead was damp with beads of sweat. "God knows if I'll be in jail by then," he said.

"Don't give up hope, John," Baxter said. "It's only been a couple of days. We're hoping they can get some new evidence."

"Yeah. Well..." He let his voice fade. He rose, seemingly too agitated to stay seated. John was shifting his weight from foot to foot. He looked even more nervous than when he'd taken the stage himself.

"Is there anything in particular you'd like me to help you with during tomorrow night's performance, John?"

"No, just try and keep an eye on everyone backstage or in the wings. Baxter can do the same. We're getting another—" He broke off, then began again, "We've got a reporter from a Colorado Springs paper coming to watch it. I'd love for the play to be flawless and get rave reviews."

"Sounds good," I said. "So should we just come in late tomorrow?"

"Yeah. Whatever. Come on, Flint," John said. "It's time to hit the sack. I feel half dead. See you later."

Baxter waited a beat as John and his dog left. "You ready to go?"

"I want to check in on Felicity. I want to ask if we should train Pippa again in the morning."

"Okay. I've got some computer work to do," Baxter said, tilting his head toward the hidden camera. He was probably going to check and see if anyone had paid attention to Karen's lemon water.

Predictably, Felicity was upstairs, seated behind a sewing machine, working away.

"Hi, Felicity. Just wanted to see how you and Pippa are doing." Pippa was wagging her rear-end. Those upright tails of theirs weren't as easy to wag as other breeds'. She was still in her Star Trek uniform.

"I was thinking I owe you both another training session. Would tomorrow morning work?"

"Oh, thanks for offering, Allie, but no thanks. I thought she did really well in *Boomtown* last night."

"She sure did. But I don't want to short-change you. I'm more than happy to work with Pippa for another hour or two."

"That truly is sweet of you, but I'm good with the work you've already put into her." She grimaced, "Now that she's not getting bogus commands from that God-damned John Morris, I'm thinking she'll do fine."

"How did you know about that?" I asked.

"John told me himself. Just today. At least he's finally seen fit to admit how terrible he's been to me."

I couldn't blame Felicity for the venom in her voice. I would have felt the same way if John had done that to Pavlov, let alone the much more serious mistreatments of his former girlfriend.

"Okay," I said. "We'll leave it at that, then. Pippa was fun to work with, so thanks for the opportunity."

"No worries," she said, "but hang on a sec. I was just finishing this up for Pavlov."

She finished sewing a seam and cut the thread. I looked closer at her work. It appeared to be a really nice vest for a dog, with numerous pockets on either side. "Oh, that's great but you—"

"I took all her measurements, so this will fit her perfectly She never struck me as a frilly, frou-frou type, so I used the dark blue fabric that's used in police uniforms...Shepherds are often called 'police dogs,' after all. And I made her a vest she can wear whenever you go on long hikes. It has room for a water bottle and a collapsible bowl, as well as food and treats. Even for a small first aid kit and so on."

"Wow, Felicity. I don't even know what to say. It's worth *way* more than her one lesson."

"Oh, I don't mind. Just take some business cards. A lot of companies produce cookie-cutter vests for dogs, but I can email instructions on how to take precise measurements and will customize this however the owner wants."

"That sounds like a great product for dog owners with expendable cash. Baxter started a really successful business making customized dog houses."

She smiled. "I remember John telling me about that. Back when he was living with me. We'd almost placed an order for Flint. I'm sure we would have, except that was right around the time he met Sally...and promptly dumped me."

"At least that's better timing than *after* you'd purchased it to match your house."

She snorted. "Thank the Lord for small favors."

"I should get going. See you later."

"Allie?" she said. "I really regret all the garbage Sam and I pulled on John. I wish we'd never sunk to John's level."

"What John did to us...messing up Flint's performances and suckering us into coming here under false pretense...was a lot worse than you using a dog whistle to distract him."

"Yeah, but still. Two wrongs don't make a right. See you tomorrow."

"Yep." I trotted down the stairs, admonishing myself for using Valerie's pet reply.

My thoughts stayed focused on Valerie. Why had she agreed to hiring me for the play? They'd already hired Sam Geller as a trainer plus a stagehand. I was redundant, and she was deeply concerned with the theater's financial bottom-line.

Although I had next to no rational reason for my suspicions, I was starting to think that maybe both Valerie and John were in on everything: Sam's murder. The poisoning. The falling lights. The drugged dog. I could only hope that our camera captured the next poisoning attempt. But what a miserable thing to hang one's hopes on.

Chapter 24

Baxter and I didn't return to the theater until late the next afternoon. We were both in a bad mood. As it turned out, he'd taken a lot of heat from the sheriff last night over my scheme to set up the poisoner to believe another dose had to be slipped into Karen's water bottle. Even though I'd considered the conversation finished, as we neared the theater, Baxter said, "We're going to need to have Karen's back when it comes to monitoring her water bottle. The sheriff said he was going to come to tonight's performance. But he read me the riot act."

"So you said. And you also said he's still going to give any evidence we can collect to the D.A."

"When and *if* we manage to video someone tampering with the water bottle, he said he'd likely view that as a strong indication that they'd arrested the wrong guy. But he pointed out that the camera will likely only record someone removing Karen's water bottle and then sticking it back in the fridge. If we're lucky. Nobody is going to unscrew the cap and pour poison in it, all the while standing right in front of the refrigerator door."

"Someone might," I grumbled.

He gave no reply. Baxter was bringing his laptop today so that, once the play began and everyone was involved in that, he could view the camera recordings so far. We headed straight to the greenroom to our hidden camera. I noted that the camera was still in place and took a seat. Baxter opened the refrigerator. Sally's water bottle was precisely where she'd left it last night.

Before Baxter could sit down, John entered the room with Flint. He stood near the door and gaped at us. "What are you doing, Allida?" he asked.

"I'm just...sitting here. You're going to be cuing Flint. I thought I might as well relax for a bit."

"When you said you'd be here tonight, I assumed you meant to help out. Both of you. With the dog."

I rose. "What do you need me to do?"

He snorted. "Look at Flint." He gestured at him. Flint was sitting beside him, his ears perked up. I saw nothing wrong with his demeanor. "He's got no spark. I need him to give the performance of his life tonight. My entire career depends on it. And you've obviously overworked him! You never should have forced him to perform last night!"

"Dude, take a chill pill," Baxter said.

"You're still on the clock, Allie," John said. "I guess I just didn't realize that you were going to throw in the towel. Hang out in the break room, while an off-Broadway director is coming here to watch my play!"

"That's great news, John," I said. "Congratulations. And Flint looks just as energetic as ever to me."

"Well, he doesn't to me! And I'm the one who knows him best!"

I was familiar with John's plight. He was anxious and freaking out. He had plenty riding on tonight's show. "Flint is fine," I said calmly. "I'll run him through some commands right now."

"Never mind. You've clearly turned on me. You've decided I'm guilty. Just like everyone else." He flung his hands into the air as if in defeat. "You can go on back to Boulder now. You'll get your check in the mail."

"John. Seriously," Baxter snapped, "Get a grip."

"*You're* the one who's lost his grip," John growled. "Just go. Both of you. You're fired."

Baxter balled his fists. "We'll leave on Sunday morning, just as we've planned. We don't work for you. We work for Valerie. If she wants to fire us, she can."

"You're such an asshole," John said. "I'm sorry I tried to help your girlfriend boost her career. I should have known better than to think you'd appreciate it."

He stormed out of the room.

Baxter cursed. He was breathing hard, his fists and jaw clenched tight, staring after John as if it was taking all of his self-control not to chase him down. I had never seen him this angry, and I didn't know what to do or say.

"I want to punch that guy's lights out," Baxter said.

"Me, too. But we have to see this thing through. For Karen's sake, if nothing else. And we still need to be able to come in tomorrow and retrieve the camera."

"No. Tell Karen to drink the bottled water tonight. I need to stay the hell away from John.

I'm going to go back to the hotel. Spend the evening with our big girl."

"Okay. I understand."

He furrowed his brow. "You need to come with me. Play it safe. There's nothing you can do tonight, during the performance anyway."

I shook my head, still alarmed at Baxter's demeanor. "We haven't had the chance to check the recording. I can't leave yet. Not while I know Karen's a target."

"Or a great actress, who set this all up."

"I trust my gut, Baxter. Karen and I are friends now."

He sighed in obvious annoyance. "I'll stay here, then, too."

"I'll be fine. Frankly, I don't think you'll be good company until you cool off."

"Fine," he growled. "I'll zip back here during the first act, grab the camera, and check its memory at the hotel. If anybody has touched the bottle, I'll alert Sheriff Caulfield by the second act. When I 'cool down,' as you put it, I'll see if you're willing to be in my presence." He headed toward the door.

"Baxter...."

He turned back, glaring at me. "What?"

I didn't know what to say. We stared at each other in silence.

He sighed. "There's safety in numbers," he said, his voice much less hostile, at least. "You can't let yourself be alone with anybody."

"We'll talk during the second act," I said. My heart was pounding once again. Maybe Baxter had anger-control problems. Or maybe *I* was being too quick to sympathize with John's anxious behavior instead of Baxter's reaction.

Baxter stood still for a few seconds, then left. I booted up his computer and logged in with his password. But within a few seconds, I started cursing myself. I had never used his doggie-cam software. I didn't know how to examine the camera's records. For all I knew, we had caught the killer red-handed already, but I wouldn't be able to find out until Baxter had examined them.

***

The curtain opened at 7:30. I had managed to follow Baxter's advice, spending much of my time with Sally and Karen in the dressing room. I'd passed Valerie only once, who'd thanked and complimented me on Flint's performance last night, spoken briefly to Hammond and Greg, but hadn't seen Felicity—or Pippa—once. I remembered she'd said Pippa would be wearing her formalwear tonight and was curious, although she might have been joking.

I deliberately watched from the wing opposite John's. Otherwise I'd be listening to his every word and would fly off the handle if he gave Flint a bad command. Halfway through the first act, everyone on stage seemed to be at the top of their game. All I could think about now was Baxter and the camera recordings.

I quietly left my post and went to the greenroom, hoping to spot him and tell him how much I loved him. I toyed with telling him we could leave now, but being honest with myself, I wanted him to agree to stay as planned and maybe have one last conversation with Sheriff

Caulfield. If nothing else, I needed to know Karen was safe. I couldn't imagine how I'd feel if I returned home, then learned she'd been poisoned.

The greenroom was empty. The camera was gone. So was Karen's water bottle.

For a moment I felt almost faint. I had told Karen to stick with bottled water. Had she ignored me?

Baxter must have taken it, along with the camera.

I called his cell and held my breath.

"Hey, hon," he answered.

"Do you have Karen's bottle?"

"Yeah. I figured either it's already been poisoned or not, but either way, Sheriff Caulfied's going to lower the boom on our sting operation tonight no matter what. I just left a minute ago. Still on my way back. I love you forever."

"Me, too. See you soon."

"Lucky me," he replied with a smile in his voice.

I felt an enormous weight being lifted off my shoulders. Baxter and I were fine. Karen would be fine. We'd put this investigation in the hands of the sheriff, where it belonged.

I lingered in the women's room, trying to level out my rollercoaster emotions. I all but literally bumped into John.

"You're still here, I see," he said. "I suppose I should apologize for flying off the handle. I'm really just trying to get through the day. Getting arrested for murder does weird stuff to your head."

"I can imagine."

"The real reason I blew up at you is because I found out you've been asking around about me...trying to take my dog away from me."

"Well, John, what can I say? I've been concerned about your treatment of Flint because of the tranquilizers. Even though I can sort of see why you felt the need to be extra cautious when the lights fell, you gave Flint a tranquilizer between acts during the final dress rehearsal. According to the sheriff."

"I already explained myself. I didn't know what else to do. Felicity had reported to Valerie during the intermission that Flint bit her."

"You never told me that!"

"That's what *she* claimed happened. I'd been talking to the actors between the first and second acts, trying to make sure they were able to keep straight their adlibbing. She showed me the injury on her forearm. Two puncture wounds on her arm where she said he drew blood."

"Why didn't you tell me about that right away?" I asked.

"Because by the next day, I realized it was likely that *Pippa* was the one who actually bit her. I think she lied about Flint because she didn't want her dog to get in trouble, but felt it would be the justice I deserved if *my* dog got the boot."

"Did you tell Valerie that, or confront Felicity with your suspicions?"

"Yeah, and Felicity held strong, so Valerie said we'd let it go this one time. She said she couldn't be certain either way."

"But the bite marks of a Pug versus a Border Collie should have been easy to tell apart."

"Maybe if we'd checked immediately after the bite. It sure wasn't obvious at a glance to *me*, almost twenty-four hours later. Meanwhile, she told me I was going to get sued if he bit anyone a second time." He stamped his foot. "Allie. I'm just trying to get through the performance. There really *is* a Broadway producer in the audience tonight. Don't wreck everything for me!"

I turned on a heel and walked away. He could have been telling me the whole truth, or he could have lying through his teeth. I couldn't tell. Maybe it didn't matter. He didn't really seem like a terrible dog owner, just not a very good one.

The second act began, but I couldn't focus and decided I'd just go ahead and text Baxter.

Anything? I typed.

Moments later came the reply:

Nobody even opened the fridge.

Seconds later he added:

Sorry, darling. You're the love of my life.

I smiled at the screen and sent back some heart emoticons. At least now I could concentrate on the performance. I had read the script so many times that I'd memorized the lines. Even so, Sally and Hammie's repartee was so engaging, I found myself laughing along with the audience.

Flint was now crossing to his third target, where Greg was going to trip over him, causing him to accidentally dump his drink on Karen.

Suddenly, I felt a distinct chill. On the stage, Flint froze instead of hitting his target and barked twice. It was his fearful bark.

"Whoa," Greg adlibbed, pretending to be so startled by the bark that he jerked his martini glass and dumped it on Karen.

"There goes John's flawless performance," I said under my breath. I glanced at John. He was hanging his head. I knew it was silly, but I whispered, "Annabelle, if that's really you, please stay away from the stage. You're scaring the dog."

Maybe it *was* just a simple draft inside a leaky old theater. In any case, I realized now that I wasn't helping Flint or John or anyone else by watching the play. I might as well investigate the source of the draft.

The backstage door was propped open by an electric fan, which was running full blast. The actors probably appreciated the cool breeze. I chuckled at my leaping to the conclusion that it was a ghost.

I stepped over the fan and strode down the steps. The breeze over the river was every bit as chilly as Annabelle Dancer's ghost, I mused to myself. Realizing how very little I wanted to listen to John bemoaning Flint's minor miscue, I grabbed my cellphone and texted to Baxter:

I want to say goodbye to Karen at intermission. See you at hotel in a few.

As I turned, I saw a shadow passing the upstairs window. That had to be Felicity. I should probably ask her about the dog bite. It would ease my mind to know that John was telling the truth about why he'd given Flint a tranquilizer.

As I started to climb the stairway to the second floor, I had yet another chill, this one so strong it felt as if I was in a freezer. Two steps later, I was nearly gasping at the heat. This time I knew for certain it wasn't a draft. Either there really was some sort of ghost that haunted the premises, or there were inexplicable atmospheric conditions in this building that could affect the temperature of small pockets of air.

I entered the sewing room. To my surprise, it was Valerie, not Felicity. She didn't look happy to see me. Apparently, I'd surprised her, and she had come here to cry in private. She swiped at her cheeks and said, "Yes?"

"Hi, Valerie. I'm sorry to interrupt. I didn't realize you were here. I saw you in the window and thought you were Felicity."

"Felicity started sneezing her head off...allergies...and went home. I've been sitting here for the last half hour. I was never near the window."

"Must have been Annabelle," I said.

"*She's* at it again?" Valerie snorted. "She's probably looking forward to my company."

I didn't know how to take her last statement. "I'll talk to Felicity tomorrow." I stayed still, weighing whether I should pretend I hadn't noticed her tears or if it would be best to show some basic compassion. This was clearly not a good time to discuss my decision to leave a day early. "Are you okay?"

"No, I am not at all okay." She glared at me. "Love problems, if you must know."

Apparently I should have opted for silence. "Sorry, Valerie. I didn't mean to butt into your personal business."

"Oh, I'm sure." Her voice was a shade below hostile.

"I hope your day improves, Valerie." I gestured at the stairs. "I'll—"

"Nobody realizes how hard my life is. No matter what I do, it's like I'm always barefoot on the sharp edge of a knife. I thought I could make this play work. Keep everybody happy. You make one stupid mistake when you're young and in love, and that's it. You're just trapped into one awful thing after another."

I cursed to myself. The words were too reminiscent of what Karen had said about wanting to forgive Greg for what he'd done to his first girlfriend well over a decade ago. Valerie had known that information firsthand. Maybe she had been somehow been complicit in Greg's committing vehicular homicide. "I'll let you go," I muttered. I turned toward the stairs, hoping to make a quick exit.

"Stop, right there," she said. "Turn around."

I turned. She was aiming a gun at me and coming toward me.

"What are you doing, Valerie?" My voice was surprisingly calm; I'd somehow half expected her to be holding a gun.

"I'm going to make you pay for ruining my life. Thanks to you, I can't make any of it go away. Everything is backfiring on me."

"Look, Valerie. I don't know what you're talking about. But whatever it is, it isn't worth taking a life and going to jail."

She cackled. "I *already* took a life, you idiot. I had to, because of John. He dug into my past with Greg. He uncovered my secret, and promised me he wouldn't share it with Greg...just as long as I helped *him* turn his damned play into a hit. I found *his* dirty secret—how he cheated Sam Geller in order to get Flint."

"I had nothing to do with any of—"

"I was going to get Flint back to Sam, and Sam was going to help bring Greg back to me. But Sam turned on me, thanks to you. *You* made him think he could earn good money training canine herders. He figured out I was trying to frame him for Sam's murder. Told me *he'd* tell Greg my secret!"

"*I* don't know your secret, Valerie, and I don't want to know. I never did anything to hurt you. I was only trying to help Flint."

She half laughed half cried. "If that's true, it's too bad for you. You wound up in the wrong place, at the wrong time. I came up here to shoot myself. All those years ago, I caused Greg to think his girlfriend was cheating on him. I got him drunk, to drown his sorrows. I told him she was waiting for her new lover on the corner. They were just friends. And I'd told *her* we were going to pick them up there. But Greg wouldn't give me his keys. Or let me get into the car with him. He spent ten years in jail, because of me. He killed a girl. Because of me. And now *I* killed a man. So I could stop him from making Greg hate me. Stop having my guilt shoved in my face. All just so that I could have the chance to make it up to Greg. For us to be together."

"You don't have to kill yourself or me. You need help, Valerie. This is too much for anyone to handle. Let me—"

"No. I'm done. But, I'm going to kill you first."

In a last-ditch effort, I gasped, pretending something behind her had arrived to save me. "Pavlov, sic her!" I cried, pointing at Valerie.

She turned to look back, and I lunged at her with all of my force, tackling her in her midsection.

We fell to the floor. I knew by the "Oof" sound she'd muttered that I'd knocked out her breath. I grabbed her arm that held the gun. Using all of my weight, I pinned her forearm to the floor. She grabbed a fistful of my hair with her free hand and yanked my head back.

She was larger and stronger than I was. I was overmatched. She was strong enough to bludgeon a man; strong enough to crush me.

Despite the excruciating pain in my scalp, I continued to squeeze her arm and force it away from me.

I felt more than heard a swift-approaching canine race up the stairs toward me. Then there was a growl and a blur of motion as Pavlov leapt over our sprawled legs.

Valerie screamed in pain. She released her grip on my hair, as well as the gun. I lurched forward and grabbed the gun, then swung around onto my knees, aiming at her.

Pavlov had chomped onto her arm. Valerie was making guttural noises of pain. She was struggling to get up while Pavlov tried to pull her away from me.

"Pavlov, release!" I yelled, aiming the gun at Valerie's head.

She continued to growl and ignored me.

"Leave it, Pavlov! Now!"

She obeyed me and backed away.

On her knees, Valerie cradled her arm, gripping it below the injury.

"Allie?" I heard Baxter cry from downstairs.

"Up here," I yelled. "Call nine-one-one. Now!"

Baxter pounded up the stairs and was momentarily by my side. "Oh, my God. Allie! Are you okay?"

I kept my eyes riveted on Valerie. I could see him drop his cellphone and scramble to pick it up. "You removed the bolts from the light fixture. Why? Just to freak out John?"

She was sneering at me, her face hideously distorted. "I thought you'd see what a bad dog owner John was. But you were clueless. You did nothing about the chocolate in the kibble. And you were the goddamned genius who realized Sally's bouquet could be poisonous, and saved that monster's life by telling everyone. The poison was injected straight into his blood stream. John would have died! Which is what he deserved! Sam would have gone to jail for his murder. Karen would be out of the picture. And Greg would still be in love with me."

"This is Baxter McClelland," Baxter said into his phone. "Sheriff Caulfield is here in the audience. He needs to come to the second floor of the Creede Playhouse. Valerie Devereux has confessed to killing Sam Geller. She tried to shoot Allie Babcock. Allie got the gun away from her. We need her to be arrested immediately." He paused. "Yes. Baxter McClelland. Hurry. I have to tie her up."

I wondered if the dispatcher would believe Baxter. It all sounded so bizarre.

"*She* poisoned John," I told Baxter. "She would have killed Karen, too, if she hadn't tasted the poison despite the lemon juice."

"Karen stole Greg from me! I've waited and plotted for years and years to get Greg back into my life! *Greg* gave her flowers!"

She glared at Baxter while rocking herself in pain. "All of you miserable, stupid people with your miserable stupid dogs!" Her words were coming out in shrieks. "It's all you think about. You and your vicious pets! You can all go to hell!"

I felt numb. Valerie's mind was so twisted, I could only feel sorry for her. Yet she'd destroyed Greg's life, killed Sam, and, yes, had done one awful thing after another. It was overwhelming just to know that there was this much misery in the world.

Baxter grabbed a shirt off a hanger. He sat her down in chair and bound her waist to the chair. She was still gripping her wounded arm.

"People like you don't deserve pets, Valerie," Baxter said.

Epilogue

Three weeks later, Baxter and I had mostly recovered from our trauma. Pavlov seemed to have recovered, too. The very last thing I had ever wanted for her was to have to attack someone. I was still having bad dreams, however, despite having been safe in my own home and waking in Baxter's arms. In time, though, those dreams would fade.

The Creede Repertory Theatre was now opening a new show at the Ruth Theater. Judging from several online reviews, *Good Dog, Blue!* was still going strong, gleaning rave reviews and an extension to what would be a twelve-week run, a two-week extension to their entire season. The mounds of publicity from the release of the director and the arrest of the theater manager had indeed helped the theater's sales.

John had sent me two bouquets (red roses) and apologized via email at least a half-dozen times. I would undoubtedly have to testify at some point in the murder trial. I'd learned through John that Felicity had been temporarily promoted to theatre manager, and all the other actors had carried on their roles, with both Flint and Pippa making excellent Blues as the need arose.

Karen had called me just to chat. We had vowed to get together in Boulder, after she'd completed her work in Creede. She told me that

Sally had permanently dumped John, and that Felicity had also made it clear that she would never get back into anything beyond a business relationship with him. Felicity had told Karen that she was truly looking forward to the play's run ending, which would lead to John leaving town for "brighter spotlights."

In his most-recent email, John wrote that he had finally realized he had been treating Flint like a commodity, but the events of late had awakened him to understand what a privilege it really is to earn the love of a good dog. He promised me that he would measure up and deserve Flint's loyalty from here on out.

He also wrote that he was getting requests for productions of his play from five different western and southwestern states. He assured us that he would love to let bygones be bygones and to cut us into the action as a dog-training team. *I want to atone for my terrible transgressions*, he wrote.

We turned him down.

Note from Allie Babcock

Leslie O'Kane is a dog lover, a certified decorator, a tennis player (though she has a caustic relationship with the net), and a hula-hoop dancer (but keeps bruising herself).

Although Leslie has been a published author for more than 20 years, she has issues with self-promotion and is in a 12-step program to overcome her fear of newsletters, blogs, and publicizing her books through social media.

Please help me push Leslie onto the next step by visiting **LeslieOKane.com** and signing up for her **New Book Alert** or sending her an email at **LesOKane@aol.com**, and, if you are so inclined, "like" her Facebook page, Leslie O'Kane Books. She also is attempting to start an interactive blog on her website about dogs and book clubs.

Lastly, if you enjoyed this book, please write a review; apparently such things help authors to sell books and encourage them to write more. If you send a copy of your review to her email she will send you a deeply felt personal thank you.

At the time of this writing, the next book in the series is not anticipated until late 2018, all five of Leslie's women's books feature dogs. In fact, the dog named Red in Leslie's latest women's novel is instrumental in the story of **How My Book Club Got Arrested**. Her Life's Second Chances books are a series only in the sense that they feature similarly strong female characters, romance, action, humor, and a dog. They are all stand-alone novels with unique settings and casts of characters. You can find these books at book retailers of your choice, or at my website, **LeslieOKane.com.** As a bonus, the first chapter of **How My Book Club Got Arrested** follows.

Foreword

Note from the Important Author

Please Read This

(Speaking for myself, I tend to skip forewords.)

Getting a book published has been my lifelong dream. Several years ago, I attended a bookstore signing at which the author was late to arrive, so the store owner led the audience in a group discussion by asking: "What do you most want to see in a book?" My answer was: "My name as its author on the cover." Although publishing HOW MY BOOK CLUB GOT ARRESTED was the realization of my dream, having my name on the cover has proved to be problematic.

Due to my book-club members not wanting to get hauled into court yet again, all of the names herein have been changed, including my own. All of the *events*, on the other hand, occurred as written and were witnessed/perpetrated by one or more of us. Most of our conversations were recorded by a prototype voice-to-text app (which, btw, my computer-whiz son designed; {my publisher didn't want me to include the name of this software program, but if you ask a computer expert to recommend the best voice-to-text app on the market today—with such first-rate voice recognition that it can identify up to eight different speakers—that will be my son's}) :).

(Okay, yes, that's a happy face, which is amateurish. I was having fun with punctuation.)

It is an understatement to say that, in my telling of this story, feathers were ruffled. Feathers were plucked and jabbed into sensitive places where no feathers belong. Countless times none of us book-clubbers wanted to believe that we actually *said* the things the app recorded. This led to a sentence-by-sentence dismantling of initial drafts of this book, even though the text and the software application that produced the text were thoroughly vetted and have been declared accurate by no less than the entire freaking State of Missouri! (I'm a bit touchy on this particular subject.)

Many book clubs are basically wine and cheese parties named after a different book each month. That sounds fun. Cheers! *My* merry band of book lovers, however, can criticize the daylights out of a book. To date, we've discussed some 128 titles and have yet to find a single book that we all held in precisely the same regard.

Imagine, if you will, how things played out when I asked them to critique a book about *them*—my beloved-but-opinionated friends who were traumatized by the very events described within said book. Are you picturing something along the lines of me as a metaphoric sirloin patty that's been dropped into a tank of hungry piranhas? If so, that's not quite right. Out of a complex need to protect one another's feelings and yet assuage our own guilty consciences, it was more along the lines of five underfed piranhas—myself included—trying to simultaneous eat themselves plus one another, along with the aforementioned metaphoric sirloin patty.

The only thing that presented an even greater challenge was when I gave my manuscript to the *sixth* member of the book club—my adult daughter. Fortunately, she handled the matter with grace and maturity. (Because I've bragged about my son's software application and I don't play favorites {which neither of them believe}, I'm joyously announcing that my daughter's singing, dancing, and acting skills have recently led to her being cast in a musical on Broadway! Yet another reason that pseudonyms were required for all concerned.)

Even though it's fair to say that the state of Missouri agrees with the narrative herein, it is also fair to say that an average of two points of significant contention regarding accuracy arose on every single page of this book from one or more of my fellow Boobs. (And, no, the word *Boobs* is not a typo. An explanation can be found in Chapter 1.) Even so, we talked everything through, and the book club remains intact.

A couple of months have passed since everyone in the group was given the opportunity to read and comment on my eighth draft. There will not be a ninth, because one of the members, whose real and fake names shall remain anonymous, threatened to strangle me—and honest to God, at this point, I'd be more than happy to provide a hemp-based (see Chapter 2) rope.

At the onset of the road trip from Boulder, Colorado, to Branson, Missouri, I had envisioned this book as a travelogue. In my capacity as a beta tester for the voice-to-text software, I requested and was granted everyone's verbal permission to record them. I kept the app running on my mini-iPad in my purse, except while recharging it at night, and my purse was usually with me. What none of us knew at the time was that these recordings would be key evidence in a trial.

And so, dear readers (assuming more than one person buys this book), here is what actually (sort of) happened. :) (My last happy face. I promise.)

Chapter 1

Having a Ball...

"Move the catsup bottle, and scoot your chairs closer together," Susan, our book club leader, instructed from the iPad screen at the far end of our restaurant table. "I can't see Abby."

"I'll just lean in front of Leslie whenever I have anything to say," Abby Preston suggested, rising enough to do exactly that and waving at Susan's screen image. I took a deep breath and blew on her wispy, sandy-brown hair. Laughing, Abby said, "Cut that out," and sat back down. After a few moments of adjusting our chairs, the computer, and the catsup, Susan said, "Let's begin."

"You sound like we're commencing a deposition," Jane Henderson teased. (Jane's a lawyer.)

"Well, she *is* wearing a *robe*," I said.

Kate Ryan chuckled. (She's kindhearted and laughs at everyone's jokes.)

"We can call her 'Judge Susan,'" Abby said.

"I'm a little nervous," Susan replied. "It feels weird talking to a screen."

Yesterday morning, Susan Tyler had fallen off her bike at CU Boulder—where she is a professor in American history—while trying to avoid a squirrel on the path. She saved the squirrel, but broke her ankle. Susan was forced to stay home from our group road trip.

Susan grinned. "Okay, Boobs, what's the first thing that hit you as you read Wilder's book?"

"This was my first time reading Laura Ingalls Wilder," I said (jumping right in per usual), "and I was really impressed. I thought it was great when Laura said how disappointed she was that Pa had missed shooting the bear that was trying to eat their pig. And that she loved bear meat. If ever there was a statement about how much times have changed in America, that had to be it."

The waitress did a double take as she passed our table. I gave her a sheepish smile. She'd cleared our plates a few minutes earlier. It was eleven thirty a.m., and this diner in Burlington, Colorado, was less than a third full. I'm sure it was strange to see four thirtyish-looking women jammed shoulder-to-shoulder at one corner of their table, talking at a mini-iPad at the opposite corner. (FYI: Not counting my daughter, Alicia, Kate Ryan is our youngest member at forty-six. The operative word in the previous sentence was "looking." Plus the suffix "ish." And possibly an iamb of poetic license.)

"I liked how Mary got to play with the pig's bladder like a balloon," Kate said. "I loved reading this book again. Wilder's language is just so soothing. It makes me want to cuddle with a child in front of a fireplace and read it aloud."

"So that's two possible activities for us to engage in before we reach Branson," I said. "Provided we can find a store that sells pig bladders. I'm certainly happy to volunteer to fill the role of the child being read to."

"I don't remember anything about a bear and a pig in the book," Jane said. She was a striking-looking woman—tall, athletic, with long, wavy auburn hair—but today her blue eyes lacked their sparkle; she looked like she had a headache. "I must have missed that section when I was speed-reading. I thought the writing was terrible."

"I found her writing style utterly charming," I replied, surprised at Jane's reaction. We typically agreed about the quality of the writing in books, if not the book's plot, characters, theme, and overall quality.

"Oh, dear," Kate said to Jane. "Maybe it was just the childlike tone that didn't appeal to you."

"No…I really think it was the crappy writing."

"So, who was your favorite character?" Susan asked, after glancing down at her notes. (Well-organized people are such a blessing to those of us who can never as much as find the same dedicated loose-leaf notebook twice in a row.) Instead of giving any of us the chance to answer, Susan launched into a lecture about Ma and Pa Ingalls' relationship.

We are the Second Saturday of the Month Book Club, also known as: the Boobs. Nine months ago, in September of last year, Susan had made a typo in our group email. Since then, we would occasionally say something like: "Are we missing any Boobs today?" which led to silly responses such as: "Left boob's here, though she seems a little flat today." I continue to suspect that my fellow Boobs were eager to do anything and everything to cheer me up in the wake of my husband's death, last August. He'd been only 57. I was devastated. We'd had a highly imperfect marriage that worked almost perfectly for us. I wasn't even sure that Susan's "Boob" in the email was unintentional; a deliberate typo a mere month after my loss was in keeping with the wonderful way our club ebbed and flowed. We were well aware of one another's faults, but we were fiercely loyal. In one of our less-than-sober moments at our annual Christmas party, we'd declared our motto to be: *Don't mess with the Boobs, because we've got each other's backs!* There were six of us in the club, counting my adult daughter, who'd joined us seven or eight years ago when she was still in high school. Now that she'd moved to Branson, Missouri, she—rather than Susan—had been the member who attended our meetings via telecommunication.

Our only rules were that the host of that month's meeting led the discussion, which consisted of asking us a couple of book-related questions about the storyline and characters. From there, we'd discuss the book, as well as our childhoods, recipes, jobs, Zumba, spouses, vacations, movies, stain removal, politics, racism, life philosophies, North Korea, God, hair, sports, cavities, gum, plastic wrap, and mascara, which would organically lead us back into an analysis of the author's writing style, and sometimes into my pet rant—new-age writers who refrain from using punctuation. That discussion would then delve into taxi drivers, Uber, grocery stores, insurance rates, allergies, swimsuits, wealth distribution, child rearing, Adele, and coconut oil, then into the reminder about the upcoming month's book club. Finally, while Susan (typically) kicked off our thank-yous to this month's host, Jane would learn, as if for the first time, which book and which hostess was scheduled for next month. Abby, in turn, would promise she'd start reading tomorrow and would complete *next* month's book. Kate would say something sweet and reassuring along the lines that there was no need to apologize, even though (in a typical meeting): 1) Jane vehemently disapproved of our next book choice, 2) Abby had gotten sidetracked from reading last month by the burbling in her condo's plumbing, 3) Kate and Alicia (my daughter) hadn't talked as much as Jane, Susan, or I, and 4) I had eaten more than my fair share of the snacks.

Getting back to *today's* meeting, however, Susan's current treatise on Ma and Pa had dabbled its toe into the changing role of women's rights and marital relationships in modern times, but then hopscotched into how moved she'd been upon seeing the actual fiddle that Pa played the first time she'd visited the Laura Ingalls Wilder Museum in Mansfield, Missouri (our final destination on our road trip). Susan suddenly broke off and said, "Whoa. I've been rattling endlessly, haven't I? Is the computer still on, or did I break its little speaker?"

"We're still listening," I replied.

"Excellent points, Susan," Kate said. "It's enlightening to hear about husbands and wives relationship from a historical perspective. You're just such an asset in our group." (Kate Ryan is from Kansas, teaches fourth grade, and is a joy to be around. She's also beautiful and has an amazing singing voice. If this book was fictional, I'd never have chosen her to appear within these pages, because she doesn't have any interesting character flaws.)

"I wonder what blind-people's dreams look like," Abby said.

Jane and I exchanged grins. We enjoyed playing hide-and-seek with Abby's non-sequiturs.

"You're thinking of Mary, Laura's blind sister?" Jane asked. "She wasn't blind at birth, so I'm sure her dreams are probably like anyone else's."

"But what about Stevie Wonder?"

"He wasn't in *Little House in the Big Woods*," I quipped. "Stevie makes his first appearance in the Little House book six, doesn't he?"

"*Little House in the Big Woods*?" Jane repeated as if confused, while Abby, speaking over Jane's voice, said, "Stevie Wonder *was* blind at birth. So does he dream about people like we do? With regular faces? Or are their features all blurry?"

"He probably hears lots of music in his dreams," Kate said.

"I kind of like the thought of Stevie lying in bed, hearing 'Isn't She Lovely?' as he sleeps," Abby said wistfully.

"All of us are sighted," Susan said, "so we can't answer that question. Somebody who was born blind but gained sight later in life could probably answer."

"Let's get back to Laura Ingalls," I said. "My favorite character is—"

"I'm going to ask Siri," Abby said.

I put my hand on top of her purse to block access to her cellphone. "Let's get her input later. Siri isn't a Boob." (I'm sorry to say that I can get snarky sometimes, and "Let's ask Siri," is one of my least-favorite phrases. That is, unless I'm driving and need directions, or I've been drinking and am in a jovial mood.) "My favorite character is Laura," I persisted. "It's just so interesting to see how loving and happy about household chores she is, without all of the luxuries and time-savers we have now. She *did* slap Mary for bragging about her blond hair, though. At the same time, I wonder how accurate her story really is. She started writing the books in her middle age, and she's only four or five in the first book."

"She's *four*?" Jane asked. "Geez. No *wonder* none of you are making any sense. I read the wrong book. I thought we were supposed to read the *first* book in the series."

"We *were*. Didn't you read my email?" Susan said, her voice a little testy. "The note in which I reminded all of us to read *Little House in the Big Woods*?"

"'Fraid not. *Mea Culpa*. I just assumed the first book was: *'The First Four Years,'* because of its title. Naturally, I thought that meant the first four years of her life."

"The title refers to the first four years of Laura's marriage to Almonzo," Susan said.

(I resisted my urge to joke that *I* thought she'd married Stevie Wonder.)

"My favorite character is Michael Landon," Abby said. "Or his character, rather. What a cutie he is! His big smile. His gorgeous hair." She sighed as if picturing the actor in front of her.

From the computer screen, Susan was forcing herself not to comment. When Susan committed herself not to say what was on her mind, her mouth became a straight line as she bit both of her lips.

"It was so touching when Mary went blind and everyone was sick," Abby continued. "She had to drag herself across the room to fetch her parents a cup of water."

"That didn't actually happen until book five or so of the series," Kate said. "*On the Shore of Silver Lake.*"

"She went blind on the shore of a lake?" Abby asked earnestly. "I thought it was scarlet fever."

"That's the name of the book."

"It's named *Scarlet Fever*?" (*Authors note*: Abby was much spacier than normal. That said, none of us were pleased with how goofy we sounded when we read our conversation on these pages; we typically get into intelligent, thought-provoking discussions. Months later, after much discussion, our agreed-upon excuse for this particular conversation is: reviewing a children's book put us into juvenile mindsets. On the off chance that we *are,* in fact, a bunch of nitwits, we also agreed to never again record our future meetings.)

Jane started fidgeting—simultaneously stirring her soda with a straw and rocking in her seat.

"Did you *read* the book, Abby?" Susan asked. "Not counting watching old episodes of *Little House on the Prairie*?"

She shook her head. "I ran out of time. I'd forgotten how we'd switched mid-month to *Little House*, from the book about the invisible light."

"*All the Light We Cannot See*," Jane grumbled. "*That* one, I read."

"It was fun to read a children's book for a change," Kate interjected. "I hope we choose to do this again sometime."

When Kate changes topics suddenly, she is sensing hostility. I glanced at the screen and saw that Susan's mouth was once again a lipless line.

"Do your students read the Little House books?" I asked Kate.

"Yes, although early readers can start on them in second or third grade."

"Sorry to interrupt," Abby interrupted, "but I need to go check on Red again." (Red's her dog.)

"Do you still have the car keys?" Kate asked.

"Sure do. Thanks," Abby answered.

"Hang on a sec," Jane said. "I think I left my wallet in the car." She swept up her Coach bag from the back of her chair and strode toward Abby. "But don't let us hold up the discussion."

She and Abby rounded the corner, chatting quietly. Jane's abrupt departure worried me. Had I been talking too much? Or offended Jane somehow? I knew Kate or Susan couldn't be to blame. Most likely, this was mere paranoia on my part. With my husband's death and my daughter's recent long-distance move, my book club *was* my family; I shuddered at the thought of anything jeopardizing our group.

"How much longer will your leg be in the cast?" Kate asked Susan.

"At least two months."

"Are you in pain?" I asked.

"Not at all. I'm on OxyContin. Thanks to the drugs, it barely even bothers me that only the three of us read the book. And that I won't get the chance to see the Laura Ingalls Wilder Museum with you."

"I'll make it up to you as best I can," I said. "I'll not only give you a copy of the printout from the Pocket Stenographer (not the app's real name) so you can read what we talked about, but we'll schedule another Facetime session when we're in Mansfield. I'll carry my iPad with me, facing out, the whole time we're in the museum."

Susan beamed at me. "That's so sweet. Thank you, Leslie."

"Plus, *I'll* text you whenever I think of how much I wish you were with us," Kate offered. "Actually, every tenth time. Otherwise, I'd be texting constantly."

Susan was getting choked up, and *my* kneejerk reaction to emotional moments is to reach for a laugh. "We'll have to insist that you sing 'A Hundred Bottles of Beer on the Wall' while you're driving then, Kate. It'll be unpleasant, but safer than texting while you're behind the wheel." (The operative word this time was *reach*; I'm well aware my remark wasn't funny. Kate chuckled anyway, rather than letting me ruminate about my lame comment.)

"I get emotional easily while I'm on such strong pain killers," Susan said, wiping her eyes. "Tell you what. Instead of texting me when you miss me, how about if you both text me when you see something that reminds you of a book we've read recently? That would be really fun for me."

"Great idea," I said, while Kate, too, expressed her enthusiasm. "Also, Susan, I might have already mentioned this, but even though they don't allow audio recordings at her theater, Alicia told me she thinks she can get permission for me to record a song or two of her and Kurt's performances."

Attending Alicia's performance was the key objective of our road trip. Her boyfriend, Kurt Winston, had taken a Freshman History class from Susan six years ago and became one of her favorite students. With some egging on by Susan, Alicia and Kurt met each other. Their second semester, they wound up getting roles in a student theater production. They fell in love. After graduating from CU, they'd stayed in Boulder and moved in together. Kurt is from Branson, and his mother had arranged auditions for them for an oldies' show. Ergo, two months ago, they moved to Branson. Wednesday—four days from now—we had primo tickets to their show.

Susan looked at Kate with an inscrutable expression; the two of them had done most of the planning for this trip, including getting us tickets to a couple of other shows. "That'd be great," Susan said. "Fingers crossed." She looked at her watch. "I can see why Alicia struggles a bit now that she's attending meetings only virtually. It definitely feels a little like you're an outcast."

"You're never an outcast to us!" Kate hastened to exclaim.

"Our unusual meeting time today conflicts with Alicia's matinee," I told Susan. "I was hoping to angle two iPads so you two could see and hear each other."

Abby and Jane returned together and reclaimed their seats. I got a whiff of what smelled like alcohol on Jane's breath. I studied her features. She'd had a nasty divorce from a husband over a year ago and was struggling. Recently, I'd tossed a piece of tinfoil into her recyclables and was stunned at the number of empty wine bottles. A prickle of worry ran up my spine.

"Red's fine," Abby said. "He was sound asleep in the driver's seat until I woke him up. It's still nice and cool in the car, with the windows rolled down a little." She gave me a quick hug around the shoulders. "Leslie will be thrilled to hear that I also checked Siri. Basically, blind people's other senses are heightened, so their dreams are about smells and people's voices and the particular sensation of their touch. But they don't have any visuals."

I had no response. The waitress came over and gave us our check, but assured us there was no rush.

"So how was *The First Four Years*?" Abby asked Jane.

"Don't get me started. Twice in a row now I've been forced to read first drafts of books by talented authors who never wanted their manuscripts to be published."

"Laura Wilder didn't want *The First Four Years* to be published?" I asked.

"Nobody *forces* us to read any of the books," Susan pointed out. "But, yes. Laura Ingalls Wilder had already died by the time *The First Four Years* manuscript was discovered, and it was her weakest book, by a wide margin. Some readers think that's because this is the only 'Little House' book her daughter didn't rewrite for her. But others think it's just not as good as the others because it was her first attempt at writing through an adult's eyes, and she might have lost all her enthusiasm by then."

"In reality, it was probably the fault of some money-grubbing agent who found the first draft and published it without anyone's consent," Jane scoffed.

I groaned. (But quietly.) "You promised we weren't going to discuss Harper Lee this week."

Jane shrugged. "At least I didn't say her name."

"But you referred to a 'money-grubbing agent' for the hundredth time since we first put '*Go Set a You-know-what*' on our book list."

Jane spread her arms. "*Somebody* has to stand up for Atticus Finch."

(As you've probably realized, *Go Set a Watchman* was our club's previous book, which Jane had failed to object to when Susan sent the email list of suggested titles for the upcoming six months. As we discovered at last month's meeting, however, Jane's deep admiration for the character Atticus Finch was a major reason she had chosen to enter the field of law in the first place. In Jane's personal opinion, publishing *Go Set a Watchman* was elderly abuse, something she cares about so deeply, she does pro bono legal work for senior citizens in Boulder County.)

"Should we continue our book club meeting," Susan asked, "or are you eager to get to wherever you're staying tonight?"

"Oh, it's no problem. We're less than four hours away from the ball—" Kate stopped, blushing slightly.

"Ooh," I said, with a grin. "The cat's out of the bag. We finally know where we're going for tonight's surprise destination. We're going to the ball, where we can dance with the prince!"

"Goody," Jane said. "I've been brushing up on my Fox Trot!"

"I *meant* to say we're only four hours away from having a ball when we arrive," Kate said.

That made little sense. Puzzled, I studied her attractive features. Kate has what poker players call a "tell." Whenever she lies (next to never) she looks over your shoulder instead of meeting your gaze. Ever since we'd agreed on taking this trip to Branson, she'd spent quite a bit of time glancing over my shoulder.

My cellphone made a noise. I knew the noise signified something other than a phone call, but that's as techno-savvy as I get regarding my phone. I looked at the screen and saw I'd gotten a text from my daughter. After a couple of swipes and screen touches, I was able to read:

Getting ready to go on stage. Can't wait to see you!

So glad you're finally meeting Kurt's dad! Xoxo

"Huh," I muttered. "Alicia says she's happy that I'm going to meet Kurt's divorced father. I sure hope she's not trying to fix us up."

"She probably just wants both families to enjoy each other's company," Kate replied. "Which brings up a good topic for discussion. The Ingalls were pretty isolated. Did you think that they had lonely lives?"

"Not for that time period," I replied, too distracted to elaborate. Kate's vision had been focused over my shoulder when she gave an excuse for Alicia being excited about my meeting Kurt's father.

Made in United States
North Haven, CT
14 September 2024